Praise for
Claire and Present Danger

"A milestone in the Amanda Pepper series . . . a must-read not only for readers who have been with the series from the beginning but also for those who are ready to jump on for future journeys."
—*The Book Reporter*

"Roberts is a witty, light-fingered writer who . . . keeps the plot humming."
—*The Providence Journal*

"[Amanda Pepper] is young, sparky, funny, tough . . . the antithesis of the grandmotherly stereotype so common in the genre. Amanda is nobody's grandmother. And, as her fans have already discovered, she's nobody to mess with, either."
—*Booklist*

"Roberts returns with a brisker, brighter tenth Amanda Pepper. . . . More substance to the mystery, more crackle to the dialogue: a notch up for the series."
—*Kirkus Reviews*

"What stands out most about Amanda is her outlook on life—the humor that carries her through the rough times. . . . The story is well-paced and the conclusion satisfying."
—*Romantic Times*

HOW I SPENT MY SUMMER VACATION
"Roberts concocts colorful and on-the-mark scenes."
—*Los Angeles Times*

WITH FRIENDS LIKE THESE . . .
"A pleasurable whodunit with real motives, enough clues to allow a skillful reader of mysteries to make some intelligent guesses, and a plethora of suspects."
—*Chicago Tribune*

I'D RATHER BE IN PHILADELPHIA
"Literate, amusing, and surprising while at the same time spinning a crack whodunit puzzle."
—*Chicago Sun-Times*

PHILLY STAKES
"Lively . . . breezy . . . entertaining."
—*San Francisco Chronicle*

CAUGHT DEAD IN PHILADELPHIA
"A stylish, wittily observant, and highly enjoyable novel."
—*Ellery Queen's Mystery Magazine*

By Gillian Roberts

CAUGHT DEAD IN PHILADELPHIA
PHILLY STAKES
I'D RATHER BE IN PHILADELPHIA
WITH FRIENDS LIKE THESE . . .
HOW I SPENT MY SUMMER VACATION
IN THE DEAD OF SUMMER
THE MUMMERS' CURSE
THE BLUEST BLOOD
ADAM AND EVIL
HELEN HATH NO FURY
CLAIRE AND PRESENT DANGER

CLAIRE AND PRESENT DANGER

AN AMANDA PEPPER MYSTERY

GILLIAN ROBERTS

FAWCETT

FAWCETT BOOKS • NEW YORK

Claire and Present Danger is a work of fiction. Names, characters, places, and incidents are the products of the author's imagination or are used fictitiously. Any resemblance to actual events, locales, or persons, living or dead, is entirely coincidental.

A Fawcett Book
Published by The Random House Publishing Group

Copyright © 2003 by Judith Greber
Excerpt from *Till the End of Tom* copyright © 2004 by Judith Greber.

www.ballantinebooks.com

ISBN 0-449-00736-7

Manufactured in the United States of America

OPM 9 8 7 6 5 4 3 2 1

First Ballantine Books Edition: June 2003
First Fawcett Books Edition: November 2004

This is for Ferne and Steve Kuhn—
despite the puns!

Acknowledgments

Special thanks and gratitude to Jon Keroes, who generously and repeatedly shared his considerable professional expertise. Any errors are mine, as is the fact that I took the information and twisted it to suit my criminal purposes.

And to my longtime partners in crime, estimable agent Jean Naggar, and amazing editor Joe Blades—thanks, as well, for making work a pleasure.

One

"ALWAYS THOUGHT IT WAS KIDS WHO WERE RELUCTANT to go back to school, not teachers." Mackenzie sat on the side of the bed, tying the laces of his running shoes.

"Another popular myth shot to hell," I muttered. "The big thrill was getting new notebooks, lunch boxes, and backpacks."

"An' I was too insensitive to think of buyin' them for you. Guess I'm not a New Age kind of guy, after all."

"I didn't get so much as an unused gum eraser."

"But you aren't actually re-entering. You did that two days ago."

He meant prep time. A duo of days designed to quash whatever optimism had built during summer. Days of listening to a lazy end-of-summer fly halfheartedly circling the room while Maurice Havermeyer, Philly Prep's pathetic headmaster, droned along with them. The difference was this: The fly's noises were interesting.

Our headmaster's spiel was stale from the get-go with the same meaningless jargon-infested exhortations to be ever more creative, innovative, and effective. I fought to keep from putting my head on the desk and falling asleep, and wondered if I could peddle copies of his talks as cures for insomnia.

He reassured us he'd be there to offer all the help and re-sources he could, but he was careful to never define precisely where "there" might be. Maybe he didn't have to. Anyone who'd worked with him knew it would be as far away as possible from the problem or question.

Two days of sprucing up classrooms, filing lesson plans with the office, checking bookroom stores against class lists, and creating colorful bulletin boards nobody except our own selves would appreciate. And all of it surrounded by the loud silence of a school without students, which was not, to my definition, a school at all.

But now, here we were. The real stuff. Back to school.

"Thought you loved teachin'," Mackenzie said.

I do, although what love affair isn't a roller-coaster ride? "It isn't that," I said, looking at a to-do list I'd prepared the night before. "It's everything converging at once." I felt stupid even saying that. It wasn't as if anything came as a shock, and it wasn't as if there were that many *everythings*. What was exceptional was how daunted I felt by my list of obligations.

I had to teach. No surprise.

I had a part-time job after school to help our personal homeland security, but I'd been working there along with Mackenzie all summer, so that wasn't out of the ordinary, either.

Starting to push things over the edge, however, was an obligatory appearance at a ninetieth birthday party for a former neighbor. Given her advanced age, I couldn't rationally beg off and promise to be at her next big bash, even though the only living creature to whom old Mrs. Russell had shown kindness was Macavity, my cat. Her house had served as his summer camp and spa, and it would have been more logical for him to attend the festivities, but I didn't see how to swing that, either.

But to really make the day require at least forty hours, I had Beth. My event-planner of a sister was thrilled by my engagement, which she and my mother saw as a victory for their side, capitulation and unconditional surrender on mine. Beth was so delighted and relieved, she was doing her damnedest to absorb me into the world of wives before I was one. At the moment, this translated into attendance at a dinner she had orchestrated and produced, a fund-raiser for an abused-women's shelter. "You'll love these women. They're the movers and shakers of the whole area," she said. She wisely left off the "even if they are married," although her point was that life went on after a wedding ceremony, and that I'd better set a date soon.

"Half my reason to be there," she continued, "is to network. There are nonprofit consultants, foundation heads, and corporate executives." People who could help build her business. Plus, it was all for a good cause and one I subscribe to—but dressing up and eating dinner as a way of helping the less fortunate has never made sense to me. Not being able to afford to go to such events is one of the few perks of living on a shoestring.

This time, I couldn't use poverty as my excuse, because Beth had comped my ticket. Besides, she was doing me an enormous favor in a few days, and being cheering section, back-up, and support for her networking attempts was a form of prepayment for what I metaphorically owed her.

Before it even began, the day cost me hours deciding what I could wear that would see me through my four lives. I settled on an outfit that wasn't great for any of them, a gray suit I'd had for years that I hoped was so unremarkable, it belonged nowhere and anywhere. The bed was piled high with my rejects.

And that's why, at 7:30 A.M., instead of being exhilarated by a new school term, I was worn out.

"If it's too much, skip Ozzie's." Mackenzie came over to where I was packing up my briefcase and kissed me in the center of my forehead.

"Ozzie's not the problem." I was moonlighting. Actually,

both of us were moonlighting. After years of deliberation, Mackenzie had taken the plunge, leaving the police force so as to attack crime from a different perspective. He was now a Ph.D. candidate in criminology at Penn. Despite his partial fellowship, moonlighting was going to be necessary for at least the next four years.

Need I say that my mother's hysterical delight in my engagement had been tempered by this switch in careers? "He had a good, steady job," she said. "Why on earth . . ."

"This is what he's wanted for a long time, and it's fascinating, Mom. He'll study sociology and criminology and law and biology—it's a great course. And then he can go into research, or teach, or—lots of things."

"It takes so long!"

Translation: How could you marry a man with no income for the next how long?

Further translation: Your biological clock is going to strike midnight before you'll be able to afford children.

"But Mom," I said. "When he's done, he'll be a doctor. Your son-in-law, the doctor."

". . . . ."

Translation: A Ph.D. in a cockamamie field is not a *doctor*.

Nonetheless, she was not that far off track. Poor R Us, and when we did the math on paying the mortgage plus luxuries like food, it seemed a good idea to bring in whatever extra cash we could. Philly Prep did not pay its teachers a living wage, unless you were living in a pup tent in Fairmount Park.

That's why Mackenzie had gotten his P.I. license and was working whatever hours he could manage out of the office of Ozzie Bright, retired cop and current private investigator, and I was working for C. K. Mackenzie. *With* him, I liked to say and think, but the truth was, *for*. I wasn't licensed, and so was more or less his apprentice, and he, my supervisor, although I'm not fond of thinking in those terms. I like to consider us a partnership, not boss and employee, or pro and peon, which is closer to reality.

Over the course of the summer, C.K. let me try my wings at everything from interviewing witnesses and new clients to clerical chores like handling the nonstop flow of papers for discovery. The words *private eye* prompted images of shady gents in fedoras and platinum-blonde dames in teeter-totter high heels. Of cracking wise and trapping bad guys.

The job wasn't exactly that. Mostly, I sat in front of a computer, or filed papers. Solo. Since our schedules seldom overlapped—I was at school while he was working, and at the office while he was in school—the "working together" part was as fictional as the fedoras, but we were definitely partners at trying to help our communal bottom line.

Besides, most of the time I enjoyed the work, and Ozzie Bright, as idiosyncratic a man as he was, was several flights of steps up from Maurice Havermeyer.

"A regular Nick and Nora, you two," Ozzie had said when we entered his lair, and who could resist that idea, either? What's better than having fun and being in love while simultaneously squelching crime? So what if N&N were stinking rich all the time and stinking drunk most of the time? And then there was their adorable dog.

On our side we had unpaid bills, sobriety, and an overstuffed dust mop of a cat.

And mostly unimaginative cases. Nick and Nora messed with big-time baddies. Our clients were mild, straightforward, and their crimes white-collar, when there were any crimes at all.

For example, finding a long-lost high school love didn't, in our case, lead to revelations that she was a serial killer we could cleverly snare. Instead, when we found her, happy, bland, and the grandmother of five, the drama was that our client threatened not to pay because after thirty-seven years, she wasn't the way he remembered her.

We'd done background searches on two prospective corporate hires, and only one turned out to have all the credentials he claimed. We'd done interviews for the defense of a man accused of sexual harassment and, to my surprise, it appeared that the case had no basis and he'd be acquitted. Mackenzie was getting a good reputation in the biz, but in truth, not quite with Nick and Nora pizzazz.

But on this particular Monday morning, neither the pressures of back to school, the duties of my part-time job, nor the pileup of unappetizing parties made my nerve ends twang. It was the other thing. "Plus, there's . . ." I couldn't finish the thought honestly. Instead, I said, "Too much."

"I haven't seen you like this before. You don't seem . . ." He stopped midsentence and laughed out loud.

"What?"

"I know about posttraumatic shock—but pretraumatic shock? You're so efficient, not wastin' time waitin' till the actual trauma happens."

"I cannot imagine what you mean." Lying again.

"There's no trauma in store, Amanda. I can't fathom why you're so worried. If we were kids, askin' their permission," he said. "If there was some big objection anywhere to our gettin' married—maybe I'd understand. We're even spared worry over whether Daddy's gonna disapprove and disinherit me, 'cause there never was a thing to inherit except my good looks and charm."

In a few short days, I was going to meet Mackenzie's parents for the first time. I'd spoken with them on the phone. We'd exchanged notes and birthday cards and Christmas gifts, and in every instance they sounded warm, welcoming, and delighted with the prospect of my joining their family. I couldn't have identified or quantified what worried me about meeting them, but worried I was. I constantly felt as if I had overdosed on caffeine, my blood hoppity-skipping through my veins and my skull expanding and contracting as if I were pumping up a leaky basketball.

"It's stage fright," I muttered. "That's a pretraumatic shock." And as close to the feeling as I could get. Would my performance be adequate? Would I get flowers and curtain calls, or be splattered with rotten tomatoes?

Their impending arrival had stirred the muck of memory, so that I recalled fleeting anecdotes, funny stories told over glasses of wine a year or two ago—anything that had to do with my beloved and other women. Now, with painful clarity, I remembered being told about a girl in C.K.'s hometown who Gabrielle, a.k.a. Gabby, Mackenzie had believed the "perfect match" for her son despite said son's total lack of interest. That part was not exceptional, but I'd heard about her because Gabby Mackenzie continued to tout the virtues of the girl back home even after her son and I were living together. C.K. thought it was funny. I might have at the time, too. Now I didn't.

I remembered everything I was supposed to have long forgotten. Every casual aside made in the past years. Every response, however terse and reluctant, to every question I'd asked. Stories such as the one about the girl back home that had been told as a funny example of how silly his mother could be.

The original context no longer mattered. I'd sifted everything out until I was left with the facts, which I examined and analyzed with the zeal of a scientist.

I remembered the girl he'd actually been engaged to, years ago. Miss Bayou High—something like that. The prettiest and most popular girl in school. In town. And rich, he'd said, treating it all as a joke. "But you've got to know, our standards were so far down, they were subterranean. Her father was a partner in a not overly successful body shop, but compared with us—she was an heiress. And a nightmare. As soon as she had a ring on her finger, she dropped the sweetness and light and turned into a harridan and as interesting and deep as the paint jobs they did on pickups."

At the time he told me this, I'd laughed and said her mistake was dropping the act with the engagement ring. As for me, I'd wait till I had a wedding band before I showed my true and ugly colors.

All in jest, and said in that phase of dating when you tell a carefully edited "all" to the new interest in your life. Now, with my new perspective on life, I think we should present ourselves as tabula rasa and never, ever write on our slates. No past, no first love, early loves, puppy loves, and no mistakes. Information has a toxic, delayed-release afterlife.

The thing was, I remembered the minor footnote to Miss Bayou High's story as well. She was ancient history to C.K. and to her three former husbands—but he'd found it entertaining that his mother still exchanged Christmas cards and occasional visits with her. That, of course, was the portion upon which I fixated, giving me further reason to fear Gabby Mackenzie. It was painfully obvious that I was not her daughter-in-law of choice, and her sweet long-distance welcomes were simply good, insincere, Southern manners.

Mackenzie had delivered his reassurances while standing in the middle of the loft, doing that peculiar side-to-side jounce in place. My in-law angst was delaying his run and doing harm to his heart and day. I had to admire him for staying around to convince me, again, that his parents were not coming north to blow this damn Yankee girl away. "Amanda, honey," he said, shifting left to right to left to right, "they're excited about meetin' you. It's no big deal to them. They've been through this kind of thing lots of times."

"I thought you were only engaged once before."

"I meant," he said, bouncing as if he were waiting for a traffic light to change, "my vast collection of siblings, most of whom are already married, some for the second time and one for the third. I'm the last holdout, except Lutie, who is between husbands rather than never married."

That didn't help. Maybe they resented dragging themselves north for a redundant daughter-in-law, and not even the right one, at that.

"It'll be fun. You'll see. We'll show 'em the Liberty Bell and Independence Hall and take a buggy ride through Society Hill and they will not only fall in love with you, but with Philadelphia, too. It's all taken care of, so relax. You've got enough on your plate today without worryin' about them, too."

"Thanks," I said. "I know you're right." That wasn't exactly true, but I couldn't bear talking about in-law worries any longer.

With another kiss, he was at the door, opening it as the phone rang. I took a deep breath, then lifted the receiver. A call at this hour could only mean disaster. Or—

My mother. "Mom," I said, and Mackenzie relaxed his vigil, waved, and closed the door behind him. "Mom," I said again. "You caught me about to leave. First day of—"

"I know. That's why I called now. I just spoke to Beth—"

We'd bought my mother a cell phone for her birthday. The sort with low-rate long-distance perks. We'd explained that she could now wait until we were awake to phone, and it wouldn't cost her any more. "I get up so early," she said in response. "There's nothing else to do at that hour."

And so she phoned. I geared up for a recital of what the day held for her between her clubs and charities, her card games and shopping expeditions. This was a woman who could devote an entire day to finding the right drain-stopper, and consider the time well-spent when she found it. Further, she loved to relive the hunt and the triumph by reciting it in detail to her daughters.

"I've got a surprise for you." Her voice had lowered to a mischievous chuckle.

I was now officially engaged, so she'd stopped sending me clippings and books about ways to meet men. Nowadays, I received domestic trivia: a soap-holder she'd discovered in her daily rounds, a subscription to a decorating magazine, a sleek vegetable-peeler, clippings about perfect weddings. I wondered what today's discovery might be.

"I spoke with Beth," she said again.

"Uh-huh." She was primed to re-create her conversation with Beth, thus doubling the pleasure of whatever tale she had to tell. I carried the phone around the loft, checking that I had the necessary supplies for the day and evening. Roll book. Lesson plans for all five classes. My annotated copies of the novels I was teaching. The key to Ozzie's office. The wrapped and beribboned gift for old Mrs. Russell, a set of Pavarotti CDs. Pavarotti was second only to my cat on her shortlist of loves. And thinking of Macavity, I checked that his dish of kibble was full. Ticket for Beth's fund-raiser.

"She said Chuck's parents are coming up."

It was my fault she called him Chuck, which wasn't his name at all. Early on, when I didn't know that C.K. stood only for itself, when I was sure they were the initials of names he wouldn't share with me, I assigned him "C" names at will. Unfortunately, during one of those guessing-game sessions, I identified my new gentleman caller to my mother as "Chuck." It was a joke, but I delayed setting my mother straight because, unlike C.K.'s parents, she wouldn't consider a set of initials a proper name.

My fault, too, for telling my sister anything about my life without considering the ways my loving mother could mess with the information when she found it out, which she always did.

Of course, this time, I'd had no choice but to tell Beth, because I wanted her involved. She was Good Family, and she'd make a great impression with her weathered stone palazzo on the Main Line, and her talents as a hostess. She was making dinner for the Mackenzies the night they arrived. That was the favor I was prepaying by going to her event tonight.

But still my fault because I'd failed to tell her to keep the entire business a secret from our mother.

"So I thought—what could be a better time than now? It's almost an omen, don't you think? It's so awfully hot here in Florida now, and this way, we'll all meet each other! Bingo! Won't that be fun? We're flying up Thursday in plenty of time for dinner, so don't worry—staying at Bethie's and . . ."

I'd missed something—the moment when I'd be asked whether this was a good idea.

Let me make it clear that I love my parents dearly. They are kind, decent people. And that includes my mother.

But when I thought of what currently occupied her mind—C.K.'s decision to turn away from his "nice, steady" job, concern that we hadn't set a wedding date, upset that the Mackenzies had produced eight children without considering what it would do to Bea and Gilbert Pepper's daughter's wedding budget—and then I thought of Gabby Mackenzie's easygoing, soft voice on the phone and her laissez-faire attitude . . .

I broke out in a cold sweat. My mind boggled. My imagination envisioned tossing these incompatible sets of people together in Beth's living room and I cringed.

For starters, my mother's relief and joy at the prospect of *finally*!—that word was always there, always with loud punctuation, as if my shelf-life expiration date was years past—marrying me off would terrify any sane person, which I dearly hoped included Gabby Mackenzie. And my father barely spoke. He knew how, of course, but to date, he hadn't found much worth mentioning.

Mackenzie claimed his parents would be sanguine, even casual about our status and plans or lack of same, but my mother could drive anyone crazy. I envisioned her arriving with a clipboard, shaking their hands, then moving on to her itinerary.

When was The Event going to be?

Where?

What sort?

Color scheme?

Who'd marry us?

Who'd—

Pit that against the Louisiana contingent, the laissez-faire let the good times roll side—

"I know you have to run, honey, so I'll say good-bye now, and we'll call when we get to Beth's. I'm so excited! Love to you and Chuck!

I said that an early morning call was either news of a disaster or my mother. I hadn't fully realized it could be both.

Two

I'M WILLING TO BET MY STUDENTS THINK THAT AT TERM'S end, I'm taken to the basement of the school, deflated via a secret valve in my foot, and stored on a hanger until school starts again.

And I'm willing to bet they accepted and believed my happy-faced expression all during this first day back to school. My real life had begun again!

They might even think I believed their feeble expressions of pleasure, or at least acceptance, at being back in harness for another full school year, spending time with me, rather than the beach, camp, mountains, videos, CDs, or computer games.

We all pretended we'd missed each other terribly, and the day flowed on, busy with book distribution, my contracts with each class, and the assignments I'd prepared. My theory is to slam them into the school mode so quickly, they're not sure what hit them. Homework the first day and no turning back.

In a school like Philly Prep, where the majority of our students couldn't—or wouldn't—perform elsewhere, it's better to be whispered about with hushed horror ("she's so *hard*!") than taken for a teacher they can easily dupe. You always can—I always do—ease up and relax the standards, but you can't tighten them once they've discovered the joy of tromping all over you.

This seemed particularly important on an enervating hot and humid day like today. We used to call it Indian summer, but in fact, it's all-ethnicities and origins summer. It is, in fact and reality, still *summer*. We invented this premature, back-to-school autumn. We fill magazines with cute woolen sweaters and bright-colored scarves when, in fact, it was a day designed to sit on a porch and sip lemonade or, better still, go to the shore. Surely not a day to find yourself back behind a desk. But while I saw children looking groggy from the heat, and I felt beads of perspiration on my own forehead by midday, nobody complained or made a case for starting school when the weather improved. That's the first-day glow.

Today was also the day to get a handle on the feel of each class, what a business would call its culture. Every class is a new and unpredictable chemistry experiment. I wish I knew the secret formula, because when the personality elements combine the right way, teaching is one long high.

This is a rare situation.

Even when it doesn't work, I remain fascinated by the mismatches, and by how nothing really changes in the basic politics of school. On this first day, the class hasn't jelled into what it will become, but the players are there, ready to adopt roles that remain the same, year after year.

I could spot the potential queen bee in each group, the future Miss Bayou High. Just as when I was in high school, she was the girl who looked closest to how girls have been told they should look. She always had great hair, however that translated this year; a slender build; clean, even though not necessarily gorgeous, features; and a self-assurance she hid under an elaborate dance of self-deprecation. If a girl is too obviously secure about her appearance, it counts against her, sets the rest of the girls against her. This is not a good situation, but it is how it is.

Boys aren't taught to be modest and self-effacing. Their

king—or perhaps duke, if The King is in another section—
can acknowledge his divine rights. Then there are the imi-
tators, the hangers-on, the king's and queen's courtiers, and
somewhere on the fringes, the serfs, the unaccepted. The
outsiders, the ones who don't fit the precut ready-made
puzzle pieces, are the most interesting. They'll someday
spin being different—another word for *unique*—into gold
or dross. They're the future inventors of obscure cyber
components, the performers and poets—and the highway
snipers.

"You're choosing the grade you want to receive," I told
my seniors. "Here are ten points you can or cannot cover
in your discussion of the book you choose." The list included a dozen analytical approaches to fiction, such as
types of conflict; *point of view, with examples*; and *the significance of the setting*—each with specific directions as to
what the student would need to do about explaining that
aspect of his book. They could choose to include six of the
points and earn an A, four of the points and earn a B, or
three of the points for a C. We didn't discuss anything less
than that.

While I handed out the sheets and spoke, the alpha determined how her group should react. Would my assignment and I live or die? Thumbs up or down?

They weren't drones, and she wasn't a dictator. But she
was *popular*, that most significant word in the school vocabulary, and she was the arbiter of what was appropriate
dress, behavior, and attitude.

A new transfer who'd obviously decided not to attempt
to belong to the popular group—she of the blue lipstick,
two rings threaded through her upper lip, and a spitting-
cat tattoo on her bicep—studied the list, deciding what
she'd do on her own, not so much as glancing at her class-
mates.

The alpha male, of course, rolled his eyes and pushed the

paper to the side as if disinterested. The assignment wasn't fair—I was forcing them to abandon cool nonchalance and actively work for a given grade level.

I gave myself a metaphorical pat on the back. My reputation for being hard, possibly even mean, was being strengthened. The first and best advice my student-teaching supervisor gave me was, "Don't smile till Christmas." I still haven't managed that, nor did she mean it to be taken literally, but it's advice I've passed along more than once.

The day meandered on. In many ways—most?—I am as beguiled and naïve as my students and I view back-to-school with an optimism close to insanity. This year, I swear, I'm going to be completely and consistently prepared. This year, I'm going to mark every single paper the night after it's handed in. This year, every nuance of the classroom will be in service of some greater philosophical purpose.

Isn't denial a wonderful thing?

Every autumn I harbor such thoughts even though I know that within minutes, my energy and efficiency will dissipate under the inexorable pressures of time and reality. Simply learning who everybody is becomes exhausting. It's sad but true that you most quickly learn the names of the troublemakers, which might be the entire point of their troublemaking. By the end of first period I knew that Bo Michaels, a big, good-looking dimwit, was going to be a thorn in my side as he burned up excess energy by being class clown.

By the end of third period, I had two more names carved on my heart, Butch and Sundance wanna-bes, buddies who had long ago perfected their two-against-the-world act. Unfortunately, there weren't any banks to rob in sophomore English, so they contented themselves with high fives, secret signals, and unsecret ogling of the girls.

The day progressed until finally, it was last period with the newest Philly Prep students, the ninth graders.

I didn't love having them at the end of the day, but I didn't have a vote in the scheduling. By this point, kids are either ready for naptime or antsy and overeager to get out of the building. But this early in the term, and this painfully new to the building, ninth graders tread softly, adjusting themselves to being low men on the new totem pole, and to finding allies among the other young'uns.

"Let's try something," I said after distributing *Lord of the Flies* and asking them to put their chairs in a circle.

"Does this count?" an intense-looking girl asked.

I spared her the near-obligatory pedagogical explanation that everything counted as a learning experience. She meant grades, and I knew how *she*—Jessica, another name immediately memorized—was going to be straight through till June.

"It doesn't count," I said, wishing I could say that in the real world when I was at risk for doing something stupid. "The book we're going to read is about a group of young people stranded on an island, and I thought it would be fun to see how you think you'd handle the situation before you see how they did. So imagine yourselves on a desert island without a single adult around."

Predictably, they looked guilty as they laughed with pleasure. "Your dream situation," I said. "Paradise. But the snake in paradise is that there's no way off the island, and all you've got is the clothing you're wearing and whatever's in your pockets. No food, no beds. The island is partly sandy beach, partly forest, partly a mountain, and partly a lagoon. How would you organize yourselves to survive?"

I gave them twenty minutes to work out a plan while I sat outside the circle, acting as secretary, taking notes on what they decided they'd do.

For a long time they looked at each other, waiting for

someone to take the lead and tell the rest of them what to do. Finally, a red-haired boy broke the silence. "If nobody else is going to do anything, I will," he announced.

"What are you," another boy asked, "the chief?"

The redhead—Mike—nodded. "And here's what we have to do."

At least five boys protested. It wasn't fair. Just because he'd spoken first didn't give him the right to . . .

The girls, to my dismay, said nothing. Along with them, I listened to polite male jousting for position, until they finally decided there wasn't going to be a chief. Instead, an untitled somebody would check the chores and rules, and that role would shift every day. For the moment, however, Mike could be in charge.

Mike assigned jobs. "Who can hunt for food?" he asked, and I tried to imagine which of these city boys knew a thing about stalking prey—and if any did, why? We recorded the names of the hunters. "Who can fish?" This produced another male squabble about whether fishing should be separate from hunting and whether the same people could do both.

The females played mute until a pale, undersized girl raised her hand (unlike the boys, who shouted out their suggestions) and said, "Can't we—I mean the girls—can't we do something, too?"

A girl on the other side of the circle who'd been whispering to her neighbors gave the girl who'd spoken The Look. I have seen it my entire life. Fashions and slang change, but The Look remains the ultimate feminine, passive-aggressive weapon.

The Look shows no emotions except, if possible, a negative one so powerful, it's like a suction pump. It's a black hole in the emotions, a blank stare, almost as if the girl doling it out were removing from its recipient both air and the possibility of human feelings.

I am sure the fabled Evil Eye was a version of The Look.

What a pity *Lord of the Flies* was exclusively masculine and these girls wouldn't necessarily see themselves reflected in it. I'd have to make sure they did.

After a moment's pause, Mike responded with Darwinian theory as he saw it. "We're more fit, is all," he said. "We're the hunters and we're the ones who will have to tend the fire and watch out for wild animals and things. It's how it is. Survival of the fittest." He held up an arm and flexed his bicep for emphasis.

So much for my new-school-year optimism.

The girl who'd given The Look, a pretty girl with sun-streaked hair—Melanie, when I checked—giggled. "Oh, but really," she said, looking on the verge of a blush, "but really, what about us, Mike? You know, the unfit ones?" She rolled her eyes and giggled again. It was the same question the undersized girl had asked, but the first speaker had forgotten the self-deprecating part, the flirting part, the accepting that the boys were the leaders part.

Weren't things like that supposed to have changed a few decades ago?

"You'll do the cooking and cleaning," Mike said. "And, of course, if there are babies . . ."

All the boys—because not a single pimply, gawky, undersized oddly constructed one of them would dare appear not to get the implications of Mike's line—laughed self-consciously while the girl who'd asked the question made yipping noises of feeble protest and covered her face with her hands.

They eventually had a plan, sloppy and incomplete, but they'd organized their anarchistic, adult-free society with provisions, laws, and punishments.

It was a nice preface to *Lord of the Flies*, a nice sense that they could run things and no sense yet of the disasters built into their Darwinian fantasy world.

And worse, no sense that they'd already seen Darwin in action. *Been* Darwin in action, fighting for airspace and the means of surviving high school, which was its own desert island with no help in sight. I had to hope that a slender, but great novel would help them deal more benignly with the process.

And now, the school day was done. Time to whip off my English-teacher disguise and become: Amanda Pepper, After-School P.I. Today promised to be quiet, more like Amanda Pepper, After-School Clerk; but I was tired, not yet reacclimated to the unceasing state of alert teaching required, so I wasn't upset to be facing nothing more taxing than filing papers.

I stopped to check my mailbox before heading out. There wasn't much except Philly Prep's homemade junk mail. I glanced at items as I removed them, and tossed them into the nearby trash can until I realized that the new secretary looked stricken by my callous disregard for her hard work. If she hadn't authored the pieces, she'd been the one to put them in the cubbies. I saved the rest for a later, secret disposal and, as a secretarial kindness, I read through a straight-faced, dead serious reminder that the next faculty meeting's focus was "Our Mandate Is Striving for Excellence." Faculty was urged to bring suggestions. The only suggestion I had, if we really wanted excellence, was to replace the entire student population, a great portion of the faculty, and, specifically, the headmaster who'd written the bulletin. The mandate might be striving for excellence, and good for it!—but if so, it was the only thing around that was. Havermeyer claimed he was upgrading the academic aspirations of the school, but so far, if you had the tuition and your kid's I.Q. was the equal of his resting pulse rate— he was in.

At the bottom of the detritus I spotted a pink While You Were Out slip that said, in a loopy handwriting with an

open o dotting the i: *Ntervu nr U 2-day? Call 4 d-tails*.
Signed with a smiley-face. I had to intuit the rest of it: that
it probably was a message from Mackenzie; that it might
have to do with work; and that it should have been delivered to me a good while back, before all those other notices
were piled on top of it.

"Sunshine?" I walked toward the new secretary. She was
here on an interim position, if we were to believe the offi-
cial P.R. Helga, the office witch, was on indefinite sick
leave. Apparently, being found in flagrante delicto with the
headmaster had made Helga gravely ill. It had certainly
had that effect upon me.

Havermeyer's immune system—at least when it confronted his own offensiveness—was iron-clad. He was still
around, although since the day I discovered them, he badg-
ered me less often and seldom met my glance directly. I
hoped Helga had a record-breaking sexual harassment case
going, suing the pants off the man—much more fun, I'd
have to believe, than removing them for any other purpose—and that she'd make so much money, she'd never
return to Philly Prep to darken my days and hoard my supplies.

In the meantime, we had a sweet, though dim, replace-
ment for the Witch: Sunshine Horowitz. ("That's not my
real name," she'd trilled, making me think perhaps her
name was actually Sunshine Jones, "but it's what everybody's called me since I was a teensy-weensy baby!")

"Miz Pepper!" she chirped. At the end of her first student-
filled, undoubtedly chaotic day on the job, she didn't appear frayed or fatigued. "How can I help you?"

I was so unaccustomed to that kind of response from behind that desk, I was momentarily speechless. "This note?"
I finally said.

She glanced at it, then winked at me. "You like Sunshine-

Brand Shorthand? I invented it all on my lonesome, and it's real easy to read, and fun, right?"

I tried to strike a casual, nonthreatening pose, but there was no place to rest an elbow or forearm. Sunshine collected tiny metal animals, all polished to a blinding gleam and heavy on unicorns. She made her office "homey," she said, by lining them up on the center divide.

"Ah," I'd said upon first encountering them. "The *brass* menagerie. By Tennessee's cousin Pennsylvania, perhaps?"

Her eyes were the pale blue of empty sky, and my quip produced as much comprehension as a cloudless vista, despite her valiant smile. "States are related?" she asked. "Or is that some kind of joke?" Her smile remained wide and hopeful. Made me feel bad for confusing her.

"Some kind of bad joke," I'd said. "An English teacher sort of joke."

"Ahhh." She nodded and gave a conspiratorial wink. Obviously, lots of incomprehensible jokes and comments had been made in her company, but I wasn't going to add to them ever again if I could help it. She was too innocently, blankly happy, and it would be cruel, like hurting a kitten.

The cure for Sunshine's saccharine self was the memory of Helga scowling, refusing to allow me a new red pencil because it would deplete her stock of them. Sunshine didn't scowl. Not ever.

She was further confirmation of the wise saying "Be careful what you wish for." If anybody ever asked for further confirmation.

"There's no name on the message," I said.

"No?" She wrinkled her nose and put a fake pout on her face. "Why is that?"

I didn't think I was really supposed to come up with an answer.

"I know! I remember! I wasn't given a name, that's why!" And she giggled.

"Maybe you were given initials?" I asked quietly.

"Could be." She shrugged and smiled. I let it go and, instead, pointed at the time on the message. The call had come in an hour and a half ago.

Sunshine beamed that smile at me and nodded, proud, perhaps, to have written down what each line on the little form required.

"It says 'While You Were Out,' but I was here the entire time," I said.

"They come from the store with that already written on it," she said. "Should I have crossed it out?"

"No, no. I meant . . . the messengers—those children who are here during the day, one or two per hour?—it's sort of a tradition to have them carry messages. Bring messages up to the teachers. It doesn't interrupt class or anything, and sometimes messages can be urgent."

She looked as if I'd given her a gift. "Thank you!" she said. "I had no idea, but now I do! Thanks again. People here are so incredibly kind!"

I walked a few steps away and turned on my cell phone. Mackenzie had a class in an hour and was probably en route, but he also had a phone, so there was a chance he could explain what he'd meant—or what he'd actually said. And maybe after that, I'd try to help Sunshine understand that she had to include information even if she couldn't turn every word into a rebus puzzle.

"I told it all to that—who was that?" C.K. said.

"I suspected as much," I murmured.

"Except the client's address and name. Didn't want to entrust anything serious."

He's a wise man.

"The woman's a block from where you are. Other side of the square." He'd upped the tempo of his sentences. I imagined him checking his watch, driving faster. "If you could do the interview, get all the information she has, a photo if you can—and more important, get a sense why she wants it. I need a feel for her."

"Fine. What's it about?" I loved the unspoken words, that Mackenzie trusted me, was ready to rely on my take on the situation, and my evaluation of what I'd see and hear.

"Need to make sure this isn't a stalker case. She wasn't all that forthcoming."

"Hasn't she seen old movies? She's supposed to swagger in, sit on the edge of your desk, cross her legs, and spill her guts or con you."

"She's got physical problems. Incapable of swaggering."

I didn't want to break the collegial mood by suggesting that a physically challenged stalker was, possibly, an oxymoron, although the concept of a stalker on a walker was almost entertaining enough to make it a worthwhile risk. "Do you think she didn't want to meet up with you in person?"

"That's what you'll find out."

I liked everything about this. About us. And about a stalker who wouldn't leave home. Must be frustrating, to say the least.

"Name's Claire Fairchild," he said. "Wants a background check."

Even better.

"On her future daughter-in-law."

End of the investigative fantasy honeymoon. I was indignant on behalf of this unknown future daughter-in-law. The back of my neck heated in vicarious outrage as I imagined how I'd feel if I found out that Gabby Mackenzie had hired someone to check me out.

"You there?"

"Yes, but I hate the idea of—"

"Of not being objective? Of taking only clients whose interests and activities dovetail with our worldview?"

Nice of him to use the word *our* while he kindly reminded me that I'd vowed to be less judgmental and to understand that few investigators were nominated for the Nobel Prize, and that the Pennsylvania P.I.'s code of ethics doesn't include "refusing to work with people whose behavior doesn't appeal to you." For some reason, they'd also left *Honing to Amanda Pepper's Personal Sense of What Is Right* off the list of licensing prerequisites. A P.I. license was a business license, not a higher degree in philosophy.

I'm familiar with all of this because more than once we'd discussed my likely need to dismount my high horse. But it had been theoretical then, and mostly a joke.

"You have time for it?" Mackenzie asked with an edge of impatience. "Sorry to be rushed, but my class—"

Of course I agreed, and I scribbled down the woman's name and address.

After I hung up, I was still thinking about pros and cons and ethics and investigating your son's beloved, and my expression must have shown my disdain.

"Everything's all *right*, isn't it?" Sunshine asked. This time, her smile was small, filled with hope, but not quite ready to commit. I hated frightening her, casting a shadow on her golden world. I envisioned the landscape of her mind with Disney-style supernatural sunbeams crisscrossing one another and, on each, a bluebird, warbling.

"Everything's perfect," I said. "In fact, I just got some good news." The good news was: This mother-in-law from hell wasn't mine.

Three

I'D PASSED THIS SOLID OLD BUILDING COUNTLESS TIMES, and many of those times, I'd stopped to admire its concrete ornamentation—cornucopias and wreaths, stone grape clusters, bouquets of roses—an unabashed stony hosanna to abundance and pleasure.

This afternoon, I didn't pause for a long examination. It was still too hot to willingly dawdle outside. The air trembled and lay low, vibrating with hidden electrical charges in the dark clouds. But even if I hadn't been hoping there'd be air-conditioned relief inside, I was eager to see Mrs. Fairchild's home, having long speculated what the pre–WW II apartments looked like.

For starters, how lush to have the elevator stop at one's front door instead of open onto a long corridor. This was Claire Fairchild's floor, every parqueted inch of it, including the blue and ruby Oriental rug outside a door that looked newly lacquered with layers of a shimmering cream. The brass NO SMOKING plaque next to the buzzer seemed anachronistic in these lush, prewar surrounds.

When the cream door was opened, Mrs. Fairchild's condo proved one of the few things that turned out to be exactly as I'd fantasized it. High ceilings, carved crown moldings, mellow wood paneling, herringboned inlay floors with more jewel-toned Persian rugs. And that was only the foyer.

"Lovely," I couldn't help but say to the housekeeper,

even though I wasn't sure whether my private eyes were supposed to notice architectural niceties.

The housekeeper was the roundest woman I'd ever seen. She was tiny and apparently pregnant with someone huge, and her unborn child occupied all the space available from her chin to her thighs. "Mrs. Fairchild, she waits for you in living room," she said. "You see no smoke sign, yes? You wear perfume?"

It took a while to sort out her unmatched facts and questions. "I don't smoke, no," I said. "I do wear perfume, but I'm not wearing it now."

"Perfume make Mrs. Fairchild sick." She turned away from me.

I followed her, amazed she could walk this briskly, or, in fact, move at all. It looked as if it would be easier for her to roll.

I wondered if Claire Fairchild had environmental allergies, although this carpeted and draped home was anything but the stark-surfaced clean room I thought such sufferers required.

The living room's street-side wall was almost entirely tall French windows that, on a nicer day, would probably have been open onto a balcony edged with a filigreed, art deco railing. Despite the gunmetal light this afternoon, the room sparked and glowed with carved and polished surfaces.

And it was air-conditioned. I took a deep breath and relaxed into it.

A sandy-haired man in his forties wearing jeans and a plaid shirt sat in a wing chair near the French windows. He looked pleasantly worn out and faded, like much-used leather, but that could have been the light. Across from him, in a matching chair, a woman, shiny dark hair framing her face, smiled at me. She was more elegantly turned out than the man, dressed in a long-sleeved blouse with ruffled lace cuffs and collar, close-fitting black slacks, and soft boots, giving her the appearance of a nineteenth-century poet. I wondered if the two people had arrived together, as they looked as if they'd set out for separate destinations.

Only then did I notice the older woman in a chair turned away from me, toward the windows and the couple. She leaned sideways, nodding and smiling a welcome. I walked over and shook her hand.

Claire Fairchild was a delicately made white-haired woman in an ethereal blue dress that looked knitted of fibers so fine, they might sigh and melt away. Her earrings matched a long strand of pearls, and both echoed the tones of her hair, and she wore dainty, impractical blue shoes meant for a night on the town, dancing.

She seemed a suitable accessory for her environment's gracious elegance. The only discordant note in the entire room was the portable oxygen tank that stood at the ready next to her chair.

"Forgive me for not getting up," she said. "I save my air for talk. Hot day like this—tried to go outside . . ." She shook her head slowly side to side. "Delighted to . . ." She paused, deciding, too obviously, how to address and present me. ". . . see you again, Miss Pepper," she finally said. "I'd like you to meet my son, Leo."

The fair-haired man half-rose and put out his hand, which I shook. "Pleasure," he said rapidly, ducking his head in a shy bow. A man apparently not overly comfortable in social situations.

"And I'm Emmie," the girl dressed like a Romantic poet said. "Glad to meet you. I'm Leo's fiancée." She didn't seem to mind that no one had remembered to introduce her.

I shook her hand. "I'm Amanda," I said. "Glad to meet you." Her smile was so all-encompassing and warm, it felt like a hug of greeting.

"Sit," the housekeeper said, not unpleasantly, pointing at

a love seat across from Mrs. Fairchild, who, in turn, gestured at the table between us, which had a French press filled with coffee. "You can go now, Batya."

The housekeeper waddled out. Claire Fairchild redirected her attention to me. Her movements were slow, and she spoke with deliberation, possibly weighing how much breath any given word required. "Coffee?" she asked, and I nodded and watched her pour.

She passed me the cup. "My son and Emma—"

"Emmie," the young woman said softly.

"Emmie, then, came to tell me they've set a wedding date."

"Congratulations." I glanced again at the poet with the radiant smile, she who I was supposed to investigate. *Poor baby.* "I wish you all the best."

Silence followed. We all knew what was missing: an explanation for who I was and why I was there.

"Miss Pepper," Claire Fairchild said, "is my reader."

"Your what?" Her son's eyebrows and general level of interest both rose.

"Reader. You know how tired I can get. She suggested reading to me, so I could close my eyes and—"

Bad choice, I thought. Bad, bad choice. Hadn't she heard of books on tape? And why would she have hired a reader this afternoon when she didn't seem tired and was handling the coffee service without stress. She could hold a book if she could fill my coffee cup.

Nevertheless, I nodded and smiled agreement. Her son and future daughter-in-law returned my smile with visible reservations, and I didn't blame them.

"We met in the Square." Claire Fairchild gazed proudly at me as if I were a precocious child or a puppy she'd discovered.

"Have you two done this before?" Leo asked his mother.

"Many times."

"I never knew you had secrets," he said with a smile that

he probably intended to indicate humor, but didn't, quite.
"I never took you for a reader, least of all for someone who
loved it so much, you'd hire somebody to help with it. What
other secrets are you keeping behind our backs?"

I could have told him a whopper of one.

Mrs. Fairchild almost laughed, as if his words had been
funny, but ridiculous, but controlled the impulse, looking
as if laughing hurt her lungs. I considered what a sad lot in
life that would be.

"Is that your line of work, then, Miss Pepper?" Leo Fairchild asked. "You're a professional . . . reader?"

"Oh, no. Wish I could be, but it's simply auxiliary funds.
We, uh, met by chance, but it's a business of sorts. I adver-
tise in that local paper—the throwaway you get? Amazing
how many grown-ups still love to be read to." I was being
a bad liar, saying way too much, embellishing the lie in
ways that could be exposed.

"What a clever idea, though," the fiancée said. "And
what a luxurious, delicious way to spend an afternoon."

"Quite different, I think, from tape-recorded books," I
said. "This is personal." Even I didn't know what I meant.
I drank more coffee to keep me from more verbal nonsense.

"Then what else is it you said you do?" Leo Fairchild
was awkward, but smart, and not easily put off track. His
concern on behalf of his mother was obvious and sincere.

"I teach school, and you know how poorly teachers are
paid, and I like reading, so—"

"What is it you teach?" He'd seemed faded and pale
when I first saw him, but now I thought he'd simply been
withdrawn for some reason. Now, his forcefulness and will
were obvious. He even looked younger. He didn't trust me.
He probably thought I was here to scam his mother, and he
didn't care if I knew it.

"English." I try to lie by telling as much truth as possible.

"Where?" he demanded.

"Right—other side of the Square. Philly Prep."

"An English teacher! No wonder you like to read, then," the Poet said. "What a nice thing to do, too. Like having a friend visit, I'd think. You must love it, Mother Fairchild." She was going out of her way to put me at ease, and of the three of them, I liked her best so far, and realized I was building a grudge against the woman who wanted this sweet woman investigated. My client.

Leo stood up, and his bride-to-be followed suit. "I hope you don't think us rude to rush off," he said in a tone that suggested he really didn't care what I thought, "but we were about to leave right before you arrived, and given that you and Mother have this . . . well . . . appointment, we'll say good-bye now."

I wished them well again, and watched as they kissed the white-haired woman farewell. Nothing more was said until we heard the front door click.

"The coffee's still hot," Claire Fairchild then said. "You could use a refill." She leaned forward to pour me a cup.

"I could serve my—" I said.

"So can I," she said carefully, continuing to pour.

I studied her, and although she was paying attention to the coffee, I knew she was giving me the same careful dissection. "Sorry about that lame excuse," she said. "But you didn't seem to have any cover story of your own."

"I didn't know what to cover," I answered honestly. "I hadn't known I'd need to cover."

"But you did well, once you knew the situation. I like that. Your story about teaching—that was a clever thing to come up with on the spot. Do you think they believed it?"

"Not really."

"Not Leo," she agreed. "Such bad timing for them to show up this afternoon, of all times. Especially with that news. Sugar?"

I declined.

"Still, maybe good you saw them. Emphysema, if you're wondering what my problem is." She passed me the cup and saucer. "A muggy day like today . . . I get out of breath." She was quiet for a while, and I adjusted down to her rhythm of speech and waited in silence, as unnatural as that felt.

"I thought this disease was a big nothing when I was warned." Her breathing was audibly labored. She pulled hard and paused between sentences to refill her lungs. "I was wrong. It's a big something."

I was having coffee with a woman being slowly asphyxiated, and I didn't know how to respond. Yes, it was a big something, a huge, deadly something. But how could I say that without sounding fatuous? I nodded, and opened my mouth in the hopes that appropriate words would swim into it. They didn't, so I shut it again, hoping instead that my dropped jaw had not signified my stupidity, but instead, sympathy and horror on her behalf.

"I'm not dying, in case you think that."

"No. I . . . That's good . . . I'm glad." I wished I could rewind the tape and go back to standing outside her creamy front door. I wanted this first meeting not to count, as my students would put it. Second time through, I'd have a ready explanation for my presence, and wise words about bad lungs. And maybe even a handle on what I was doing here.

She sipped coffee, then put down the cup. "I expected a man," she said. "I spoke with a man." She sounded as if we'd pulled a fast one, swapping an inferior product for the real thing.

That didn't endear her to me, but I wasn't about to be sidetracked. I fired up my speech center again, and strengthened my backbone. "I work with Mr. Mackenzie," I said. "We're partners."

I was glad she had challenged me, because I get a kick saying things like that out loud.

The soft noise of her breathing filled the room while she decided whether I was telling the truth, and even if so, whether she found me acceptable. "I suppose you'll do," she finally said.

The incapacitated fragility, while real, barely covered a will of steel and a temperament to match it, and it was so forcible, I could almost see the metal shimmer through her skin, like an undercoat of armor.

She cleared her throat. It seemed a major production number. Then she spoke again. "The problem is, my son is getting married."

I was sorely tempted to ask whether her son also considered his impending marriage a problem. He certainly hadn't looked that way, taking his future bride's hand, speaking in the plural about leaving. But Claire Fairchild had hired us, so I used my mouth to sip coffee, not speak. Java in the mouth, in lieu of foot.

"Let me restate that. The problem is not the *idea* of marriage." She paused, breathed in and out, and continued. In a way, it was nice. There was time to consider each sentence already spoken, and to plan the following one. It made for efficient, thoughtful and, most of all, meaningful, communication—or should have. "The problem is his fiancée," she said.

I nodded, waited, then had to prompt her because she apparently considered that enough. "And why is she a problem?"

Claire Fairchild planted a blue-eyed permafrost stare on me. It was more efficient than the air-conditioning in lowering the temperature. "I don't know who she is. Appeared from nowhere. Nobody knows her."

I was appalled, but not entirely surprised. This was traditional Philadelphia, the city of Who Are Your Parents?

For the benefit of non-Philadelphians, the translation of Claire Fairchild's so-called problem would be: Nobody in Philadelphia—nobody in the right echelons of Philadelphia families—knew this woman's family. Therefore, nobody knew how to rank her, and nobody knew whether she could be given her social green card.

But that attitude was an infamous part of the Philadelphia of long ago, when your ancestry mattered more than who you yourself were. Do not ask for whom the Liberty Bell rang. Those people were tone deaf.

This was the twenty-first century. Claire Fairchild's words and attitude lowered her score on my estimation-o-meter. I worked at keeping my expression neutral, but I felt sorry for that sweet-faced woman in her deliberately Romantic clothing. She'd so obviously wanted to please.

"I know what you think." Ordinary words, but she made them so forceful, I almost believed those icy eyes had, in fact, penetrated my skull and seen my guilty ideas. "You think I'm a snob." Pause to breathe. "That I'm talking about social status."

"I wasn't—I didn't—" But of course, I was. I did.

"Understandable. I might have taken it that way myself."

I am a talkative woman, often too much so, and seldom tongue-tied, but the nearly palpable force field surrounding this woman had the power to freeze my lips together and to turn off the pilot light in my brain. I waited for her to clarify what she meant.

"I might have," she repeated, "but it would be ridiculous. I'm not that sort of woman."

When I didn't respond, she sighed. "I've never wanted for comfort," she said. "Not socialites, however. Not from a famous family. No pedigree. Leo made the real money."

I avoided her laser stare and kept my gaze on an invisible spot between her head and the wall behind her.

"You're surprised."

I was going to deny that, but then I wondered why I should.

"This place? It would have been beyond my means, but Leo bought it for me. Always kind to me, Leo. He takes good care of me." She sat regarding her patrician hands and long fingers before she spoke again. "Not good to leap to conclusions. I'm not the stereotype you've decided I am." She looked at me, the eyes still frostbitten, but a small, nontaxing smile on her face as well.

"I assure you—" I began.

She shook her head slightly and wagged her index finger, dismissing whatever protests I contemplated.

So she was a smart woman and she'd read my mind, and I'd been wrong. But in that case, I had a new and equally nasty motive for investigating that young woman. Claire Fairchild's son had made the big time, and the only woman in his life till now had been Mama, who wasn't ready to become the second-best woman in his life.

She sighed, as if she'd again read my mind. Time, then, to switch gears. Tackling straight-on questions and answers might dispel some of the tension. The room had become as charged as the storm-awaiting air outside. "Why don't we—"

"Are you clear on my motives?"

I looked at her directly. "To be honest, not at all. You told me what wasn't your reason for calling me in, but you haven't said what was, or what you do want."

"Because you jump to conclusions. Make assumptions." She lifted a hand and indicated the room, the world in which she lived. "It's not about money, either. . . . I have everything . . . more than I need."

"Good, then. But . . ." And I waited, finishing off the coffee.

She seemed hellbent on outlasting my silence, and she won.

"Why don't you tell me what this is about," I finally said. "Unless you really want me to read you a book."

"Seems nice, doesn't she?"

"Emmie? Very much so."

She nodded. "She is nice . . . always. . . . Leo's a brilliant mathematician and electrical engineer. Socially?" She shook her head. Her physical motions were minimal, energy saving, but her concern for her son was nonetheless clear. "Naïve . . . gullible . . . late-bloomer . . . an innocent in many ways."

I already knew that, simply by meeting them for a few minutes. I wanted her to get to the point. I had seen that Leo Fairchild wasn't Mr. Sophistication. What I hadn't seen was what was wrong with beautiful Emmie—or why Claire Fairchild was on the warpath. But people reveal themselves when they ramble, even when they require frequent pit stops for ingathering breath, so I stayed silent, professional, I hoped, and worked to maintain bland approval on my face. I wanted to register, not react, like movie P.I.s, which, along with mystery novels and a word or two from Mackenzie, comprised my training manuals.

"Why are you silent? Ask me things."

Maybe I was wrong. Maybe it was shrinks who weren't supposed to approve or disapprove of anything. Still, you wouldn't think somebody who could barely breathe could be so belligerent. "I did ask," I said. "You haven't answered."

"You think I'm a meddling old crone."

"Of course not! I—"

"Where's your handle on reality, girl?"

"What?"

"Pay attention! I *am* meddling."

I couldn't help a small smile. She was honest, I'll give her that. I admire self-awareness, even when what you're aware of is that you're dreadful.

She was a miserable troublemaker—and, yes, a major-league meddler—and I liked her, which was frightening.

"The problem is, I'm a chronically ill meddler," she said. "That's why I'm hiring you to meddle for me."

I no longer liked her, and I wasn't overly fond of me, either. I'd sold out to the enemy, was doing its dirty work. Was betraying my entire species: quaking fiancées facing malevolent mothers-in-law.

My emotions rode the seesaw, and I didn't know where they'd come down—except that on this first day back to school, I'd have to give myself an F for remaining professional and uninvolved.

Four

"OKAY," I FINALLY SAID, PULLING ON MY INVISIBLE
private-eye cloak that would make me tough and strong-
jawed. "What's up? Why am I here?"

Mrs. Fairchild raised her eyebrows.

"I'm not asking you a metaphysical question."

She grinned. In another setting, at another time, she
probably could be fun. But now, the grin flattened, and
vertical creases—canyons, really, they were so deep—
appeared between her eyebrows. Frowning was not a re-
cently acquired or unfamiliar expression. "I need to know
who she is." She leaned forward in her chair, examining me
as best as she could, and avoided the point yet again. "You
look too young for this kind of work."

It was a statement, not a question, so I let it ride. Besides,
I wasn't all that young. Thirty-two is old enough to have
this job. Any kind of job, in fact, except president of the
United States. But given that Mrs. Fairchild was treating
her fortysomething son as if he were a helpless, innocent
boy-child, it followed that she probably thought of me as
being in the late fetal stage. "A first question, then. What's
Emmie's full name?"

She raised her eyebrows this time. "When I introduced—
didn't I say?"

"She introduced herself, and only said 'Emmie.' "

"Well, then. That's part of the problem. You see?"

I did not. I tried to imagine how the nickname and/or the omitted last name could so offend this woman that she'd call in private investigators, especially since Leo had also been introduced with only a first name. Since the only theories I could envision involved more bigotry than I could manage, I stopped imagining.

"Cade," she finally said. She looked as if she was waiting for a reaction so she could spring. "Calls herself Cade."

Calls herself? As I called myself Pepper, and she, Fairchild? I ignored the slur and moved on. "I know she said *Emmie*, but is that officially Emma?"

She shrugged and simultaneously shook her head. A half-hearted body language "who knows anything at all?"

But we were discussing a first name, not something generally subject to interpretation and misconstruction. "Ms. Cade's name seems to distress you," I said. "Why is that?" I could have recited amazing names I have seen on the Philly Prep list of students, names that would highlight Emmie Cade's ordinariness. Offhand, I remembered students named for geographical sites including Morocco, Paris, and Verona, semiprecious gems (I was particularly fond of Lapis Lazuli O'Brien), climactic conditions including a Hurricane Waters, and Sirocco something or other; and one name that was not only odd but included punctuation: X-tra Stein. I always wanted to know the story behind the poor girl's naming, and I had to believe that despite the fancy spelling and having a dash of her own, the Steins were not overeoncerned with X-tra's self-esteem.

Mrs. Fairchild would have appreciated the names, but I wanted her to keep believing that my story of a day job teaching was a clever ruse and, in real life, I was her full-time investigator. She appeared to be a woman who would not be happy with someone who was not only female, but who had to stop sleuthing in order to grade spelling exams.

I cut to the chase. "What troubles you about her? What do you want us to look for?"

She lifted both hands, palms out, as if to defend herself. "Who is she? That's the trouble." She seemed eager to make herself clear no matter how many sentences and pauses it took. "That's what you have to find out. She's sweet. Friendly. Fine first impression."

Did I have to point out that I needed a problem, and she was giving me an endorsement?

Then, after another long pause: "But—out of nowhere."

And we were back to the starting line. I drained my coffee cup on that one because otherwise, I'd have had too much to say. The "nowhere" business grated on my nerves. Where was someone supposed to appear out of? Was it necessary to send trumpeters and heralds in advance? Courtiers to inform the court of where you've been, so it won't be labeled *nowhere*?

"Do you mean she's a recent newcomer to Philadelphia?" I finally asked.

"A year. Less."

That was the sin. Of course. An outlander. An alien. I could see the movie marquee now: *She Came from Somewhere Else!* Thousands of tiny Claire Fairchilds fleeing in horror.

"Rented a house in Villanova. Joined the cricket club. Charitable groups. Right circles right away. Met Leo at a party. Moved here, into this building. Engaged to my son."

"She lives here?"

She pointed her index finger upward. "Upstairs." She lifted her eyebrows. "She said the suburbs were no place to be single and childless."

Moving to Leo's mother's building, lovely and unique a place as it was, did seem a rather obvious positioning of the troops for the major assault.

Nonetheless, she was right about living as a single in the

suburbs. And even if she moved to the city so as to be more visible to Leo, so what? All's fair, they say, and so far, this newcomer sounded pleasantly—dully—ordinary. Maybe a little tawdry—a gold digger. But Claire Fairchild had said this wasn't about money. And in any case, while it might be more interesting for her to have put her energy into ending world hunger, if her goal was marriage to a wealthy man, then she'd demonstrated expertise and wisdom, and had been out front and honest about it. My mother would have revered her, wished she'd been her daughter, and before I had attached myself to my significantly unwealthy man— would have wanted me to make Emmie Cade my guru and life guide. Maybe I didn't want her as my new best friend, but, so far, she sounded as unworthy of investigation as it was possible to be.

Maybe we were having a semantic problem. I tried to fig- ure out what Claire Fairchild actually meant, to force out specifics about the *nowhere* business. "Has she told you where she lived before she moved here?"

"In her way."

"Meaning?"

Mrs. Fairchild required several deep breaths before continuing, and then her words were spaced with pauses. "Emmie talks. Chatters. Smiles. Answers. Laughs. Very merry. Open-seeming."

The significant word, apparently, was *seeming*.

This time, Claire Fairchild leaned over and lifted her cof- fee cup and sipped at what had to now be a lukewarm brew. She carefully returned the cup to the table before speaking, and I wondered if she had a repertoire of dis- tracting actions to take her listener's—and her own—mind off what a strain it was to keep up a conversation.

She looked at me directly. "Later, you realize, she didn't say anything."

"I think I understand."

She pursed her mouth, but decided to be clearer. "Where she grew up? She says . . . father was executive. Changed companies. Moved a lot. Lived in Atlanta."

Something tangible at last. "That's a start." I wrote it down.

"And Bridgeport. Austin. Fargo."

I looked up. Mrs. Fairchild's mouth had tightened. "Gotcha," she was saying, as if I were her enemy, as if we weren't supposedly working in tandem. "Chicago," she said. "Los Angeles. Cleveland." She tapped her index finger on the arm of the wing chair. "Many schools, too. Talk. More talk. Funny stories, but . . ."

"You mean that ultimately you realize she never mentioned what companies her father worked for?" I asked, hoping to spare Mrs. Fairchild a bit of air. "Or a specific school?"

She nodded. "Or dates. Or neighborhoods. Los Angeles!" Both of her hands rose and spread apart to show the daunting size of L.A., the meaninglessness of not being more specific about origins.

I thought about the beautiful woman in the poet's blouse, her graceful gestures, that flash of high-wattage smile, her free-flowing compliments about my supposed job. I could imagine her speaking at length and saying very little, but saying it in a warm and delicious manner. Was she accidentally or deliberately offering conversational cotton candy?

A woman could babble out of nervousness when confronted with the formidable Claire Fairchild. Or she could have a conversational style based on the idea that nothing about herself was all that interesting or important, so above all, she shouldn't bother listeners with specifics. Instead, she'd aim to entertain, amuse, and turn the conversation to other topics and other people. What, in fact, could be a more traditionally feminine philosophy than to feel that her purpose was to make the listener happy? Maybe she'd been taught to behave that way.

Nothing Claire Fairchild said necessarily triggered suspicion. I'd had friends—short-timers passing through Philadelphia—whose fathers worked for I.B.M., and they'd referred to the initials as standing for "I've been moved." Things might have changed by now, but that's how it was for a large segment of the nation's children, and for a long time.

Plus, I knew people who were congenitally vague, avoiding specifics as if they were tainted. They intended to be clear, they thought they'd been clear, but I nevertheless had to ask, "Do you mean . . . ?" Poor communication skills, not anything malicious.

"Did she say where she lived right before she moved here?" I asked.

"Near San Francisco."

I must have frowned, thinking what *near* might mean in researching a person's tracks.

"Yes," Claire Fairchild said. "Vague. I ask, 'where?' She says . . . 'Gosh! You know Indian Cliffs? Little town, a way out? I was near there.' Always places nobody's heard of."

I wondered whether Claire Fairchild had ever traveled, whether "places nobody's heard of" was accurate, or a reflection of a stay-at-home, unsophisticated woman. Not that I knew where any "Indian Cliffs" was in the Bay Area, either, but I was the perfect example of someone who hadn't—yet—gotten to travel.

"Then she talks about the baby deer by the front door, and the fox that ran by." She paused and bit at her bottom lip, remembering.

I nodded encouragement.

"The story's charming. And over. Nothing . . . definite. Ever." She looked up toward the scrolls on the crown molding and sighed. Then she looked at me, and her expression was solemn.

"So you called us." I still didn't get it. Emmie Cade sounded ditsy. Besides, one look at Claire Fairchild's unforgiving eyes, and a woman in love with her son had good reason to blur what might be a less than stellar, educated, or straight-and-narrow past. I'm sure I'm not the only adult female who has adventures and experiments in my past that I'd prefer be kept quietly away from prospective in-laws.

And there was the issue of how powerful Claire's hold was on her boy, how much her opinion would matter. As witness her having hired me.

"I could use more information," I said. "All I've got at this point is her name and a last address somewhere near San Francisco."

Claire Fairchild rolled her eyes. I had no idea why.

"For example," I asked, ignoring the theatrics, "has she mentioned a college?"

She shook her head. "Here's what I know: Her birthday is August first. Same as Leo's."

That was cute.

"Or so she says."

"And her age?"

A slow head shake this time. " 'Much younger than Leo!' she said. Seemed wrong to press her on it. On anything. Finally found out she's thirty. Widowed. College?" She shook her head in her abbreviated, energy-saving manner— one turn left, one turn right—and continued in her telegraphic stop-and-start manner. "Parents died. Small plane crash. No siblings."

Fortune was not smiling upon me. My first solo flight and I, too, were going to crash. So far, I had found no visible inroads to Emmie Cade's background. "Did you talk about the wedding?" I asked.

She looked miffed. An intrusion into her personal life, I suppose, as if inviting me here weren't precisely that. "They only announced it today. That's why they were here. I told you," she said with mild indignation. "*Two weeks* from now."

"So you said. Not much time. That's why I thought you might have discussed a guest list. Bridesmaids? Maid of honor? Out-of-town friends or—"

"Only the date. Small, of course. Tiny. No attendants I know of. No list."

I took a deep breath and considered. "Did she ever say what brought her to Philadelphia?"

Mrs. Fairchild was silent, considering. Then she shook her head. "Her friend, I think. Victoria. Nice girl."

"You've met her?"

She nodded. "Knew her before Emmie. Leo's friend. Knew Emmie back when. Bumped into each other again in San Francisco last year."

Good—an actual way to wiggle into Emmie Cade's past. "Do you remember Victoria's last name?"

"Baer, but Emmie sometimes calls her Smitty. Maiden name Smith, I guess. Victoria's divorced."

"You said school friend. Is Victoria Baer perhaps a college friend?"

She raised her shoulders in a gentle shrug. Her expression was worth a thousand words, or at least thirteen: *Did you expect anything more concrete than that? Didn't I say she's vague?* Then she returned to spoken language. "Emmie called her a school friend. But . . ." She sighed and lifted her shoulders, reverting to world-weary body language. "Emmie's vague about college. She quit, anyway. No degree."

Another easy source moved back into the shadows.

"Got sick, she says. That—whatever you call it. Students get it. My day, called 'the kissing disease.' " Her mouth curdled again. She knew how Emmie had contracted her illness.

"Mononucleosis," I said. "A virus." Not that it would be okay in Claire Fairchild's cosmos if her son's intended had gotten an illness that involved the transmission of bodily fluids.

"Didn't go back. Talks about getting a degree now. Why not? She doesn't work."

"You said she's widowed. Is her income from her dead husband?"

Claire Fairchild lowered her eyelids and almost subliminally raised her shoulders.

Maybe Victoria Baer would be less vague. Or at least tell me the name of her alma mater.

"That ring." Claire Fairchild tilted her head and nodded toward my hand on the arm of my chair. "Are you engaged?"

I nodded.

"Pretty."

"It was my fiancé's grandmother's." The small sapphire encircled by tiny diamonds didn't particularly look like an engagement ring, which was one of many reasons I loved it, but apparently Mrs. Fairchild was ever on alert for signs of impending matrimony.

"Will it affect your attitude?"

"Toward what?"

"My . . . this investigation."

"Why would it?" Though I'd never admit it, I knew the answer, and, I suspect, so did she. And the answer was yes, definitely—it already had prejudiced me against her. She'd notched up all the dreadful mother-in-law clichés by calling in auxiliary troops with which to persecute a girl. She'd have frightened and repulsed me even if I myself were not engaged.

"You know his parents?"

"I'm about to meet them. They live out of state." *They're going to appear out of nowhere,* I wanted to add, *and how about that?*

"Do they know you?"

She wasn't making sense. "As I said, we haven't met."

"Do they know normal things? Your name—"

"You know that about your son's fiancée."

She shook her head.

So that was the problem with the name. She didn't believe it was real.

Not that she said so. She aimed her iceberg eyes at me and said nothing.

"Mrs. Fairchild?"

She seemed to pull herself back from the far horizon. "I didn't decide to investigate out of the blue."

"Of course not." The velocity and emphasis with which I lied were improving with practice.

"But that's what you think."

My lies were fast and loud and failures.

"I don't do things like hire private investigators."

Need I mention what a rush that sentence gave me? Forget her imperial attitude. She believed I was what I said I was, even though I barely believed it. She'd handed me my credentials. I felt knighted by the queen.

"I don't care what you think."

The thrill was gone. "It's your dime, Mrs. Fairchild, but if I'm on the wrong track—or if you think I am—maybe you could be more helpful about rerouting me. More precise about why you decided to hire me—"

"I didn't."

"Us, then. Hire us."

She had a wide variety of lip-poses. This time, she pushed her chin forward and pulled her mouth tight, regarding me again with her freezing gaze.

I'd about had it, especially if *it* meant coffee, in which

case I'd had about too much of it. "While you're thinking," I said as I stood up, "could you direct me to a powder room?"

She pointed toward the entry and to the right. Even though I'd asked to leave the room, I felt dismissed.

The apartment was spacious, with a hall leading off the entry. I passed a full dining room, its long table ready to seat ten, and then I saw the door she'd mentioned and opened it.

Except she hadn't meant this door, because I found myself in a narrow room lined to its high ceiling with shelves heavy with china and glasses on one side, and boxes and bags of rice and grains on the other. Traditionally, a butler's pantry, I believed, but at the moment, a housekeeper's refuge. I'd nearly tripped over Batya, the super-pregnant dumpling, who sat on a low step stool, crying.

She looked up at me, a tissue pressed to her nose, her eyes swollen and red-rimmed.

"I'm sorry," I said. "I thought this was the—" What did it matter what I'd thought?

Batya clutched her belly and looked away.

"Are you all right?"

She flashed a bitter look at me. Okay, it had been a stupid question. People who are all right don't huddle, crying, in a butler's pantry. "Is it—is everything okay about the baby?"

She looked down at her pregnant belly, as if surprised by it. "Yes, why . . ." She shook her head and retreated into herself again.

We were in a social situation that might be described as awkward. Having intruded, discretion—backing off and making an exit—seemed polite. It also seemed inhumane. Was I to behave as if I'd noticed nothing? "Can I do something for you?" I asked.

She shook her head back and forth, vigorously. "No," she whispered. "No. Please. I handle this."

I heard fear, but also a real plea for me to leave her alone. "Okay, I'll—"

She put up a hand. "Wait—please, miss—don't say to Mrs. Fairchild."

"Say that I—" I didn't know how to finish that sentence. Somehow mentioning out loud that she was crying in the butler's pantry made it worse. "—saw you?"

"Yes. You did not see me, yes? Please, is important."

"Sure," I said after a pause. "But are you positive there isn't something I could do?"

"Nobody can help me. Nobody on the earth."

"I could try." I knew I should back out of that pantry and remove this scene from my mind. This really was none of my business. Or was it—in the way it was everybody's business? There are no parables of the Half-Assed Samaritan who asked politely, then backed off.

"If you say to her I tell you anything, it makes worse. That you saw me cry? That makes worse." She drilled her words into my skull with her eyes and intensity. "*She* makes worse."

She. My client. She who gets upset about women's names and intimidates the investigator she hired.

"Two years I work for her," Batya said softly. "Two years, day and night. I live here. She says, 'Batya you are best. Stay with me.' My aunt, she watches my baby."

My surprise must have shown, because Batya's baby was inescapably, hugely here.

"Other baby," she said. "He is two years, but he needs medicine." She shook her head, as if forbidding that child's sickness to be true. "I see him Sunday only. She feeds me, gives me room, I buy his medicine, but . . ." She grimaced and shook her head.

"Money?" I whispered. "She pays you, doesn't she?"

She didn't look at me now. She shrugged, and looked away, and I had to lean close to hear her say, "Not so I can live somewhere else. Not so I can live with him. She say that is all she can pay. She is widow on—how you say— always the same money."

"A fixed income?"

"Fixed. Yes. She says someday, when she dies, she is leaving me money. Is all big lie. Mr. Leo, he's rich. He gives her everything. She gives me nothing."

I looked at her, an eggplant-shaped woman, face wet with tears. "And now this," I said softly. "Are you crying because of this baby?"

She looked up at me and sniffled. "For both babies. I ask Mrs. Fairchild for more money. Only what other people get. Is fair, what I ask. I work hard for her. I cook, shop, clean, help with the sickness. I take good care." She put her hands protectively around her belly.

I thought of how many positions there were like this one, how many ill and elderly people could have used Batya's services. It would be easy enough for her to quit, to find a new job or accept public assistance. Unless . . . "Are you a legal alien, Batya? Do you have a green card?"

She looked up at me, her mouth open and her eyes wide and wild. Her worst fears had been realized.

"I'm not going to tell anybody. I wanted to know what she . . . Is that it?" The threat of deportation is a powerful form of blackmail and, apparently, of keeping virtual slaves from fleeing.

"My husband left. Disappeared. Mrs. Fairchild, she says it doesn't matter. Is my fault." She clutched her belly and rocked.

"Don't panic," I said. "Let me find out what can be done. Just take care of yourself and your baby and don't panic— and I won't say a word to Mrs. Fairchild."

"Or to—"

"To anybody. I promise."

"But she—she—" She shook her head and was silent.

I tiptoed out, the echo of that *she* hissing through my brain.

Five

WHEN I RETURNED TO THE LIVING ROOM, CLAIRE FAIRchild looked as if she'd fallen asleep. I stood near the entry and cleared my throat by way of announcement. Her eyes opened and she adjusted her torso to a more upright position. I suspected that once, before parts of her went bad, she'd had ramrod posture.

"Don't sit down," she said.

Fired? Like that? I formulated a protest, feeling as humiliated as the frightened housekeeper had been, except my emotions immediately steamed and mutated into anger. Enough of this woman's imperial attitude!

"The desk." She pointed. "Bottom drawer."

As almost always, I was glad I'd held my temper. I didn't hear arrogance in her voice. I heard exhaustion. It had probably been a busier than normal day already, with her son's visit and, as added psychic strain, his announcement of a wedding date to a woman she wanted investigated. Me. And, from the appearance of it, earlier on, a confrontation with her housekeeper.

I went to the small desk—what was called a *lady's* desk because it's easier to say *lady's* than *useless, undersized, and intended for trivial, inconsequential tasks*. It was narrow and delicately formed of pale wood inlay. I opened the lower of its two shallow drawers.

"On top," she said. I extracted a plain manila envelope

CLAIRE AND PRESENT DANGER

and held it up. She lowered her head in a nod of acknowledgment, then, wiggling her index finger again, indicated
that I should bring it over.

I handed it to her and sat down on my assigned love seat.

"I thought I was being too . . . careful . . . putting it
there. He drops over. Lucky today."

So there was more to this than a snit about inadequate
story-telling skills, and we were finally getting to the point.

She slowly unclipped the envelope and extracted sheets
of paper and photographs, all of which she let sit on her
lap. "I worried," she said. "Not right, how she says nothing. How determined she is. Moving here. But I called because of this." She checked one of the papers on her lap,
then passed it to me.

The top of the page was dominated by a drawing of a
skinny-necked insect with huge eyes and saw-edged front
legs, an unreal creature from an inept science-fiction film.
Below was a message written in a collage of different-sized
print from what looked like newspapers and magazines. I
had the sense of being back in an old movie. Given computers and clip art, nobody had to cut up newspapers to remain anonymous. This was the *Antiques Roadshow* of
crime. I read the message:

> the PRAYING man TIS! lookS devout but LOOKS lie!
> sHE eats its mate when sex is done.

"Did this come in the mail?"

She nodded.

"Do you have the envelope?"

She shook her head and frowned. At herself this time, I
trusted. "I remember. From New Jersey, somewhere."

"You couldn't have known," I said, wondering why I
was trying to spare her feelings. "In any case, this could

mean anything, about anybody or nobody. Most likely, it's a prank. I don't think it should worry you. Somebody plucked your name from the phone book—"

"Not listed."

"You know what I mean. Somebody found your name and address. For starters, it's on the wall downstairs, next to the buzzers. This isn't necessarily anything, and its meaning—it doesn't make sense."

"Then this came." She passed a second sheet that was again crudely fashioned out of snippets of print, some words pasted on letter by letter. Letters were clipped from shiny magazine stock, others from newspaper headlines or advertisements.

Would not YOU Feel More InFORMed IF! you Could read THE Independent Journal?

I looked up at Mrs. Fairchild. "Sent from Altoona," she said. "I remember."

"What's it mean? What's this *Journal*? The sender doesn't sound bright, to put it mildly."

She shook her head and passed me a third page that had only a date, about fifteen months ago. "From Chicago." The envelope was clipped to a page dominated by an illustration of a praying mantis.

It made me sad that the detailed drawing had been hacked out of a library or textbook, just for the sake of this ill-intended mailing. I knew that defacing books was not the problem I was supposed to be considering, but all the same . . .

The message read:

PRAY NOW! Don't wait UNTIL It's TOO late & YOU are tHE prey!

I was ashamed of myself for noticing—and worse, being pleased by—the fact that we were dealing with a literate crank, because *it's* and *too* were properly spelled. I guess you can take the English teacher out of the classroom, but et cetera. "Is this the end of it?" I asked.

She shook her head. "Six so far. Every three–four days."

"Since . . . ?"

"Last two weeks." She passed me the fourth:

Nothing is free xcept some murderers.

Dollar signs of various sizes dotted the page, and the name *Independent Journal* was repeated, accompanied by a date.

"Mailed from Baltimore," Mrs. Fairchild said.

"Did you check out that newspaper? Find out where it is?"

"Went to library." She made a small gesture toward the window. I understood. She meant the library snuggled at the edge of the Square. She could walk there, though judging her strength, it would occupy the major part of the day. "Batya helped me."

"Does she know about the threats, then?"

"Batya knows everything. I can't do . . ." She sighed. "Batya knows."

Then pay her a living wage, I wanted to shout. Stop blackmailing her, threatening to have her deported.

"Librarian found the paper. Outside San Francisco."

Where Emmie Cade last lived.

"Librarian said it has no . . ." Her brow wrinkled as she tried to remember something. "Archives!" She nodded. "No online archives." Her voice was weak, and she paused more often, but seemed determined to get everything out and onto the table. "But—"

I thought I knew what she wanted to say. "They have them on file, and we can request articles."

She nodded. "You'll find them."

That seemed an easy-enough task. "Did you report these notes to the police?"

"What would I say?" I had put the pages on the small table beside the love seat, and she glanced at them. "Looks like kid stuff." She stopped and breathed quietly, silently, for a minute, her eyes lowered. Then she looked up at me. "Wouldn't have called you, except . . ." For the first time, she seemed unsure of herself.

"There's more, isn't there?"

Her face contorted, and she looked near tears as she handed me another page with a copy of the newspaper article the earlier mailing had referred to.

To my surprise, the article had nothing to do with Emma Cade. "Who is Stacy?" I asked, because that was the name below a blurred picture—a copy-machine copy of a mediocre newspaper photo.

"Emmie. Stacy. King. Cade. Who knows what else?"

I looked at the shot of a woman, a mourner obviously taken by surprise. Her face was misted behind a veil, and one arm blurred as it rose to shield part of her face. She wore black. Only a brooch—a twisted, abstract outline of a heart—broke its severity. The woman was identified as Stacy King, widow of noted sailor Jake King.

The text was unsettling. It managed to make clear, in oblique and nonlitigious ways, the confusion and suspicion surrounding Jake King's death. Apparently, he'd been everybody's favorite regular rich guy. He'd been a dot-com entrepreneur when the going was good, smart enough to pull out reams of money in time. But being a land animal was only his day job. His soul lived on the water. Many fellow members of his yacht club were quoted as being incredulous that he'd had any accident, let alone a fatal one.

According to them, Jake was practically drown-proof. He'd been exceptional, an avid sailboat racer and all-around expert seafarer, and nobody could understand why, on a calm spring day, he'd pitched over the side of his boat, half naked, not wearing the life vest he always wore, and drowned.

"It was the heat," the widow was quoted as saying. "The wine. I warned him, but he loved fine wines, and it was his party." Her take on the accident sounded weak and unconvincing.

"Jake was lots of things, but not a reckless sailor," his ex-wife, Geraldine Fiori King, also an expert sailor, was quoted. The article semi-obliquely referred to a long and nasty divorce that followed Jake King's meeting the lovely young Stacy. "He respected the ocean and bay," the first Mrs. King said, "and the only time he took his vest off— well . . . you know . . . let's say to go to sleep, okay?"

An investigation was underway. I thought of the lithe young poet-woman I'd seen within the hour. "Are you positive this story and this Stacy has anything to do with your son's fiancée?"

She passed over the two photos she'd earlier pulled out of the manila envelope. One showed two young women, smiling into the sun. One, in a broad-brimmed hat trimmed with daisies, wore a halter top and a softly patterned long skirt that showed the outline of her legs through its translucent material. Her feet were bare. The hat was good for her skin, but bad for recognition purposes, as it shadowed her features. Her companion held her hand up as a visor, almost as if she were saluting the photographer. She wore a man-tailored shirt, sleeves rolled up, and tails tucked into a pair of belted, tailored slacks and deck shoes. She reminded me of my sister and all my sister's friends.

"That's her, too. This past summer. The halter girl. The other is a proof."

"The other woman? Proof of what?"

She shook her head.

I understood. Not the other girl, but the other photo, and not evidence of anything, but a photographer's proof.

"Leo thought maybe an engagement announcement." She took a few slow breaths before starting again. "She didn't like any of the shots. So, nothing in the paper, but . . . I still have proofs. Must return." Finally, a clear image of the young woman I'd met today. Emmie Cade, a.k.a. Stacy King. I didn't know why she hadn't liked the portrait unless she truly didn't want a clear image of herself anywhere. The photographer had captured her delicate beauty and the exceptionally warm smile. She didn't look as if she were posing. She didn't look capable of artifice of any sort. Instead, she looked as if she were transparent and the viewer had a view straight into her pure heart, catching her in a moment of joy.

I would have pressed my case that this woman wasn't related to the one in the news story, except that Emmie Cade wore the identical, unusual brooch of metal that had been hammered and twisted into a semiabstract image of a heart.

"You know," I said, "despite whatever initial confusion there was at the time of that news story, and despite these anonymous messages, the law found her innocent or she wouldn't be here. This feels like maliciousness. Somebody who's furious that she's finding happiness again. Or somebody without any real reason, just a desire to make trouble."

"I hope so." She looked at me, head slightly tilted, challenging me to say she was lying. Oddly, I believed her. I couldn't remember anyone else about whom I'd had such a mix of positive and negative emotions, all at the same time.

"That's why Leo isn't to know about this," she said.

"What if—they're probably just an evil-minded prank, but if there's any real threat—"

"Not till he's married, I think. No point before. No money till then."

"And that marriage is taking place in two weeks?"

"I can't let it. Not until you"—she gestured toward the pages—"What I'll do is get sick. Today. Near death. Delay wedding until you . . ." She squinted at me, as if close-reading my expression. "I'm pretending sickness," she said. "I look worse than I am," she said. "People think—they'll believe, but I'll be around for years."

"Of course." If force of will had anything to do with longevity, she'd outlast me.

"When we know what's true, I'll recover. Up to you."

I nodded, painfully aware of how many people's happiness, and perhaps lives, now depended on my nonexistent investigative expertise.

"Until then . . ." She put her finger to her mouth.

She was being remarkably considerate. She was suspicious with cause and worried on behalf of her son, but unwilling to taint his relationships—with his fiancée and with her—with her fears.

"He's happy," she whispered, underlining and emphasizing my thoughts.

She was a complicated woman: a considerate and worried parent, a meddling, autocratic harridan; a woman with a sly wit and an imperious attitude, Batya's inhuman slave-keeper. All of the above and who knew how much else?

Her daughter-in-law-to-be was all charm and grace, mildly ditsy and vague and/or a conniving gold digger and murderer. So far.

This wasn't what I wanted. When I read fiction, I wanted characters as complicated as they are in real life. In real life, however, particularly in this real-life new job, I wanted no ambiguity. I wanted a comic book world, with 100 percent bad villains and my good guys spotless. And while I was at it, I wanted X-ray vision and the knowledge, flat out, whether to like or trust somebody or not.

I put the studio portrait of Emmie Cade into my briefcase along with the anonymous notes. I paused as I added the snapshot of the two women smiling into the sun. "Do you know who the second woman is in this picture?"

"Victoria. Victoria Baer."

"Does she live in the city?" I would have staked my day's income that she did not. Given that Emmie's first rental was in Villanova, my bet was that her one friend in the area lived nearby in the suburbs. Besides, she looked Main Line. She had that classic look, so understated as to be barely audible, reflecting the utter fear of flashiness or trend-following.

She looked like my sister Beth's wardrobe.

"Bryn Mawr," Claire Fairchild said.

I'd find Victoria Smith Baer in a flash. Even though she and Emmie Cade would be younger than Beth, I was willing to bet I'd get a leg up via the suburban matron's six degrees of separation. The hardest boiled gumshoes relied on confidantes, pipelines, and snitches. Those are guy words for gossips. I knew gossips.

"Then that's it for now." I briefly outlined whatever I could think of as to when we'd report back to her, and while I spoke, I tidied the pages she'd given me and the photographs. She passed me the manila envelope and I was ready to refill it when I remembered something. "Didn't you say you've received half a dozen of these notes?"

She nodded.

"I have five." I recounted to be sure.

She pulled back in surprised confusion and shook her head.

I looked around and didn't see any more pages. Then I looked inside the manila envelope and saw it. "It got itself stuck."

She watched as I pulled it out, then put her hand to her mouth and nodded.

This page was different, red construction paper, onto which black bold oversized letters spelled out:

AND THERE'S MORE DEAD!!!!!

That was all. The letters looked clipped from happy ads. This one got to me viscerally. I looked up and was startled to see a smirk on Claire Fairchild's face.

"Hate that, don't you?" she said.

"What's that?"

"Having to change your mind." She squinched up her mouth, but couldn't control the slightly malevolent grin.

"About what?"

"Witches and crones and meddlers. Evil mothers-in-law."

"I have no idea what you're talking about, ma'am." I stood up. "I'll let myself out." I didn't want to summon the sobbing Batya.

Mrs. Fairchild's moment of triumph passed along with the mild smirk. She looked more delicate than ever and she'd aged during the visit. "I'm afraid," she whispered. "Afraid of what that means. That there's more dead. Is that in the past or—"

"Please try not to worry," I said as I made my exit. "From now on, we'll take care of this."

I could say that—and almost believe that—because at the time, I had no idea of what any of this meant.

Six

Back outside Mrs. Fairchild's building, bidding adieu to the ornate scrolls, cryptic gargoyles, and the vaguely antebellum swirls of balcony rails, I understood that I wasn't going to be the next centerfold for the Sleuth-of-the-Month Club.

Other than that, I knew nothing. Hadn't a clue. Literally.

I walked toward the office in a deep funk. This wasn't what I'd anticipated. All summer long I'd worked under Mackenzie's supervision, and had done well, he said. But this was my true maiden voyage, my test flight. I'd expected to interview the client and leave bursting with ideas as to what to do next, but at the moment, all I drew was a blank.

Background searches can be routine, and I'm sure that's what C.K. thought this one would be. Unfortuately, that assumes the investigator has a few salient facts about the person being investigated—beginning, perhaps, with her actual name.

Instead, I'd been given a blank wall and told to read the writing on it, and in this case, the moving finger had moved on so quickly, not even fingerprints were left.

Maybe being a private eye, even a part-time one, wasn't such a hot idea. Much as I loathed the idea of admitting my incompetence, much as I loved the idea of our partnership, push had now come to shove, and look who was falling down. Perhaps it was time to restrict myself to dangling participles and pronoun case. It was possible my mission on earth was not solving crimes, but disabusing people from saying, "He invited John and myself." Or, "Between you and I."

Surely preserving the Mother Tongue was as important a public service as doing background checks.

On the other hand, we needed additional income, and pronoun usage wasn't going to generate it. The question remained: How could I track this creature of murky past, floating names, vague antecedents, no relatives, and no known jobs or schools? And how to do it subtly so her fiancé is never made aware of my investigation?

I stopped, mid-Square, and considered what I did have.

A birth date, August 1, thirty years ago. If, in fact, I believed that cute coincidence that she'd been born on the same day as Leo.

I didn't have her Social Security number, nor did I have her last address, but I could get a place-name, now. Surely a town would be named somewhere in the records of Jake King's death, and I could work from there.

I had a news story, a possibly fake birth date, and a studio photograph. What I didn't have was an idea of how best to proceed. I wasn't eager to ask Ozzie, who was gruff at best, if he'd deign to speak to me, nor did it seem adult to go home and await Mackenzie's wisdom like a pitiable, helpless flower of a girl—the hothouse variety that isn't native to Philadelphia.

"You all right, young woman?"

Bad sign when the person offering to help you is a bent-over old woman at least fifty years your senior. "You look dazed," she said, her gray eyes circled by worry-wrinkles. "Something hurting? You need a doctor?"

I assured her I was fine, thanked her, took a deep breath, and reminded myself that I had resources. I had my brains

and, for once and probably the last time till June, I didn't
have a paper to mark or a lesson to prepare. That's about
as free as this woman gets.

I passed Philly Prep across the way and thought about
the abominable Sunshine and her ability to look on the
bright side even when there wasn't one. Hard as it was to
swallow, I had to be more like her and focus on the posi-
tives.

I had the name of Emmie's local friend and former class-
mate and she most likely could give me a lead into Emmie's
origins. Where she'd gone to school at some point. Her actual maiden name. And I had the newspaper story, the
newspaper's archives. If the death of Jake King was as big
a mystery as that article made it out to be, there'd be other
stories, more information, especially about the widow. A
coroner's inquest. Perhaps a trial.

For now, I'd assume that after all the fuss over Jake
King's death, Emmie had opted to take back her maiden
name. That didn't explain the Stacy-Emmie switch, but I
didn't need her first name for the Social Security death
index. I was looking for her father's name, and Cade didn't
seem that common a surname.

I wasn't down for the count yet. By the time I reached the
office, I was reinvigorated. I needed to be, because Ozzie
Bright—whose name did not reflect truth in advertising—
was never overjoyed to see me, and was always less than
helpful. He'd welcomed Mackenzie, on any basis, because
Mackenzie could walk and chew gum at the same time,
plus, he understood computers. Ozzie could make neither
of these claims.

He wasn't a misogynist; he was more of what was called
"a guy's guy," comfortable working with men. I'm sure
that in his secret heart, he referred to me as "that dame."
And dames had no place in his office, except as clients.

Ozzie was tolerated, however—more than tolerated, accepted fully, and recommended by his former associates on the force—because while he was still wearing a uniform, he'd suffered an "unfortunate accident," the details of which were never discussed, except that they involved a weapon and a never-to-be-disclosed part of his anatomy. The silence surrounding Ozzie's condition was a prime example of male bonding, but a female couldn't help but notice that whenever it was obliquely referred to, all the men in the room murmured, "Poor bastard."

His cranky and stubborn ways, his frustration and ineptitude with electronics, the basic tool of today's private investigator—all that was greeted with the slow, sad shake of the head and an almost saintly level of tolerance. I didn't expect much of Ozzie, except that he'd let me do my thing without interference.

Which is what I did. "I'm only here for"—I checked my watch and estimated the time I had between now, the party at my former neighbor's, and arrival at the Bellevue—"a half hour," I told him. He didn't bother to hide his relief.

Not everyone's listed on the Social Security death lists. Some people belonged to private pension plans, a group that included lots of teachers, in fact. But it was highly probable that a corporate executive—if Emmie Cade had been telling the truth about that—would have paid in.

I looked up Cade.

First big surprise: There were over two thousand. I suppose that did, in fact, mean it wasn't an overly common last name, but the numbers were nonetheless daunting. Still, I hoped that among all those names, I'd narrow it down to logical dates and find the woman and man with the same place and date of death. Her parents, my plane-crash victims.

The list was alphabetical. I had to pick a letter and click on it, which meant I couldn't do a visual check through the alphabet, and I couldn't retain whole lists in my head wait-

ing to find a date-mate elsewhere. Ninety-five names and I
was still in the A's.

Two hundred and still counting and I was still in the B's.
This wasn't a great plan.

Maybe Emmie was named for one of her parents. Six
hundred names in, I reached names starting with "Em."
Emmas and Emmetts, Emmers and Emogenes, Emersons
and Emorys.

This was no help.

I realized at some point that Mrs. Cade—still assuming
that was Emmie/Stacey's actual maiden name—might have
been a schoolteacher, or unemployed and not on the list
at all.

For too long, I nonetheless doggedly continued, eliminat-
ing Cades who'd died before the seventies—before they'd
have had a chance to father Emmie. And then, I realized I
was still looking at too wide a selection, since if she'd
moved around through high school on her father's corporate track, that meant he had to have lived into her teens. I
pushed my cut-date into the mid-1980s.

If I lucked into a set of names, I'd know where they died,
and when, and I could check a local newspaper. A plane
crash would make the news, or there'd be at least an obit-
uary, but I had to be lucky. Some entries didn't even list a
last residence or place of final benefits.

I was not lucky. I wound up out of time, with only a
headache.

I quickly packed my things, and bid adieu to Ozzie, who
grunted back. Feeling ever more frayed and sweaty, wilting
in the oppressive humidity, I made my way through the
streets, up to my former neighborhood. I was struck by a
tidal wave of nostalgia for the row of tiny homes on the
narrow cobbled street. Nothing much had changed since
I'd moved. In fact, nothing much had changed since Benja-
min Franklin probably rode a horse down this street.

My old house had been rebuilt, maintaining its Colonial façade. It looked to be in the hands of loving tenants, with its cherry-red window box overflowing with geraniums. The hitching post on the curb had been painted to match the flower box and the front door.

The street was still too narrow for easy passage of cars, impossible for parking. All was as it always had been: houses intended for servants, people who walked, not for cars, which had to be parked on a more modern street or rented garage.

There it was in all its glory. Cute, photogenic, inconvenient, and cramped—and I really missed it and all the people who'd been my neighbors.

I entered the crowded home of my friend Nancy Russell and her mother, a woman whose first name, as far as I could tell, was *Mrs.* I had never called her anything else, except behind her back, when she was *Old Mrs. Russell* or *Nasty Old Mrs. Russell.* Or worse.

She has been a longtime burden for Nancy, who, luckily, has a strong back and a sufficiently strong income to hire caretakers much of the time.

In all her ninety years, Mrs. Russell has never had time for most of humanity or even for domestic animals. She believes both species scheme behind her back and exist only to spread disease and plan her downfall.

Except for my cat, Macavity. She adores him and believes him the exception to all her rules. Until she grew truly enfeebled, she was—at her request—the proprietor of Old Mrs. Russell's Cat Camp for Macavity Pepper.

I would have brought him were it not for this crazy day's schedule, I explained to both Nancy and her mother. Given that Mrs. Russell is deaf and refuses to wear her hearing aid, explaining anything to her is strenuous. Aside from arthritic knees and hips that now kept her in a wheelchair, and the hearing loss, she was still forceful, emphatic, and tyrannical, and she made it clear that if it didn't involve Macavity, she wasn't overexcited about my presence.

I gave her the Pavarotti CDs. She'd put on her hearing aids for him. I knew she adored him, and I knew she wouldn't admit it. And then I made my way through the crowd.

In truth, I, and probably everyone there, had stopped off en route to our real lives on behalf of Nancy, not her mother. We were here to salute and celebrate her dutifulness and goodness of heart. And also, to secretly, or at least privately, commiserate. Her mother had been a mean-spirited dictator her entire life, and had only moved in with—or on—Nancy when her health was, in theory, failing. But that had been fifteen long years ago. Apparently, Old Mrs. was going for the longevity gold.

It was fun to catch up with local gossip about squabbles among my former and new neighbors. As always, wars began over anything, from one homeowner's decision to paint his shutters screaming chartreuse to a raid on another's illegal backyard crop. The people who'd bought the house I'd once rented had paid a fortune, Harvey Weiss said, escalating everybody's real estate appraisals and taxes. Nobody paid him much heed, not even his petite, preternaturally calm wife, who, as always, stood beside him, rolling her eyes at his utterances and saying nothing except, "Oh, Harvey."

"But the thing is," Carlie Hopper added, "they turned it into a showplace. Every nook and cranny just so, with the right hue of paint—they used color consultants—and the perfect piece of furniture. And the day the last accent piece was put in place, they split up."

All this and more was presented like an ongoing chorale—the neighborhood news vendors, cranks, complainers, and gigglers singing their predictable parts. Carlie Hopper found the marijuana bust the funniest thing, while Harvey Weiss found it further proof of the decline of Western Civilization as he did the very idea of chartreuse shutters. His wife rolled her eyes. "Oh, Harvey," she murmured.

Nothing much had changed. Everything set off Harvey, especially me. When you live on the same block as an obsessive-compulsive who thinks the world's already too messy, and who also is slightly paranoid and in love with conspiracy theories, and then your house explodes, you've definitely crossed his bottom line. Not that it was my fault—no chemistry sets in my basement—but that didn't matter. I'd made a mess on his street, and worse, I'd picked up my cat and left the mess behind.

I smiled and listened, learning that Peggy O'Neil's fifth-grade daughter was now bald because she'd wanted to bleach her hair but, not quite getting the concept, had used laundry bleach.

A young man at the other end of the block—this was told sotto voce and we all leaned close—had pierced places you didn't even want to think about, but which he, most definitely, wanted to discuss.

Someone's son had gone off to study hideous contagious diseases in Africa, causing everyone to shudder at the dangers he faced. Harvey, of course, demanded that he be quarantined far from the street before he was allowed back on it. "No telling what he'll be carrying on him, or in him," he said with customary emphasis.

"Oh, Harvey," his wife said. I wish for once she'd say what she meant by that, because I really couldn't tell, which, of course, was her intent. Was she expressing awe or disdain? Was the end of the sentence really "—get lost!" or variations thereof? Was she asking him to pipe down, or praising his worldview?

"Amanda, you didn't hear the news, did you?"

The speaker was Pris Shoemaker, an astoundingly dull drama queen I tried to avoid because that's the way she spoke. You could almost hear kettledrums in her background, insisting that she carried dire news. And she didn't want to lessen the impact of her message by actually saying it. Instead, you had to do the Pris Shoemaker dance.

"Hear what?" I was supposed to say.

"I nearly fainted when I heard," she'd then say.

"Heard what?" I'd say . . . and so forth and so on ad nauseam.

She delighted in, wallowed in, the shock and degree of emotion she could produce—even if it turned out to be irritation and anger. I vowed to show no emotion now, no matter her news.

But this time, she was among people who knew her style, so the woman next to her jumped in and said, "About Lily? She's—"

Pris rushed to the point without requiring prompts. "—in the hospital. She"—Pris lowered her voice, although everyone else in the circle already knew what she would say—"tried to kill herself."

"Oh, no!" The rocket of feeling that shot through me negated any promise to show no emotions. I adored the appealing Lily. She looked like one of those girls who grow up to be supermodels, the girls nobody believes were ever less than stunning. Right now, aside from the dark-rimmed glasses she always wore, she was all arms, elbows, and wild auburn curls. Someday she'd be willowy. Right now, she was skinny. And funny, and smart in school. What on earth had possessed her?

"Gave everybody quite a scare, but I think she'll be okay. She's in treatment. The whole family is."

"She always seemed a happy kid," I said. "What happened?"

"Who knows?" Pris said. "They say she left a note that said she wasn't popular. That nobody liked her. She's in sixth grade, for heaven's sake!"

Despite the generalized murmur of concern, Harvey saw one little girl's breakdown as another crusade for America. "Don't anybody tell me that it isn't proof we're not going right to hell," Harvey said. "If they don't grab guns and mow each other down, then it's like this—kids driving each other to kill themselves. And adults are no better. It's like—it's like—why don't you talk about the Feders and the Washburns? I'm sure seeing them as a daily example didn't help Lily."

"Oh, Harvey," his wife said.

"For Pete's sake—don't act as if—"

I didn't need to ask what Harvey meant, ridiculous as it was as a motive for a child to try to destroy herself. The Feders and the Washburns were our street's Hatfields and McCoys. Nobody knew the origin of their feud, only that it never ended, and given that they lived on a narrow street of homes with common walls, and went to work in suits, the fighting took on subtle guises. Window-box plants wilted and died and the demise was blamed on the other side. Halloween pranks went out of bounds and involved spray paint on front doors. Windows broke. Phones rang in the night.

And one or the other side complained to whomever would listen. If either of those families was in the house right now, I was sure they were complaining to someone.

"Feder killed Washburn's sapling," Harvey said.

I shook my head. "Come on. Everything that happens is blamed on the other one. Hurricanes and heat spells. Stuff happens, that's all."

"Sure, but grudges like they've got—they never die. People are meaner than ever. It's a fact!"

Things Harvey felt always became facts. If he said so, then the fact was, people were holding more grudges today than they did fifty years ago. I also knew what the next step in his reasoning would be. It was always the same.

"It's the pollution," he said right on cue. "It's the stuff we're poisoning ourselves with. Makes us crazy."

"Romeo and Juliet's families managed to keep a feud going in unpolluted air. And how about Cain and Abel?"

Harvey snorted disdain and waved my comments away. "You shoot industrial waste up into our—"

I looked at my watch, said, "Oops!" and backed away.

Harvey and Pris and eternal feuds had cured my nostalgia for neighborhoods lost. I made my way to Nancy, who knew I couldn't stay long, and we made a date to get together soon. She was a good human being who'd built a career importing tribal artifacts and jewelry. It had involved lots of adventures and opportunities to be away from her mother. But on the domestic scene, she'd spent way too long with the wrong man—a married wrong man who, after fifteen years, was still promising to leave his wife any minute now.

It's fairly awesome what stupid things smart women do about the opposite sex. What lies we listen to and tell ourselves. Nancy could drive a hard bargain with an Indonesian hill tribesman and she could argue price with someone in the markets of Morocco without knowing either one of their languages, but she never once understood Mr. Wrong's lies. She had her part-time man, her full-time mother, and a few good trips a year. Maybe that made her more contented than she chose to let on.

As for me, I was feeling overblessed with lives and people. The day already seemed at least a week long, and I could barely remember its beginnings. But I had miles to go before I could rest. Still ahead: Beth and an evening of eating for a good cause.

It almost made me want to hang around Harvey a little longer.

Seven

I HEARD THE EXCITED DIN WHILE I WAS STILL IN THE ELE-
vator, and I admit to a frisson of terror before embarking, a
reversion to a nearly forgotten childhood shyness. It didn't
feel easy facing a roomful of women I didn't know, women
with cash reserves and a sense of privilege I didn't have. I
immediately credited the unseen crowd with a sophistication I in no way shared, and to make matters worse, that
gloss suddenly became the only important quality a woman
needed. It was a variation on the showing-up-naked-onstage
nightmare. I had shown up unpolished.

I knew my all-purpose suit was grossly wrong, my shoes
impossibly out of fashion, my haircut inferior. Not a one of
these things had mattered to me twenty minutes ago when,
in fact, I was feeling pretty fine, nor would they in a few
hours or the rest of my life, but they did right now.

Maybe this was an aftereffect of hearing about Lily's at-
tempted suicide, because it was a very junior high sort of
anxiety.

I took a deep breath and stepped out of the elevator.

The women were attractive, well-groomed, affluent looking, and animated. They were undoubtedly lovely people
I'd like to have met one at a time, but wedging my way into
a crowded party of strangers is not my favorite leisure-time
activity. What conversations I manage taste like Styrofoam

bonbons—light, bland, and indigestible. With all the generalized good-natured cocktail chatter and glitter of dress up, enormous parties seem more about maintaining the appearance of having a good time than actually having one. I often wonder about the faces on the society pages, the people who make merry nonstop, sometimes for a cause and sometimes simply to overcelebrate an opening, a birthday, a launching, or just their own wealth—night after night with the same people. Only the outfits change. Do they love one another that much? Find one another endlessly fascinating?

Another of life's mysteries I never expect to unravel. But it wasn't a mystery why I was here. I'd escaped such events most of my life, but I hadn't escaped family obligations or sisterly affection. Along with two of her friends, my sister Beth had followed her bliss, turning her homemaking and entertaining organizational and creative skills into a package called As Needed: Event Planning and Coordination for Individuals and Corporations.

The business had been slowly building, but tonight's event was its biggest coup, not only because of the event itself, but, Beth had explained, because of the contacts it could provide.

None of that would have dragged me here. Nor would Beth's assumption that these events were part of "growing up" and facing my future as a serious—i.e., married—woman. That attitude would normally get her nowhere except in trouble with me, but this time, she'd followed that imperious declaration with one that did touch me.

She was nervous. A lot was at stake. I wasn't sure if my role was as her groupie, nursemaid, cheerleader, or witness, but here I was because Beth matters to me.

The cause was worthy. The funds raised tonight and at other events would build and maintain a battered-women's shelter and counseling for its inhabitants. I not-so-secretly believed everybody would be better off if we each wrote a check, stayed home, and read a good book, but for reasons I cannot fathom, I am not the boss of the world.

So here I was, feeling very much the peasant at the palace. Everyone else seemed hyper-happy—waving, greeting, kissing both cheeks, and chattering away in small groups. Most of the people I know don't travel in Beth's circles because the tab is too high for our paychecks. Beth likes to pretend that our differences boil down to her *Mrs.* versus my *Ms.*, but they go deeper than that, way down into our wallets. That wasn't going to change at whatever point Mackenzie and I set a date and were wed.

I hadn't a clue as to how I could mingle my way into the circles. I was regressing even more, back to about fourth grade now, watching the popular clique at recess. I couldn't stand this for too long.

I didn't have to. Within seconds, as if she'd been waiting for me—and, given her nervousness, maybe she had—Beth, the world's best hostess, was at my elbow, practically thrumming with tension as she steered me toward women dressed in chic ensembles and shoes that hadn't had to get them from dawn to this point. "So far, so good," she said, her eyes on the room, not on me. "Marilyn even got me—us, I mean, you and me—at the table I wanted."

"Of course she would. You guys arranged this shindig. Why wouldn't you sit wherever—"

"We don't do the seating chart. How could we? She used gentle suggestions after she tested the waters."

"What are you talking about?"

"The politics. Where you put people is all-important for their egos, their wallets, their friendships, their enmities—it would be like my arranging the seating for your wedding."

That wasn't anything I'd thought about till now, but considering how readily relatives who didn't speak to each other came to mind, quickly followed by friends who had once been coupled with other friends' current mates, I decided not to pursue this thought, which didn't even include the hordes otherwise known as the Mackenzie family. "Actually," I said, "it might be nice, if ever we need to do that, of course, to have you do it."

"Huh?"

"Never mind. I'm happy you're sitting where you want to be." Not that I understood why it mattered. She'd be next to me, and wasn't that the entire reason I was here?

I wondered if amphetamines could be made airborne and pumped through air-conditioning, because not only Beth, but everybody here seemed overly delighted with everything: ecstatic to see one another, enraptured to be in this room, all but twirling with anticipation of this lovely evening. Bottom line was: They were women who probably knew one another, saw one another elsewhere, and were gathered together tonight to eat and listen to a talk about the problem of spousal abuse. Was that really the stuff of the ear-piercing level of merriment—and that included Beth's controlled hysteria at being seated at a specific table. "Who is it you're near?" I asked. "The guest speaker?"

Beth's expression suggested that I ran my knuckles on the carpeting while I spoke. "Of course not!" she said. "She's at the head table."

"Then who—"

"This woman who consults to nonprofits. What is there to consult about with groups like that except how to get more money? She's very successful and the absolutely perfect contact. You're sitting next to her because it would be too obvious if I were."

Her transformation from carpool mom to business magnate was nothing short of amazing, even though Business

Beth's skills had been obvious during her stay-at-home phase.

"If you're obliquely warning me to behave, so that I don't mess up your prospect, I'll try my best," I said. "I remember about not making rude noises, not eating with my hands, not talking about politics or my sex life or yours—but I can't remember the rest. Tell me."

She made a big-sister fake pout and fake-elbowed me in the side. "It's good for you to meet these people," she said, switching out of her tycoon mode.

Luckily, I didn't have to endure the cocktail hour for long. I'd arrived late and had about ten minutes to meet a sprinkling of women and discuss how great the weather had been until today, how wretched it was today, how hard it must be to teach what with how bad kids were and how bad the world was.

All predictable, impersonal, and quickly finished, but even in that short period, my smile muscles were going for the burn.

"I'm so glad you came," Beth said as we went to our table.

I felt a pang. She'd implied that I'd had a choice.

"It's great having you as a sister," she went on. "Your life is so exciting. I feel as if I get vicarious points 'cause I'm related to you."

Since, as far as I knew, where Beth and my mother were concerned, the most exciting (and only significant) thing I'd done in the last thirty-two years was become engaged, I was astounded by her remark. Then I realized she meant my after-school job and that she, too, had been brainwashed by Hollywood. When we had more time, I had to find out what she envisioned me doing. It would probably be along the lines of what I'd imagined—back-alley crime and fast-talking men, not a wheezing old woman with a sobbing servant, or long lists of deceased Cades. And that was an exciting day, as compared with the ones where I simply organized papers and entered data on the computer.

We reached a table draped in celadon cloth sparked by cobalt blue napkins and white dishes. Each table had a bonsai tree as a centerpiece. "Is that symbolic?" I asked Beth. "You know, like how we stunt the growth of those we beat up?"

She laughed. "It's pretty, and short enough to see over."

"Well, whatever . . . those battered women sure know how to throw a party."

Beth closed her eyes in exaggerated disgust with me. But I continue to have my problems with these events, so that I considered the beautiful table furnishings and wondered how much Beth had paid to rent them, and how much furniture or counseling that might have bought a battered woman.

I wanted parties to be about having fun with people you already or might grow to enjoy, dinners to be about eating and socializing—and charity to be from the heart, and about the recipient, not the donor.

The table slowly filled, and my sister introduced herself, and me, to each newcomer. Two women walked over together and settled down. "She's Kay, I'm Fay. We rhyme," the one in violet silk announced, insisting on shaking hands clear across the table, which made for a long, painful experience and a new appreciation for the diminutive bonsai. Her friend Kay opted to nod and smile instead.

Millicent somebody joined us and said she worked for the sponsoring charity, and a Dorothy also sat down, barely got out her name, then folded her hands and looked away from us all, as if completely disinterested.

"I'm Vicky Baer," the well-tailored newest of the newcomers said as she sat down beside me.

I missed a beat before I managed what felt like a normal smile and nod, but inside, I was all gasps and exclamation points to the point where I was afraid to look at her directly.

I was as hyperastounded by being seated next to this woman as Beth had been at being placed at her table, and I couldn't believe that we'd both been intent on finding the same person. I tried to keep my jaw from dropping.

She was the woman in the photograph, the one in tailored slacks and shirt. The one who'd dressed like Beth. The one I'd planned to find via Beth's Main Line tendrils. And here she was among her peers, in her natural habitat. Not all that remarkable—and yet, completely astounding. It took my innards a while to stop turning cartwheels.

"Glad to meet you," I said, after identifying myself and hoping the time lag between Beth's introduction and my response hadn't actually been months, the way it felt.

"I think we've met before." Beth said to Victoria Baer across me. And she went on, charting where their paths had crossed, friends they had in common. In short, establishing her credentials as a part, however remote, of the same social circle. I barely heard the specifics because I was too busy concentrating on what I'd say and how I'd say it when I had the chance. I reviewed the great empty page I had on Emmie Cade and where her old pal could fill in the blanks. I debated how much I could ask, and considered the downside of asking too much.

I thought about what I already knew. They'd met at school, though at what stage in their schooling, at what school, I didn't know. I had to steer the conversation around to matters educational.

And at that point, I realized Vicky was saying that she was a consultant to nonprofits, and my sister, possibly afraid of showing her business hand and seating plan by responding with her own profession, chose that moment to include me in the conversation.

"I'm so sorry," she said to me with exaggerated party manners. "Didn't mean to talk right across you. Everybody—this is my sister, Amanda." Only Vicky Baer and the pale, smiling, silent creature on her other side could hear. The silent woman was also nameless. She'd whispered something inaudible as she'd seated herself, and since then, she'd nodded—silently— at anything anyone said. She nodded now, her smile implying that of all the names Beth's sister could have had, mine was the best, pure music to her ears.

Beth rolled on, possibly believing that her duties that evening included emceeing the event itself. I relaxed. This was going to work out amazingly well, and I was delighted that I'd come. "Amanda's keeping quiet like this because—" Beth said.

End of relaxing. I tensed up, hoping against hope that she wasn't headed where I feared.

She was. "—she's a *sleuth*. Be careful what you say or do!"

And like that, my sister had taken my amazing, serendipitous proximity to Victoria Baer—my incredible good fortune—and blown it to smithereens.

Did she think P.I. stood for Public Investigator? I kicked her under the table.

She looked at me in honest surprise, then moved her feet, as if that had been her fault. Then, her humor restored, she winked. "She's entirely too modest," she told the table in general.

"Excuse me?" Victoria Baer said. "It's so noisy in here. What was that? What did you say you did?"

"Fact is, I didn't say—"

"A private investigator. Isn't that a hoot?" Beth's voice had climbed to new eager-anxious hostess heights. "You know, like Miss Marple."

"She wasn't a—"

"Okay, like Columbo."

"He was a cop." Not that I cared about her imagery. I

cared about how she'd wrecked my stroke of good fortune, and I wanted to throttle her.

Violence wasn't going to get me anywhere. Surely I could rethink the situation, turn this to my advantage or at least neutralize the damage. Sure, the bad news was that Vicky Baer would now be suspicious if I moved beyond table-talk pleasantries to anything specific. But given bad news, wasn't it a cosmic necessity, then, for balance's sake that there be good news, too? I was hard-pressed to think of what it could be, until I reminded myself that Beth hadn't told Victoria the precise facts I needed to know.

Of course, that was because Beth didn't know them, but all the same, I clung to that. Victoria Baer didn't know me, and the odds of bumping into her again were slim, so I could return to plan A and ask away.

Most of all, Vicky Baer didn't know that her friend was being investigated and would have no reason to imagine such a thing unless I stuck both my foot and leg into my mouth.

"She's modest about it," Beth said, still replying to Victoria Baer's question, which, I was sure, had been polite conversation that didn't warrant a dissertation. "I don't know why." She smiled, or at least bared her teeth, waiting for a response I truly couldn't muster. The things I could think of would have broken my promise to mind my manners.

"Truly," I finally said. "I help out in an office a few hours a week. I file papers, but Beth has me confused with Sam Spade." Ha-ha, laugh it off, forget about it, please, Ms. Baer.

"Or Emma Peel in *The Avengers*," Fay—or Kay—said from across the table. "I always loved the way she dressed."

"That's precisely how it is. And how I dress, too," I agreed.

"It sounds exciting and . . . dangerous," Victoria Baer said.

"Filing? The only dangers are paper cuts and being bored to death."

She smiled politely and, as two more women joined us, completing the table, the conversation turned to them, much to my relief. Except, of course, that at the next lull, Beth again felt the need to introduce me to them as her sister, the shamus. Time to either gag my sibling or take over the conversation myself for damage control. "Beth doesn't want you to know that my actual job is quite ordinary and seldom glamorized by Hollywood productions. I teach high school English. Now you know the dull truth, and please don't think less of Beth because of how boring I am."

"Teaching's probably more dangerous than we thought your other job was. Kids today." The speaker was one of the newcomers, an elderly woman with unnaturally black hair through which her scalp showed. I wonder when "kids today" became shorthand for how drastically the human race was in decline. I suspected that the phrase was one of the first the Neanderthals expressed.

"They're not that bad," I said.

"Everything I hear, I read . . . where do you teach, then?" I told them.

"A private school," the black-haired woman said. "No wonder."

I took that as the perfect cue. I sat further back in my chair, withdrawing from the table-wide conversation, and turned my attention to my left. "To tell the truth, I sometimes dread saying where I work, because so many people are hostile to the very idea of private schools, and I understand their point of view. I do. Free education and public libraries—access to information and knowledge, how to use it—that's the basis of democracy, if you'll forgive my getting on the soapbox."

Ms. Baer raised her eyebrows and shrugged a "what can you do with people who don't like whatever—but don't take my sympathy to mean I'm wildly interested in this topic, either" sort of gesture.

"I gather you're not one of the people in the antiprivate schools camp," I said as a salad was placed in front of me. The greens gave me something to poke and cut so that I didn't look too eager for information.

"It would be hypocritical to attack private schools, because I attended them from kindergarten on," Vicky Baer said. "And I deal with them professionally now. I consult to nonprofits that need to find ways to raise funds."

"Really? That would certainly include the private schools I know," I said. "Your work sounds like fun. Or at least, if it's not, you're not stuck in that school forever."

She'd been toying with her fork, but I could almost see through her skull as she recategorized me from ignorable dinner partner to: Contact. She put the fork down and reached under the table. "Here," she said. "Let me give you my card. And I have a brochure that explains more of what I do. In case your school ever . . ."

I wonder what percentage of cards exchanged in this random, optimistic, and hopeful way ever result in a sale or a job, or even a phone call. I certainly had no clout with either Havermeyer or the trustees about how or through whom they should raise money. And yet turning down a card seems a deliberate insult, like blatantly saying, "I am not interested in you and I have no desire to know how to reach you."

She groped under the table and, at one point, grabbed my ankle. "Sorry," she said. "It's gotten wedged—" And then she pulled out a pocketbook that might have been a briefcase, or was both things. It had pockets and flaps and zipper compartments, but nonetheless, as she lifted it, the contents spilled onto the table, the floor, and me.

Vicky Baer looked crestfallen. Her façade of professionalism wasn't quite as smooth at the moment, and she
seemed profoundly stunned. I, on the other hand, am so
used to my mask of competency shattering that I can almost take it in my stride, apply emotional bandages, and
put myself back together. Vicky, however, lowered her lids,
shutting out the sight of her possessions, then she opened
her eyes up again and, lips tight, carefully replaced a lipstick, a small bottle of aspirin, a telephone, electronic cal-
endar, and compact, while I transferred a miniature staple
gun, a roll of quarters, a vaporizer, a tin of breath mints, a
small unopened packet of tissues, a black felt-tip pen, and
an unused packet of plastic file tabs.

"There are times you're really relieved that no men
are around, aren't there?" Beth asked from the other side
of me.

"I didn't want to carry an actual briefcase tonight,"
Vicky Baer mumbled. "I thought this would hold it all, but
I forgot to zip the top when I sat down."

I wanted to tell her that it was all right. That everybody
on earth had upended a purse, and nobody cared.

"Oh, God, even this. How did this get in there?" She
lifted a rawhide dog chew—used—off the floor and, frowning, dropped it back into her purse along with a white plastic square I recognized as containing floss. Then she
smoothed her skirt and sat up straight. "My dog," she said,
glancing at her watch. "That was a good reminder, I guess.
I'll have to go see to him in a few minutes."

I looked around and she shook her head. "Poor Bruno's
in the car," she said. "All safe, windows open, in case
you're worrying. His joy in life is the car, and he's a well-
behaved creature, so, since he needs regular medication, it's
easiest to take him with me when possible."

Beth made sympathetic noises.

And then, Vicky Baer remembered her original mission and unsnapped a compartment of the bag and handed me one of her cards, satiny and impressively embossed v. s. BAER, INC., IDEAS UNLIMITED, and underneath, ECONOMIC CONSULTATION TO NONPROFIT INSTITUTIONS. The card was clipped to an equally lush, heavy-stock brochure.

"I'll pass this on," I said. "My school's fund-raising efforts are pretty lame."

"Could I see your brochure?" Beth asked, and Vicky Baer, recovered from her faux pas and, recognizing interest, perked up. "Here, have your own. You don't have to share."

Then I, too, remembered my original purpose. "That private school you attended—was it one of ours? I mean here, in the city?"

"Eventually. I lived in Ohio," she said. "Till eleventh grade, and then I was here, at Shipley."

A prestigious school on the Main Line, but Emmie Cade hadn't lived in these parts till now, as far as we knew. Cleveland, however, had been a stop along the corporate route. "Good school," I said. "A lucky move, although I suppose that's provincial of me. Your Ohio school might have been just as good."

She shrugged and nibbled a leaf of frisée.

"Did your family move around a lot? I've had students whose parents relocate almost every year, and sometimes it creates problems. Any advice?"

The salad was crisp and deliciously dressed, and after a moment, when Ms. Baer appeared to have decided against speaking again, I turned to Beth to congratulate her. "This is terrific," I said. "Pretty room and tables and great salad."

Beth beamed when Vicky came out of her silence to agree that this was indeed a fine event. She'd decided to speak, after all, but just as she began to talk about her schooling again, Beth decided it was appropriate to admit that she had organized tonight's fine event, and that yes, that was her business and she had a card, too, and would Vicky want one?

I started to kick her again under the table, but she wouldn't know why I was doing so, so I controlled myself while the two women smiled and nodded and calculated how much business the other might generate for her.

Finally, Vicky Baer remembered my question. "The thing is," she said, "I have no wisdom to impart because *we* never moved. I did. My family stayed in Ohio. I lived with a cousin here till I graduated, then went off to Cornell. It was all my decision." She returned to her salad, and I to mine.

I had what I'd needed. Emmie Cade had never lived in the area before. Cornell had not been mentioned, but Ohio had. I could find out what school Emmie had attended in Ohio through Vicky's transfer records and then, her parents' names, her address, and her former and possibly next address as well. I had a friend who taught at Shipley and I was betting she could help me out with the innocuous but meaningful information.

"Did you study fund-raising? Is there such a major?" I asked.

"Not that I know of. I majored in biology, believe it or not. I thought maybe I wanted to be a doctor, but . . ." She shook her head. "Other options seemed more appealing, at least at the time." She smiled at the memory of her young and presumably naïve self. "You know, the whole she-bang—husband, white picket fence, and two kids." She flashed another, possibly insincere smile, then looked down at what was left of her salad. "Unfortunately, almost the same day as I was married, I realized that none of those things appealed to me. Now, I'm single and in love with my job and my dog, and that suits me fine, and I still don't want to be a doctor. How about you? Why did your sister say you were an investigator if you're an English teacher?"

"I am both, but truly, the so-called investigation work is part-time, and almost one hundred percent clerical work. I'm helping someone out, and it's nothing like in the movies. Beth likes to tease me about it, and she was including you in the joke this time." I busied myself spearing a reluctant piece of roasted red pepper. "Was it difficult, moving to Philadelphia?" I asked. "I met a woman who told me this is a tough place to be a newcomer."

"The City of Brotherly Love isn't?"

"Apparently, you have to be here a few generations before the love turns on. Or so I hear."

"It wasn't particularly hard on me," she said. "Probably because when you move into a school situation . . . And I was living at my cousin's, so I was a part of an established family. And my ex's family's been here for eons, so when I married and moved back here, there wasn't a problem."

"Guess that's it," I said. "That woman who said it was a tough city is grown and our age, and I don't think she has children—they sometimes make it easier. You can always join the PTA."

Vicky Baer wasn't interested, but until the speaker got up on the podium, her options were pathetically limited. She had the nodding silent woman on her left, and she had me and, sporadically, my sister, who was working hard to appear disinterested. So mostly, Vicky Baer had me, and she listened, and even if she didn't pretend interest, she didn't dump her salad remnants on my head and tell me to shut up.

"I always feel personally responsible," I said. "As if this is *my* city—in more than a symbolic way, and I'm in charge of making it nice for new and old-timers. I wonder if there are newcomer groups to help people like her along."

"Where does she live?" That was Beth, jumping in— meaning she was monitoring our every word no matter what else she seemed to be doing—and, as always, eager to be helpful. Or maybe this time, simply eager to be in further conversation with the consultant without seeming as if that was her intention. Every sentence she uttered, despite its actual vocabulary, could be translated as: "I'm not blatantly soliciting your business, though you could be of incredible help to me, and I hope you've noticed the exquisite discretion and tact that I bring to the jobs I am assigned."

"Not far from you," I told my sister. "In Villanova, I think."

Vicky shifted in her seat to allow the waiter to remove her salad plate. He was as good an excuse as any for letting me know how little she cared for my chatter.

But there was Beth, bless her. Beth, who could not seem to stop talking. "I know really nice people near her in St. David's—and a lovely book group in Radnor. Book clubs are a wonderful way to meet new, bright people. Give me her name and maybe I can help. I don't want to give her the wrong idea of this city."

"I think I wrote it down," I said. "My memory . . ." I began to reach under the table, then sat back up. "I remember—Emma Cade." I didn't want to say her silly-sounding nickname.

Beth had taken out a small notebook and now, she wrote the name down. "I hope she's in the book," she murmured.

I turned to include Vicky Baer in the conversation, or to look as if I were. I wanted to check her expression, and I was gratified. She looked like Macavity when he thinks he's heard something crawling in the walls. If her ears could have become erect or swiveled, they would have. "You look as if you were about to say something," I said.

"It's Emmie, not Emma. I know her. And she's not in Villanova. Not anymore. She's in Center City. Right off the Square."

"Really? I must have missed . . ."

"Good, then." Beth snapped shut her red-leather-covered-notebook. "You were worried about something that isn't a problem at all."

"You know her," I said. "Amazing. Cliché or not, it really is a small world."

"Six degrees of separation and all that," Vicky said. "The Main Line isn't that big, then you break it down into age groups, it approaches tiny. How'd you meet her?"

I decided it was okay to have met Claire Fairchild. "At her future mother-in-law's place," I said. "How about you?"

"I knew her back in high school."

"Shipley? I thought she said she was new to—"

"In Ohio. She arrived in tenth grade. She called herself Mary Elizabeth then. M. E. Her initials, not Emma."

I couldn't help but think of all the Emma-related names I'd scanned this afternoon, of all the time I'd wasted.

"I didn't see her again till college—"

"Two schools, then. Cornell, you said."

She nodded. "—she called herself Betsey in those days. Then she dropped out and we completely lost touch until a year ago, when I bumped into her in San Francisco. She was calling herself something else again. I don't know why. She somehow needs . . . disguises. Anyway, now she's here, so we see each other sometimes."

"You know, now I'm remembering more, and the fact is, she said she moved here because she knew someone—that must be you."

Vicky Baer frowned. "Me? Moved here because of me? Like I said, I knew her, but not like that. That'd be frightening, to be responsible for somebody's cross-country move. She must mean somebody else." She looked at me. "It's like with her names. She's got an imagination. Take everything she says with a grain—or a bushel—of salt."

Two things were apparent. First, Vicky Baer didn't sound like much of a friend to Emmie Cade. She seemed, in fact, barely interested in her. Second, I hadn't thought my pitch all the way through. I should have come up with a better hook than the lonely newcomer angle, because now we were out of material and prompts.

I ate chicken and tried to avoid its fanciful packaging. The chef, in a fit of insanity, or misogyny, had created a chicken something or other, dripping butter and cream and wrapped in puff pastry. It was a given that two out of three—if not three out of three—women in this room were on diets and every one of us picked at the concoction, protesting politely, pretending not to eat the forbidden parts and failing utterly because they tasted so good. This time, when I looked over at Beth, my expression was, at best, quizzical.

"I did not make up the specifics of the menu," she said. "The woman who did looks like she has a metabolic problem, and kept saying that everybody had paid so much for this dinner, she wanted it to be special. So live it up— tomorrow, we diet."

Given all the food that was going to be returned to the kitchen, I was relieved that we weren't raising funds for the homeless or the starving. I turned back toward Vicky. She was a disciplined woman, and her dinner was largely untouched, but she wasn't a subtle woman. She showed her displeasure and abstinence from fattening food and, possibly, from further conversation, by folding her hands in her lap.

I couldn't let my font of information dry up this way. I

turned to Beth and whispered. "Ask me something—anything—about the newcomer I met. Or newcomers, or—"

"Why?" she whispered back.

I shook my head. "Just ask—I'll explain some other time."

"But I . . ." And then she got it—or thought she had, and unfortunately, it was the same thing in the end. "Ooooh," she said. "You're—" Her eyes darted toward Vicky. "—but you can't—*her?*—I can't believe she—"

"Not her. No. But—ask, okay?"

She nodded, and I turned back to Vicky Baer, who looked abstracted until she noticed I was angled toward her and became alert again. "Sorry—I was lost in thought," she said. "And it wasn't worth a penny, so don't try to bribe me."

"I never would."

"Amanda," my sister began.

"That woman, Emmie," Vicky said at the same time. "Why would she tell you she was—"

"—is there a Center City version of a Newcomers Club?" Beth continued. "Do you think—"

I put my hand on Beth's knee and squeezed.

"But you—"

I pressed her knee again. She winced. But she also stopped talking.

"—lonely, or having problems?" Vicky finished her question. "She's engaged. Leo knows lots of people."

"You know what," I said. "She hasn't been here long, and she's engaged, so she probably knew her fiancé before she moved here. I'll bet *he's* the one person she knew and that's what she meant."

Vicky shook her head. "She was married, you know. Widowed not that long ago, in California, right before she moved here." She laughed, though it wasn't a particularly happy sound. "Besides, I introduced her to Leo. At a party at my house, so I fear, by default, I must be the person she meant. And you're right. It's been a whirlwind affair, but you know, when a man's ready, he's ready. And it was certainly high time for Leo. It's nonetheless amazing that Emmie Cade so quickly got herself through the poisoned brambles."

"Meaning?"

She looked at me as if deciding what to say, how honest to be. "His mother," she said. "I hope I'm not out of line—you said you met Emmie at Mrs. Fairchild's, and I don't mean to say anything against the woman, but . . ." She shook her head and grew quiet, poking her fork into the puff-pastry crust around the chicken.

"I don't really know her," I said, stepping carefully, hoping an explanation for how I do and don't know Mrs. Fairchild would form as I spoke. "We . . . the school is having a 'good-neighbor' campaign. You know, heading off at the pass the kind of complaints you get from people who live nearby, so . . ." I let it go at that, and hoped Vicky Baer's need to express her opinion was stronger than my ability to come up with a reason I needed to hear it.

She raised an eyebrow, and put down her fork. "Claire Fairchild is nice enough—unless she thinks you want a piece of what is hers. That applies to her possessions, which includes her things, of course, her money, and most of all, her son. She's destroyed every relationship Leo ever had, and I know this from personal experience."

"You and Leo?"

She made a mock pout. "Let's just say she wasn't exactly a help. My point is, there's no reason to think the old lady won't destroy this one, too. Poor Emmie. You'd think it was time for her luck to change."

"She's had a bad mother-in-law before?"

"Just a virulent variety of bad luck. Her last husband drowned. That was horrible. And I understand that her first husband was a general rotter. Of course, Emmie was pretty wild herself. Ran off during her freshman year with a guy . . ." She seemed a little lost, remembering.

"Her first husband?"

She shook her head. "Just a passing fancy. Then I lost touch. The rest I only learned later on, when I bumped into her out west."

Two marriages behind her, then, not one. And a third waiting in the wings, and she was younger than I was. A prodigy.

Vicky gave in to hunger and pulled apart a dinner roll, slowly eating a segment of it.

"Bad luck indeed," I murmured, noticing that somehow, my chicken en croute was nearly gone. "She's awfully young to be marrying for the third time."

"There was a near fourth," Vicky said. "An engagement. But he died in a motorcycle accident two weeks before they were supposed to be married."

Two husbands, a third pending, two violent accidental deaths, one by motorcycle, one by drowning. I couldn't help but remember that red paper with AND THERE'S MORE DEAD!!! on it.

"The fates seem lined up against poor Emmie," she said. "She's a bad luck girl. I don't know how else to describe it."

We both sat in silence, Vicky chewing her single bite of dinner roll, when we heard a tinkly version of the opening of Beethoven's *Fifth*.

"My phone," she said. "Sorry. I forgot to shut it off. I'll take it outside." She checked her watch. "Be back in ten minutes," she said. "Might as well go water, walk, and medicate Bruno."

I sat there thinking about what she'd said. I agreed there was bad luck aplenty in the story I'd heard, but I wasn't sure whether it was aimed at Emmie Cade or whether she held the franchise for bad luck, and she was the one doling it out to the hapless men who crossed her path.

Eight

"GOOD WORK," MACKENZIE SAID WHEN I TOLD HIM ALL I'd found out within a few hours of meeting Mrs. Fairchild. "Especially with next to nothing to go on. But don't count on coincidence striking twice. Or ever again in this lifetime."

I knew that, but I tried explaining why the evening's find had been lucky, but not exceptionally coincidental. It had been more like finding a bird in its expected roosting spot. "As soon as I saw her photograph, I was going to get Beth's Main Line tom-toms in action. The surprise was that it went from thought to actuality without any action in between. A miracle."

His nod of acknowledgment slid toward nodding off, his head lowering toward his open text for Quantitative Methods in Sociology, his hand still holding his pen, resting on his notebook. I had glanced at the book and found it largely unintelligible, and all through our mutual descriptions of our varied days—his classes and his work with Ozzie, my classes and ditto—he'd rubbed his eyes, stifled yawns, and insisted he wasn't tired. Now he snapped back up, cleared his throat, and said, "What's next?"

"Check with Shipley and find out Vicky's Ohio school, call there, see when Emmie—who I think was Betsey then, but I'll check—attended, her address, parents' names, if she transferred in or out, then from and to where—whatever else I can find out. Forwarding address, I suppose. Maybe something will lead to the first husband—the rotter. Or the fiancé who was killed. Can I say I'm considering hiring her and doing due diligence on her résumé?"

He shrugged. "Most people don't check back to high school."

"They might, since she didn't finish college. I don't want grades or anything personal, just her stats. Would Cornell have records of however long she was there?"

He nodded again, though he was so tired, that was a dangerous bit of body language, too tempting on the downward motion. "Don' forget the San Francisco stuff."

Embarrassing not to have already mentioned it. It was so obvious as, possibly, the real smear on what's-her-name's record. I appreciated the gentle, nonsuperior way he'd mentioned it, as if anybody would have needed prodding about it.

"—the marriage records," he was saying. "Maybe mention of how that first marriage ended. An' the transcripts of the inquest. I'll start that in the mornin', before class." He leaned back and stretched his arms. "I am beat," he said, standing up. "So—what's your take on Ms. Cade?"

"In person? Absolutely charming. It's only all this . . . confusion surrounding her."

"Con men—and women—have to be charmin'. It's part of their basic equipment kit."

I nodded acknowledgment. "Creepy, too. First of all, she said Victoria Baer was her great good friend, or that's the impression I got from Claire Fairchild. But that seems a gross exaggeration. Makes me wonder how stable Emmie Cade is, how tight her grip on reality is. She said she moved here because of Vicky, but Vicky acts appalled by the idea that she had anything to do with it. At best, she acts as if they are casual acquaintances from way back—a year of high school, a year of college, a surprise encounter in San Francisco, and no more than that."

He yawned and opened his eyes close to bug-eyed wide, trying to appear alert.

I pretended his ruse had fooled me, so I could justify continuing. "Mostly, I don't get it about the name changes, not to mention two dead guys. She's been awfully busy on the romantic and death front for one young woman."

"Or she's a total flake with amazingly bad luck," Mackenzie said.

"I don't much believe in luck. Except when it seats me next to the person I'm looking for."

THE NEXT MORNING, BEFORE I WAS FULLY DRESSED, LET alone en route to school, the phone rang.

"Has to be your mother," Mackenzie said from across the room. He'd been up for at least an hour and was already studying. What a good student he was. Wish I had him in my class.

"That didn't take deductive powers," I answered.

"Maybe they're calling off school because of the rain," he said amiably. Above us, the skylight drummed with water and had been since a massive electrical storm around midnight.

"Maybe they've changed their minds and aren't coming," I said.

"Let us hope."

I took a deep breath and lifted the receiver. "You said you'd explain," the voice said by way of greeting.

Beth? She really was mutating into our mother at an ever-accelerating speed.

Mackenzie returned to his coffee and studies.

"Explain what? When did I say . . ." I could only find one of my favorite black shoes, and I looked at Macavity suspiciously, though he was far too indolent to drag a shoe under the bed. I held the phone between my shoulder and cheek and got onto the floor to search. The cat stood next to me, peering in the same direction. I wondered what he thought he was looking for. It's pathetic and loveable when cats pretend to know what's going on. Then he gave up, lay down on his back, figuring that since I was in the neighborhood, maybe it was for a belly rub.

"Don't act naïve," Beth said. "I'm your sister—not a spy—and you know what I'm talking about: Vicky Baer. You asked me to keep her talking last night about newcomers, or that newcomer. You said you'd explain. Were you or weren't you investigating her?"

"I told you I wasn't." I'd spotted the shoe in the absolute midpoint under the bed. The impossible-to-reach point. I stood up and went in search of a broom with which to snag it. "Am not."

"Then why did you ask me to ask about that newcomer when we'd finished talking about newcomers?"

I kept quiet because the only honest answer was that I'd asked because I was an inept idiot, who behaved as if Beth had no brain or sense of curiosity.

"You owe it to me." This wasn't a familiar Beth. Perhaps this hard-edged tone was part of Business Beth's new wardrobe. "I'm hoping to do business with her, so if there's some dark secret I should know about, then . . . then—I should know about it!"

Macavity saw the broom and took off for the other side of the loft. I got back down and poked at the shoe with the handle until it was out the other side, and said only, "There's no secret—network her like crazy. You're safe."

Beth was silent for a moment, digesting this and not giving up. "Then it has to be because she knew that newcomer you met," she said. "That Emmie Cade."

"Apparently." I'd forgotten that Beth had written down the name. And then I heard what I'd dreaded—that nearly silent *oh!* where Beth figured something out, most likely that I hadn't met any newcomer who babbled about her life to me. I was about to say something to hold her off at the pass—as soon as I thought of what it was, when she dropped the entire matter. Maybe I'd been wrong about her powers of intuition.

"You don't have to tell me a single thing more—I understand. But don't act like your job's so unglamorous, like you're a clerk and nothing more," she said, making me wonder what she thought she understood. "And, since I have you on the phone, what do you think of the Emory mansion?"

"Excuse me? I've never heard of them, let alone visited their home."

"The family died out years ago, and their house is used for events. It's beyond gorgeous, and it'd be perfect. I'm going out there this morning, to check it out for a corporate party. Anyway, it's about thirty minutes outside—"

"Nice, Beth, but I have to get to work. Good luck with the Averys."

"Emorys! Aren't you even interested?"

"Of course I am. I love hearing how you put things together, but right now, I haven't even had coffee and—"

"I mean for you! For your wedding."

"What wedding?"

"Aren't you ever going to set a date? What's wrong with you? And then you're going to let me help you with it, aren't you? It's what I do, and you have to think ahead, way ahead. This place gets booked—"

This was way too weird for a dark, rainy morning, but since she was already scratchy about Victoria Baer, I had to tiptoe around this. It took another solid five minutes to extricate myself from the conversation and to extract a promise that she'd say nothing further about this mansion or my wedding date until so requested. But for fear of making

something more important to her than it already was, I
didn't extract a similar promise about last night's dinner
conversation. The less said, the better, I felt. I wanted her to
forget about it, and mentioning it would only make it seem
still more important. I could only hope for the best. After
all, she didn't know Emmie Cade, so I couldn't envision
any problems ahead.

A learning experience, I told myself. That's all it was. A
lesson in the perils of speaking before I thought through all
the possible consequences.

WE WERE INTO THE SECOND-DAY SLUMP, OR THEY WERE.

American ingenuity and business sense has made sure
there are numerous perks about back-to-school. Kids get
new clothing, new supplies with delicious designs and covers. Even assignment books, designed to list the hated work
they'll have to do—even those are cleverly packaged. First
day back, everything from head to foot is new or newly
washed. Back to school is filled as well with nonconsumer
benefits, like seeing people after a long summer's absence.

Twenty-four hours later, the student body's collective expressions reflect a sense of having been duped, as in some
primitive cartoon series. Fooled again, though they aren't
sure how it happened this time. They can't blame this one
on the teacher. They were party to it, but now, it's the second day of forever, and their shoes have scuffs and no matter what teen idol is on the cover of the assignment book,
its blank pages are all waiting to be filled with things they
don't want to, but have to do.

A lot of heavy lifting ahead.

Perhaps they even remember that they didn't see those
other kids all summer because they didn't particularly
want to.

They looked at me with inarticulate desperation, as if I
could help them, or at least explain what had happened,

but of course, I was a part of the problem and not its solution. Anyway, I knew it would get better, and I also knew that they'd probably felt just as robbed and cheated by summer, which was never the two-month dream of bliss they'd envisioned.

To balance things out, my back-to-school malaise was gone, and I felt glad to have shifted gears and to be in my element again. We all have our own ways to delude ourselves, and mine was to believe—again—like my own variation on that hapless cartoon character: this year would be different. I had three preparations for my five classes, had planned out the year, and was positive, despite all past evidence, that not only would the students enjoy the challenges ahead, but so would I. And of course I'd work efficiently, gladly, and promptly, papers returned almost before the students handed them to me. And when they looked at their compositions and my comments—they'd get it. They'd change. They'd think coherently, make clear points, learn new words, and thank me for my incisive advice. And while we were at it, they'd fall in love with books and reading and ideas and self-expression.

I was basking so comfortably in this pedagogical hallucination that I smiled back first thing in the morning when I arrived, dripping wet despite my umbrella, which had turned inside out, and Sunshine said, "And aren't we glad that heat wave's over!" It wasn't a question—it was a command to be joyous. "And isn't this just the most perfect day for studying?" she continued. "Mother Nature herself is saying, now kiddies, forget about that lazy summertime you had—it's back-to-work time!"

It was still pouring, the skies so low and menacing, I anticipated forty days and forty nights. My umbrella was ruined, and I was drenched, but so what? I borrowed a smidge of Sunshine's attitude and added it to my dizzy belief in the new school year. I'd dry out. Life would go on.

And I didn't particularly mind, though I wasn't overly amused, either, when Bo Michaels avoided committing to any book at all for his report by falling off his chair and pretending to have a heart attack. I had tagged him as class clown the day before, but today, drenched in the milk of human kindness and teacher-blindness, I tried to avoid classifying him, labeling him in any negative way. Instead, I determined to focus on why he needed to make a fool of himself.

And third period, I was able to ignore the still-subtle shenanigans of Butch and Sundance. I knew, even in this strangely manic mood of mine, that they'd soon be problems needing attention, but for right now, they were simply vaguely amusing, testosterone-poisoned adolescents.

Gilding my benign-teacher float was the afterglow of having done well with my first assignment for C. K. I loved the day. I loved my capabilities. I loved my students. I loved Mr. Mackenzie.

I should have known that every calm precedes a storm, and giddiness during a storm precedes God only knows what. At noon, while I was checking that all the seniors, including Bo the Clown, had indeed chosen books, a messenger arrived. That did not, however, seem bad news. In fact, it was good news, proving that Sunshine was educable. She now understood the relationship between messengers and messages.

Apparently, her deciphered message meant that one of my ninth-grade parents was downstairs, wanting to meet her daughter's English teacher. *1ts 2CU* Sunshine wrote. I struggled with the *1ts* until *wants* became clear. Little Office Sunshine had signed her note with an oversized smiley-face with an exclamation point for a nose. A *really* smiley-face. I had my first tremor of less-than-joy, but it had nothing to do with the message, only the person who'd written it out.

Ten months of unsolicited, inept rebus puzzles and jolliness lay ahead. I had to find a way to depress her.

But aside from that, I took the note and the visiting parent as a sign that things were indeed improving. Perhaps our standards were rising, as Havermeyer claimed. This woman could have waited until parents' night and I could have gotten more work done, but I wasn't ready to object to an overinterested parent after years of complaining about the other sort, the ones who dumped their screwed-up children on us as if we were an all-purpose repair service. While we patched in literature and history, we were expected to also toss in ethics, etiquette, and psychological soundness.

So I walked downstairs to meet Mrs. Lawrence, expecting a pleasantly nervous mother who wanted to tell me something special about her child. A talent with words, a shyness she'd like me to notice. Problems at home.

And I tried to remember her daughter, one of the new students in ninth grade. I thought she was the pretty girl with streaked blonde hair and an aura of confidence, and wondered what her mother's special worry would be.

Sonia Lawrence was a striking woman, dressed in a navy silk blouse and a fawn-colored suit with shoes to die for. She carried her raincoat on one arm, and held a folded umbrella, and neither the sky nor either of those items had allowed one drip on her. Her hair was the same sun-streaked blonde as the student I'd picked, so I thought I'd been right.

"I hope you don't mind this unannounced intrusion," she said, "but my office is nearby, and I had an unexpected break. The school told me you had a prep period now, so I hoped I could have five minutes of your time."

Nobody on earth has ever braved a storm to make a five-minute optional personal trip. I should have gone on alert, but why? It was the second day of school. I hadn't had time to commit grave offenses. "Why don't we sit on the benches in the entry," I suggested.

"But I'll only take—"

"It's more comfortable," I said, and she followed me to the carved wooden bench near the front entry.

"My daughter Melanie is in your last-period class," she said once she'd settled herself.

I nodded and smiled, waiting for her to define what was special about Melanie, aside from her striking good looks and what seemed inherited self-confidence.

"She brought home *Lord of the Flies* last evening."

I nodded again.

"I realize that it's something of a classic."

I was getting tired of nodding.

"The author's famous."

"He won the Nobel Prize." I had to hope that if it was good enough for the Swedish Academy, it was good enough for Mrs. Lawrence.

"In these times," she said, "do you think you're being sensitive to the traumas the children have been through—the entire nation has been through?"

I waited for her to continue, to make sense, and when she didn't, I sighed, then spoke. "Mrs. Lawrence, I honestly don't know where you're headed. It's a rich, complex book that's also approachable, a wonderful study of many things the students come to understand—mass hysteria, mob psychology, various approaches to life, civilization and what it might mean, the potential for evil in—"

"That's precisely what I mean. Why present our children with more evidence of human evil? Do you think that's sensitive in these times?"

The second *sensitive* in one minute.

"I understand that the term *lord of the flies* is a translation of the word *Beelzebub*—the devil himself." She looked triumphant, convinced she'd scored a point.

I still wasn't sure of the game.

"Don't be mistaken—I'm not a religious fanatic. I'm not a book burner. I am nonetheless quite upset at the idea of my daughter being forced to read about young boys who wind up committing murder. Perhaps in years gone by, Miss Pepper, but in these times, I find this book to be in poor taste."

"I appreciate your input, but I think it's more important than ever to encourage thought about how we behave, and why. And about violence and hatred—"

She put one well-manicured hand on mine. "They've had enough. Haven't you read about the traumatized children? You're standing by with a whip, to inflict further pain."

"Don't you want Melanie to learn to think? Isn't that what keeps democracy alive—citizens who think? It isn't so much the specific content of any given book as it is what she's going to take from it, and the unit plan has them learning—"

"I don't like what they're learning. They're learning that people can revert to savagery in the blink of an eye. To murder. That they can choose a scapegoat and destroy him. Is that who you're saying we are?"

"Excuse me—I didn't write the novel. And the author isn't saying anybody in particular is any particular—"

"I know how that novel ends. The rescuers are at war, too. The adults are just as cruel, aren't they? That's his point, isn't it?"

"Perhaps one of many points."

"The adults are just as capable of moral relativism and violence, aren't they. He's saying—and you're saying by teaching that book—that everyone is basically rotten. We're animals under a thin veneer of civilization."

"No. Not so. Not everybody in the book—"

"Thank you for hearing me out. I don't want my daughter reading this, so perhaps you'd better think about this some more. In these times—we're at war, Miss Pepper. You have heard the president, haven't you? We're at war against evil—and you're teaching your students that everyone is evil."

"No. If we don't think things through—"

"Even children."

"—people are *capable* of evil, out of fear, out of mass hysteria, and—"

"It's not only insensitive and an incorrect view of mankind, it's unpatriotic at a time like this. I'll get back to you on this."

She stood up, smiled, took my hand to shake, and said, "Thank you for taking time with me."

And that was it. She was out the door. This was an entirely new line of attack and criticism, and she wasn't finished with me. But what frightened me most about Sonia Lawrence was her efficiency. She'd delivered her message, her warning—or threat—her reasons for her feelings. The frightening part was that she'd done it in precisely five minutes.

This was a woman who meant every word she said.

Now I, too, was into the second-day slump.

Nine

"INSENSITIVE! SHE SAID IT MORE THAN ONCE! SOMEDAY, every single book ever written will be on a forbidden list," I fumed. "It's either sex, or historically accurate but nowadays-offensive racial words, or the hint of subversive political leanings—or—or—well, now, *insensitivity*! She all but accused me of being a traitor to my country!"

Mackenzie looked mildly sympathetic. Ozzie, over in his corner cubicle, didn't even look up. I wasn't sure that Ozzie had ever heard the word *book*, let alone read one. He was the man for whom TV and beer were invented.

Not that I'm insensitive to TV-watching beer drinkers. Some of my best fiancés are to be found in that group now and then.

And in truth, even Ozzie has another great passion, and that's for speed. In others. He himself is slow-moving, except, I gather, when he's on his motorcycle. He loves it, and anyone or anything that physically taxes itself to the limit. "I like fast," he's said repeatedly, explaining himself in typically terse fashion. And the office illustrates that in a style that would confuse most viewers who didn't understand the theme and mistook his lair for old-fashioned sloppy.

The portion of wall I'm near at my desk is layered with pictures of champion racehorses, the Concorde, an ad for a Jet Ski, photos of Lance Armstrong, drawings of greyhounds, and motorcycle-related icons. Ozzie does not discriminate—if it's fast, he likes it, pinning up posters and magazine pages as they appear and appeal to him.

To the best of my knowledge, this is the one place on earth that defies the laws of gravity and here, what goes up never comes down. I suspect that small, blind life-forms breed between the images, but I'm not going to check it out.

"You ask me," Ozzie suddenly said, though nobody had, "you have two choices. Either tell her to go to hell—"

"An appealing idea," I said, "but it then involves my finding another job."

"—or change the book. It's school, it's work, and does any kid care what the book's called they have to read? In fact, does anybody care?"

"I care. I know it's not the best school in town, but I care. These kids aren't stupid. They—including her daughter— are capable of thinking about the potential for evil, about choices, about mob violence—about the book I've assigned. How can they vote and be part of this country—she pretty much called me *unpatriotic!*—if they don't learn how to reason things through?"

"Jeez," Ozzie said. "It was only a suggestion." He turned back to his computer, more convinced than ever, I feared, that talking to women wasn't worth the breath it took.

"I should have taught math," I said. "Math teachers don't get harassed. Nobody tells them that algebra is insensitive, or calculus unpatriotic."

"There's the small issue that you aren't fond of mathematics," Mackenzie said softly. "In that case, you'd be miserable because nobody was tryin' to stop you."

"Then history," I muttered.

"Subject to interpretation and reinterpretation," he reminded me. "But speakin' of history, both political and personal, reminds me. You sufficiently decompressed now to consider Emmie Cade?"

"I've been working on it." Mackenzie had been out

checking real estate records—another thing I'd have to learn about. And while he was gone, I'd been finding out what I could about Jake King and his widow, holding on to my anger about Sonia Lawrence and all the well-dressed ignoramuses with whom I had to deal. Then Mackenzie appeared, and I exploded. Because I could. If for no other reason—though there are many other reasons—I'd marry the man because he knows when it's time to stand back and let me release my steam valves.

I was calm again now, and grateful. "I've called my friend at Shipley, and she's going to check out Vicky Baer's school records, find out the name of the Ohio school. The records are archived somewhere, and she needs to contact the person in charge. Plus, I've been reading through the *San Francisco Chronicle*'s archives for last year. I typed in *Jake King* and last year's January through December dates and came up with seven hundred and forty-two mentions. Much of it concerning royalty and sports teams. I never realized what a popular surname it was."

Mackenzie nodded. I felt let down. I'd expected more recognition of my labors, although I couldn't have said what: a gold star? Roses flung at my feet?

"Forget to put a plus between the words?" he asked softly.

That didn't deserve an answer. Of course I'd forgotten. Of course the slogging labors were due to my forgetting. But I had gotten information about Jake King, ace sailor who "could read water," according to friends who'd sailed with him.

He had been a champion racer in half a dozen Pacific contests, and from what I read, everybody loved him except his ex-wife, who didn't consider Jake's death any reason to lessen her fury toward him.

And reading between the lines, noting what wasn't on the page, nobody was overly fond of Jake's actual widow.

People were quoted—without attribution—as having been at the funeral and memorial service "for Jake" or because they "loved Jake." Some expected quotes were notable for their omission. Nobody remembered to express sorrow for the bride-widow.

The article said that the widow King was the former Stacy Collins, and that as Stacy Williams, she'd been an actor. I wondered, then, whether there was a Mr. Collins, or a Mr. Williams? Mary Elizabeth. Betsey in college. M. E. or Emmie now. Stacy. Cade Collins Williams King. Who else? It felt more like games with lights and shadows than actual name changes.

"I did some stuff today, too." He didn't have class on Tuesdays, but had been home studying most of the day, I'd thought. "Got you a stack of faxes from the *Chron*."

"You know somebody in San Francisco?"

"More a six degrees of separation thing, like your sister and the Main Line matrons would have been. Guy I know left the force, went out to do security work, mostly with Silicon Valley people. But he knew somebody in the city, who knew somebody at the *Chron* an'—lots about your lady. And the guy's ready to put together all the legal records if you want them."

"Like that?" I couldn't believe it. Yesterday, finding anything out about the woman calling herself Emmie Cade seemed daunting. Today, even if I'd spent all the intervening time polishing my nails, we'd have her background, thanks to Mackenzie's contacts.

"Bottom line is, the lady never has been arrested, let alone gone to prison. A lot of smoke, but no fire."

"Meaning?"

"After—what shall I call her? She's got half a dozen names."

"Emmie. Live in the moment. That's who she currently is."

"Okay. After Emmie moved here and was gone from

Marin, the *IJ*—that paper that had the big article about Jake King's death—ran a feature on her. A reporter there— spoke to him today—spent a few months gathering background. Apparently, maybe because of rumors started by Jake's ex-wife, who didn't get any money when he died, people were convinced Emmie killed him and got off scot- free, and then somebody knew somebody else in Austin, where she was engaged to the motorcycle man and knew that there was talk about her in Texas, too. It prompted this guy to dig into her past."

He passed me five pages of faxed news story. The photo at the top of the page showed the same sweet face and smile I'd met yesterday. This time, future-Emmie wore an abbreviated wedding veil that poufed around her head but didn't cover her face.

The headline said, "Out of a murky past—and gone again?"

"She disappeared from there?" I asked.

"No forwarding address, apparently." Mackenzie leaned back, satisfied with himself. "That motorcycle accident bothered folks. It was somewhat weird and thought to be a suicide, which nobody could prove, but that didn't stop them from blamin' it on her. This fellow, Collins—"

"One of her names. But they weren't married, right?"

"Right. But he bought a house with her, jointly, with sur- vivor's rights, and he'd rewritten his will so that Emmie— who was Stacy Williams then—got his estate. Not vast, mind you, nothin' like Jake King's, but vast enough to use as a jumping-off place for the next husband-hunt."

"I am so confused. When was Collins? Before or after her other marriage?"

"After it. Husband number one was—is—he survived her—William Stacey. Most people take their husband's name when they marry. His last name. She did that, but changed her first name to Maribeth."

"Which is really only a variation on her given names."

He shrugged. "Still, who takes her husband's name after a divorce? She was Betsey before she married him, Maribeth Stacey durin' the marriage, and Stacy Williams—his name backward—afterward."

"And Stacy Collins by the time she met up with Jake. I wonder how she ever remembered who she was."

He grinned. "An', may I say, according to the gossips who consulted with that writer, she walked away from William Stacey with a handsome bundle as well, and that despite rumors that she was having entirely too much fun on the side durin' the marriage with another rich guy who loved giving expensive gifts. A married rich guy. The woman has a talent for other people's money. Then she comes here and snares another one."

"It could all be gossip," I said, glancing through the long article.

"Far as I know, nobody sued about that article," Mackenzie murmured. "I asked."

"She might not have ever known about it." I skimmed over comments about Betsey's—or Stacy's—or Maribeth's flirtatiousness, and what you'd call the step beyond flirtatiousness. Open approaches to "men of substance," as the writer put it. Between marriages she'd made requests for loans while she was getting started with acting, for start-up money for a business that never materialized, for short-term help while she had a cash-flow problem with vague "trusts." I looked up at Mackenzie. "Nobody I'd want my son to marry."

"Well, as I hope to co-create any son of yours, let me go on record sayin' me neither. But—here's the point: When you strip away the innuendos and the theories and the suspicions, what do you have? A woman with a bad rep, whose morals are less rigid than we like. A woman whose love of money might be greater than her love of men, but that's not for sure. Remember—our question was only: Who is she?"

I took a few minutes to go through the articles, making notes to which I added what now felt like the pathetic crumbs I'd gotten from the computer today and dinner the night before, and then I was ready to read off the list to Mackenzie.

"According to this article, and to Vicky Baer, she was born Mary Elizabeth Cade, daughter of Michael and Patricia. Born in Chicago, moved all over the place. Attended a series of schools. I know that one of them was in Ohio, where she met Vicky Smith, now Baer."

"Do you think Mrs. Fairchild needs quite all that?"

I had no idea what or how much a client wanted. If I'd hired me, I'd want every single thing I could dig up. "She was still Mary Elizabeth then, and their paths crossed again at Cornell, where she called herself Betsey and stayed only a short while. In Mrs. Fairchild's version, she got mono and didn't come back. In Vicky Baer's version, she ran off with a guy. Might be that both are true. Anyway, she never graduated from any college. She married William—Billy—Stacey when she was twenty-one, moved to Atlanta, where she called herself Maribeth Stacey. They had an ugly divorce, many rumors of an extramarital affair or two—on her part—and she walked away with money."

"And unpaid loans."

"Then she moved to Austin and Geoffrey Collins, motorcycle man." I considered his name. "I don't think of Geoffreys with a G as Harley types."

At that, Ozzie turned his head, and I nodded. "He died in an accident, Ozzie," I said.

"That proves she's no good, then," he said. I wasn't sure if he meant Emmie of the many names or Geoffrey's motorcycle, but I plugged on.

"Geoffrey had a car dealership."

"He should have driven what he was sellin' other people to drive," Mackenzie said.

"Are you saying nobody has accidents in cars?" Ozzie snorted his derision of slow-moving four-wheeled vehicles before he returned to his work. A chemical corporation paid him a small annual stipend to do background checks as needed, mostly for job applicants, who apparently lied alarmingly about their academic and work backgrounds. Emmie might be vague about her past, but as far as I could tell, she hadn't lied. Except, perhaps, about killing a person or two along the way.

"You were sayin'," Mackenzie prompted.

"The car dealership. Right. Guess who inherited it, then sold it? And guess when that legal document had been worked out?"

"Ten minutes before his accident?" Mackenzie suggested.

"Close. Two weeks. Guess she didn't want it to look suspicious. By now, she was trying to act, and called herself Stacy Williams—her ex-husband's name in reverse. You wonder how she managed her I.D. cards and drivers' licenses. Acting didn't work out, and I guess she figured new name, new chance, so she took Geoffrey's last name, even though they'd never married. Now she was Stacy Collins, and she moved to the Bay Area, met and married Jake King. They were married as soon as he could divorce his wife. He apparently got sole custody of his ketch—a seventy-five-foot ocean-going aluminum yacht."

Ozzie turned at the words and nodded his approval. "You have any idea how much a thing like that would cost?" he said softly. "This is a well-off widow indeed."

They were married aboard the boat and then sailed off to Tahiti. Six months after their return, during an anniversary celebration aboard the boat, the man who could sail the Pacific, continent to continent, drowned on a sunny, calm spring day. Despite a boatful of people, no one had seen the accident, nor could anyone explain it. Repeatedly, mention was made of his expertise. "He could have been in the Olympics if he'd wanted to," one person had said. And there endeth the western newspapers' report because their trail got cold. She was gone.

The article said she'd told people she was going away for a short while to "heal" after Jake's death, and it wasn't until the Kings' home was put on the market, six months later, that people realized she was gone for good. No forwarding address, no further contact with former neighbors and acquaintances.

No close friends, apparently. A few who said they'd felt close to her—until she came on to their husbands.

"At which time she drops Jake's name and appears here as M. E.—or Emmie—Cade, with, once again, the cash to rent or buy the right place in the right neighborhood, meet the right people at the right clubs and charities, and catch her a new one. Did she ever hold an actual job, or try running the businesses she borrowed money for?"

"The article didn't mention any occupation except home-wrecker and fortune-seeker. She said she'd been an actress for a while."

"Great. One of the untraceable jobs, unless she's listed with Equity. And she won't be."

"Odds are against it," I agreed.

"She'd have a story for it. Never made it that far, didn't get the parts that would qualify. Waited tables, waited for a break. Moved on."

"Which could be exactly what happened. It certainly wouldn't be unique—and might further the desire to find money instead." I looked at my notes from the day before. "She did interior design in Austin, too."

"Again, nearly impossible to prove or disprove. Given that we have no evidence of her being trained for that, you have to hope she paid her dues to a professional organization. A lady has a sense of style, good taste, a retail sales number, and affluent friends she'll shop for, and sometimes, like that, she's got a new title. How do you trace her through that? Besides, once she had her first nest egg, she probably didn't need an actual job."

"It looks good to seem to be living off a trust fund," I said. "It's attractive—literally. Money goes to money. If it's obvious you don't need it—you're given full access to it." I took a breath and considered the woman's sketchy past and the reason Mrs. Fairchild had hired us. "I wonder why the person who sent those warnings about the praying mantis didn't send this story instead. This is so much more damning."

C.K. pulled at his right earlobe. That unconscious gesture seems to pull a switch in his brain. Someday, when we're both in rocking chairs, and he's had so many good ideas, one of his earlobes will rest on his shoulder blade. "Maybe that person didn't know about this article," he finally said. "Somebody who doesn't live in Marin County, who never knew the paper wrote about Ms. Cade."

"Somebody with a never-ending hate for her? Like the person who told the reporter the rumors in the first place?"

He nodded. "A Texan, wasn't it? Remember, that story came out six months after Jake King died, when the house was sold and Emmie Cade—or Stacy King, as she'd been— was long gone to places unknown."

"And we'll never find out who that person was, right?"

"Doubt it. Newspaper confidentiality about sources."

"But none of the postmarks were from Texas."

"A mystery," C.K. murmured. He didn't seem that concerned, though it remained significant to me.

"So what next?" I asked.

He looked at me without saying anything, as if he was

waiting for me to say something more. It's always a pleasure to contemplate his fine features and shocking blue eyes. They are such an acute blue, you want to search for bluer words—azure, cerulean, cobalt—except they aren't cobalt, they're lighter and brighter. They're so blue, you'd notice them from around the corner.

But at the moment, I wanted him to teach me this business, and he wasn't, so his eyes were simply blue, and annoyingly amused, and I wasn't into gazing upon them much longer. "Manda," he said softly after too long a pause, "it's okay."

"Meaning what?"

"C'mon. You don't have to play the ingénue, the apt pupil, the disciple. My ego can handle your charging forward on your own. I'm countin' on it and proud of you for it."

"I don't understand a thing you're saying. In plain English, what would an experienced investigator do next?"

"No need to ask me that. Suppose you gave an assignment to research a question about *Lord of the Flies*, and your smartest student finds the stuff she needs and writes it up. What should she do next?"

Oh. That.

No. "I can't call her up and tell her this," I said. "Not now!"

"Why not? It says who Emmie Cade is and was. That was the assignment. If she wants more, she tells us so, and we continue."

"She hired me twenty-four hours ago, and I barely did a thing—you did it."

"The newspaper in California did it, and that's called research. How different is it from the databases online? You thought it would all be nosing around with a magnifying glass?"

"I thought it would be—different."

"Sometimes it is, but the thing is, this is now. What else does Claire Fairchild need to know before she decides to tell her son about his intended? Do you think she needs more?"

"What about the identity of the letter-sender?"

"That wasn't what the client requested. Ms. Cade has no arrests, no records. I checked. A speeding ticket outside Austin, but that's about it. What's left to find out?"

It seemed hasty, unprofessional, slipshod. Too easy.

Mackenzie laughed out loud, a sound I usually relish and savor, but not when I'm the butt of the joke, and I knew I was this time. "Had a mechanic like you once. Every job, no matter how small, took a couple of days. Finally, I said, 'If I pay you the same exorbitant rate you charge for three days, could you have my car back in an hour?' He could and did, and said he didn't want me to think what he did so well and quickly was easy, was all, so he kept the car in his garage those needless extra days. That's what you think we should do. Hold back on the information so she thinks it was harder to get."

It sounded shabby when he said it that way, but indeed, that was not far from the feeling I had.

"Instead, dazzle her with our incredible professionalism."

"*Your* professionalism."

"We're a team," he said softly, the blue eyes back to their indescribable color. "A little dumb to be competitive on this, isn't it?"

"I'll write the report," I said. "Leo Fairchild is going to be furious. Vicky Baer said his mother had ruined all his previous romances. And now this one, most likely, as well."

Mackenzie shrugged. "I don't know that this will ruin anything. This is all—"

"I know. Rumor, speculation, and ever-increasing assets." I turned to face my computer, but Mackenzie put a hand on my arm.

"Claire Fairchild's worried. Her son set a wedding date. She's playin' sick to stop his plans until she hears from you. Talk with her. Today. Now. Phone her, tell her the facts, and that you'll send a written version and copies of the news stories, and so forth, later—if she wants anything around where Leo might find it."

"She wanted—wants—him to be happy," I whispered. "I think this information is going to make her very sad."

"Gonna make a lot of people sad," he said.

For reasons I couldn't have fully explained, except for the nonstop barrage of bad-mouthing Mary Elizabeth Betsey Maribeth Stacy Emmie Williams Stacy Collins King Cade had received, I thought about sixth grade, when for a few months, I was labeled a slut. It was a laughable, pitiable choice of insults, because puberty was taking its good old time with me, and while I can't say I'd never noticed boys, or suspected that someday they'd interest me, they didn't yet matter much, and I am not sure I even knew what the word *slut* meant—except that it was a bad thing to be. But somebody, for some reason, decided I was too something that annoyed them, and stories circulated, took hold, and grew. A time of torment, of prepubescent hell.

Luckily, the next year we moved into a neighboring district and, like that, my bad reputation evaporated to the point where I sometimes missed it.

But since then, I try to question labels. C.K. was right. Everything we'd read could be angry, hurt, or jealous rumors that had calcified over time, taking on weight and solidity and mistaken for historical truth. Of course, the woman had fed the negative fires with her inappropriate flirting and unpaid loans. Maybe she lacked character and was in fact a bad bet for Leo Fairchild. Or maybe she was too pretty, too delicate, too attractive to too many men, and she was the designated *slut* the way I had been in sixth grade, with as little basis.

"Look at you," Mackenzie said. "Frozen to the spot."

"No, I'm going to—"

"Tell you what. I'm starving and I have a lot of reading tonight. Why don't we both call it quits here for today and head home?"

I was all for delaying contact with the Fairchilds. "Great. I'll tell her tomorrow, I promise."

He shook his head. "We can stop off and tell her in person on the way. She's a worried woman. Deserves to know. And the rain's stopped. It'll be nice—we'll take a walk."

"Both of us?"

"Like I said, *we*."

"That'll make her happy, even if the report doesn't. She was disappointed when I showed up, because she'd talked to you—to a man. She'll feel she's getting her money's worth."

"Even though we did it in twenty-four hours," he said.

Our office is on Market Street, close to where the cityscape begins to slide off whatever downtown pretenses rule elsewhere. Almost nobody comes to us. We deliver instead, and often, it's completely a matter of phone calls and e-mails without any face-to-face. But if anyone did visit the office, they'd feel right at home in the old detective movie of their choice as they'd climb to the second-floor space Ozzie rented. The glass-paned office door felt like a window into the past. We were next to a dance studio—social dancing, not ballet. When business was good, the walls reverberated with Latin and swing rhythms. The proprietors, an angry couple in their fifties, often chose to bicker at the top of the stairs. They wore formal wear day in and day out, she in ridiculously high strappy shoes, and he in a tuxedo bought when he was at least two sizes smaller. The shoulder seams tended to split, and facing material popped out until his wife noticed, glared, and used one dagger-nailed finger to push the stuffing back inside. This evening, we had to circle around them. His stuffing was showing again.

The rain, finally over, had cleansed the air, and we had a pleasant, relaxed walk to Claire Fairchild's solid fortress of a home.

Batya opened the cream-colored front door to the condo, her eyes once again, or still, swollen and red. She held her hands under her gigantic belly, as if to keep it from falling onto the floor.

"Do you remember me?" I asked. She didn't react quickly, but she finally nodded.

"This is Mr. Mackenzie, who spoke with Mrs. Fairchild on the phone. We'd like to talk with her now."

"No, no." And in case we didn't understand those words, Batya shook her head.

"I know she's under the weather, but she's expecting us."

"She is not. No. She can't—"

"Honestly, it's okay. She won't get mad." The pathetic housekeeper was still terrified of her employer. I tried to calm her fears without telling her too much about why we were here. "Actually," I said, "she's waiting for us. She expects us. She may not have told you, because she thought we'd take longer, but—"

Batya shook her head to the point where I feared it might wobble off its moorings. "Stop. No. She isn't—can't—"

"Five minutes is all," Mackenzie said. I was sure that would do it. He has a way of wrapping his words in Southern gauze that makes them acceptable, but no less strong. It always works.

Obviously, distraught Eastern Europeans do not comprehend how attractive that accent is supposed to be. *"No minutes!"* Batya said. "Mrs. Fairchild can't see you, can't hear you—not you, not nobody. Mrs. Fairchild—she's dead!"

Ten

BATYA'S ANNOUNCEMENT LEFT ME BREATHLESS.

"Steady there," Mackenzie said.

I was astonished, but not faint. Nonetheless, "Water," he said to Batya. "And she'd better sit down." Before the housekeeper could respond, he steered me in, his arm around me, bracing me.

"I'm fine! What are you doing?" I whispered, my back to the watching Batya.

"Indulging my curiosity." Mackenzie seated me in the same love seat I'd occupied the day before. I tried to look dizzy.

Mackenzie shook his head. "You'd better sit down, too," he told Batya. "In your condition. Rest, please. You've already had a bad shock. I'll get you both water."

"Yes," she said, propelling herself into a hard-backed chair against the wall. Once on it, her feet barely touched the carpet. She'd need help getting off without tumbling forward, and I wondered how she managed when she was alone. "Is awful," she said, eyes wild. But once he'd left the room, she had no conversational bon mots to offer, so we sat in an awkward silence until I put my head back and closed my eyes, opening them only when I heard the slosh of water.

C.K. held two glasses. I sipped mine and mimed calming myself down.

"I'm sorry we've intruded at a time like this," he said softly.

Batya fanned the air with her hand. "You okay now?" she asked me, and I nodded. "I was afraid. Maybe I have two heart attacks here."

"Is that what happened?" Mackenzie asked. "Mrs. Fairchild had a heart attack?"

She nodded and sniffled, arched back until she could reach a pocket, and extracted a crumpled lump of overused tissue, then blew her nose. "Like that." She snapped her fingers.

"I thought her problems were with her lungs," Mackenzie said.

"Mister," Batya said. "I am not doctor. I wake up when emergency comes pounding and they say looks like heart, and later, that's what Mr. Leo tells me. That's what doctors tell him."

"Wait—paramedics arrived when you were asleep?"

"Wakes me up, yes. Pounding, banging—they would break door if I didn't let them in. Scared me. Like secret police, like—my own heart—" She forgot she was holding a glass, and she pressed her hand and the glass to her chest and spilled a goodly portion of it onto herself.

"Was someone else here, too?"

"Nobody. Me. Only me."

"You think Mrs. Fairchild called the paramedics, then?"

"Who else? Except she is unconscious when they get here. They say for some time. Hour, more. Makes no sense, but is how it is. Maybe rescuers come slow, like take an hour?"

"What time did they get here?"

She blinked her swollen eyes, looked worried by the question, then silently debated it before nodding. "Midnight?"

"And was she still alive?" Mackenzie asked.

She shook her head.

"Near the phone when she . . ."

Batya winced.

Mackenzie opted for euphemism. ". . . passed on?"

Batya shook her head and looked down at her belly, not as if she wanted to gaze upon her unborn child, but as if she didn't want to meet our eyes. "She was on bed, but half off, too."

Trying to reach the phone? I was over the initial shock, and now I felt her death as a great pressure on my own heart. What an ironic pity, to think you were pretending to be sick, when unbeknownst to you, you were, in fact, fatally ill.

After a beat too long of silence, Batya looked up at us. "She said she felt bad, but I didn't know so bad!"

"Nobody's blaming you," Mackenzie said softly.

Batya didn't look convinced of that.

"People have heart attacks without warning."

"Is not my fault," she said. "Mr. Leo, he tells me to go to bed. He says everything is fine. Later—I can't hear so much in my room, way back there. She has buzzer to get me." She shook her head. "What am I doing now? No job, and Mr. Leo, he says I was supposed to take care of her! He says this to me today, after she is dead."

"Let's back up a bit. He told you to go to bed. That was last night, correct? He was here?"

"Everybody is here. Was train station. They come, they go . . . I don't feel so good now and so much back and forth and Mrs. Fairchild sick like that is too much. Not my fault. Mr. Leo, he saw how tired I was and he say, go to bed, Batya. I lock up."

"Everybody?" I asked.

She nodded. "Mr. Leo, two times. First, he comes himself. Later, he comes again with the lady."

"Emmie? The woman he's engaged to?"

"Her." She blew her nose and sat still for a while. "But the other lady, the friend, she comes, too. After him. Before them. I am good housekeeper, but with the baby and my worries right now—"

"What other lady, Batya?" Mackenzie asked gently.

"Miss Cade's friend, Mr. Leo's friend. She's here before." She looked at us. "With the animal name."

Mackenzie glanced at me. "Ms. Baer?" I asked. "Here? Last night?" The same night I had dinner with her?

She nodded.

"Do you know why?"

She sighed. "I say Mrs. Fairchild is sick. Is late. She says not so late—is maybe nine-thirty. A minute only. Needs name. She wants make rain. Crazy."

Mackenzie raised an eyebrow and checked to see if I knew how women affected precipitation.

"A shower," I said. "She wanted to give Emmie a shower." Nice. Odd, too, because she'd said they weren't that close. On the other hand, the timing suggested that she'd known about the wedding date and it had only been set that day. Emmie must have phoned her—maybe the call Vicky got at dinner, the one she took outside, when she gave her dog a potty break. Maybe my fabricated tale of the newcomer with no friends had prompted the desire to be kinder toward bad-luck Emmie.

I was getting lost on a side trip, and I pulled myself back to the present, in which Mackenzie was asking questions, almost as if he were still a homicide cop. Batya, perhaps used to being questioned by strangers in her homeland, didn't seem to realize we had no right to be in the apartment, let alone to interrogate her.

"What time was Mr. Leo here?" Mackenzie asked. "The visit when he told you to go to bed."

She shook her head, held up her wrist. "No watch. Too swollen. Maybe nine-thirty?"

"Was Ms. Baer still here?"

She shook her head. "Maybe ten. Too late, yes? Kills his own mother coming here middle of night."

"And you went to sleep, yes?"

"I go to my room."

"So you don't know when he left."

"You have baby. See how you sleep near end of the pregnant. This is why I am tired."

"Are you saying you heard them leave?"

"I leave my door open a while. I don't sleep at all."

I wanted to ask how that was so when she'd already said she couldn't hear a thing from her room "back there."

I knew Mackenzie had caught the discrepancy as well, but he was incredibly polite. He smiled and looked concerned for Batya's welfare, and for all I know, he was. He has a way of asking a question that almost makes the words invisible, almost makes the person he's addressing think they've thought them up themselves, that the topic is precisely what they want to talk about. Even when he has to ask the question several times. "Do you know what time you heard him leave?"

"I hear door. I hear them in hallway, talking, then door. Not so long after, he tells me go to bed."

"Ten o'clock, then?"

"Something like. A little later, sure. Yes, sure, because now I remember. My show ended, so I turn off TV."

"And his fiancée was with him the whole time."

"This time, yes. This his second time here last night. Third time here for day. He comes first with her in day, then alone after dinner, then later, with her again. Then they leave. I didn't trust about door. He was angry, maybe he forgets to lock. So I check. And I check her, too."

I was glad I hadn't asked. Her door had been open and she'd been actively listening until she knew the door was locked and her employer was safe for the night.

"Mrs. Fairchild?"

She nodded. "She was okay. Sitting in bed, says she's going to sleep. I thought she would cry, he is so mean to her, but no. American children . . ." She pursed her mouth with distaste. It was hard for me to think of fortysomething Leo as a child.

"How was he mean, Batya?" I liked the way Mackenzie pulled her name in, often enough—but not too often—softening its edges so that it was a gentle and friendly tap on the shoulder.

"His own mother is sick in bed, but still, they shout. No—*he* shouts. Never her. It hurts too much." She tapped her chest, showing us where it hurt Claire Fairchild. Then she tried to lean forward, toward us, as if to confide, but only her head jutted out while the rest of her stayed in place behind the belly. "I not listening. Understand? I not do the . . ." She cupped her hand to her ear. "Never. But Mr. Leo is so loud."

"Could you hear what they were saying?"

She shrugged. "Noise. Angry. Words that don't make sense."

"Like what?"

"About wedding. And something—crazy. I don't know. First he asks about *reader*. I think he says 'reader,' but my English . . ."

Me. They were arguing about me, about my transparent excuse for being there. The temperature dropped precipitously, and I shuddered.

"She say something I don't hear because I never—" Again, the cupped hand to the ear.

"Of course not," Mackenzie said. "But sometimes, people are so loud, you can't help but hear. Even in a big apartment like this one."

She nodded. "I have work, always work. I don't listen behind door. And she talks soft. Normal. But he's so angry

then, so loud, and he says 'you'—he means his mother—
'hire' or 'fire,' I can't make out, 'the pie.' Fire the pie?
Maybe should be bake the pie? Hurts my head, crazy talk,
so I stop listening, finish dishes, he leaves. Then, I think I sit
down, have tea—but the Rain Lady comes. The wolf."

"Baer. Did she stay long?"

"Not very. I am so tired then from carrying trays, opening doors . . ."

"How did Mrs. Fairchild seem then?"

"She say sick. Maybe her heart hurts, she doesn't tell me
such things. I am servant."

"Did everything seem normal about her? Did she eat
much dinner?"

Batya looked at us both as if we were dangerous, as if a
wrong answer might trap her. "She never eat much. I carry
that heavy tray and . . . no. Not much."

"More or less than usual last night?"

"Same."

Either the answer was one she considered safe, or the
simple truth, since Claire Fairchild had not truly been any
sicker than was normal. Except: She died.

"How long do you think Ms. Baer stayed?"

"I have no watch," Batya repeated. "Who knows? All I
think is why so many people this one night when she is
sick? And me—I can't lay down until they go. My back always hurt now."

"Did she stay a long time, or not long?"

"Maybe not so long. But then Mr. Leo is back, and Miss
Emmie. And she brings flowers!" Batya slapped her forehead as if that was mind-boggling news. "Big yellow and
red flowers."

I could picture Emmie Cade in a lace-trimmed blouse
and layered chiffon skirt, nearly hidden behind a huge bou-
quet. Flowers signaling peace, a truce, an end to mother–
future-daughter-in-law hostilities.

"Flowers make Mrs. Fairchild sick!" Batya said indignantly. "No perfume—no flowers. She knows!"

But so did Leo. Why, then, did he allow Emmie to bring them? I almost asked, but Mackenzie did something with the muscles around his eyes. Not exactly a squint, but a clear cease-and-desist message. I wondered how he did that, and whether I could successfully imitate the expression.

"I put them in kitchen, where Mrs. Fairchild never goes. Should have put outside, in trash, but my back . . ." She pulled and twisted the fabric of her sleeve and sighed. "Maybe their smell kills her?" She snuffled, but her eyes stayed on us, deciding how we felt about her guilt.

"I doubt that," Mackenzie said. "Too far away." He spoke with great scientific assurance, as if the potentially lethal impact of floral perfumes had been the first subject in his doctoral program, and he'd gotten an A on the final. "You did the right thing, making sure Ms. Cade went in without her flowers."

Batya looked at him sideways, checking for expression, then at me. "I did right thing," she repeated. "Yes."

"And when you took the flowers, what did she do?"

She raised her eyebrows and opened her eyes till there was white all around the pupils, and put her hand to her mouth. When she was convinced we understood the gesture, she relaxed again. "Like that. *Sorry,* she says. *Forgot.* Then she goes in."

"To Mrs. Fairchild's bedroom," Mackenzie prompted.

Batya nodded. "By self. Soon, he goes in, too. Both in there now. Wear her out. Too much company for sick woman. I go in and tell them no, she not well, and they say, 'Just a minute. I be there just one minute.' Everybody says it and nobody is just a minute except his girlfriend—"

"Emmie Cade."

"Yes. Her. She is still upset about flowers, and when I say

must leave, she does. She waits in living room. He says I should go to bed, but I listen because they make Mrs. Fairchild sicker. Then they leave and later, people bang on door and she is dead." She wiped at her eyes again with the exhausted lump of tissue.

I sat holding my water glass, listening to them, admiring how Mackenzie had finessed our way into the condo and into Batya's confidences. I remembered what he'd told me about successful con artists. He, too, could have had a lucrative life of crime because he had the ability to adopt a guileless, completely convincing persona while he lied through his teeth. I wasn't sure that was a great trait in a prospective husband. He also made it easy to forget to question his presence, and I think that would be true even with a more sophisticated person than Batya, a person aware of niceties such as civil rights.

They spoke, but a voice inside of me did as well, and it wouldn't stop. Claire Fairchild was nowhere near death, it said. Something is rotten here. She told me she could fool them all, and she was right. Somebody believed she was that sick, or believed everyone else would believe it, and killed her.

I heard as well a counter-voice, challenging my assumptions, asking the simple question: How? Nobody was there when she died, and there were apparently no signs of violence, or they would have been noted. How could it be anything but a natural death in that case?

Certainly, death arrived with a snap of the finger, and people keeled over taking everyone by surprise. But until proven otherwise, I was sure that a woman doesn't investigate a shady future daughter-in-law, a possible killer, fight with people who are outraged and threatened by the investigation, intimidate and threaten her servant, then abruptly die of natural causes without provoking suspicion.

"Is there something I can do for you?" Mackenzie asked Batya. "Are you here alone?"

"Batya is alone in this world."

But not quite as desperately so as she'd been a day earlier. Batya was now free. Nobody was blackmailing her anymore.

Mackenzie didn't have to prod this time. Batya answered the question. "I cannot leave house alone. No. And Mrs. Fairchild, she says . . ." She looked at us, one at a time, and bit at her bottom lip.

"Go on," I prompted. "It's okay. Whatever it is, it's okay."

"She say if she die, she leave me money. Because I take good care of her. I am poor woman . . ." She had run out of tissue and, this time, she lifted her shoulder in an attempt to blot her tears. "Two babies, one sick, please God new one should be okay, and what? What then? My husband is disappeared and now Mrs. Fairchild, too." Mackenzie fished around in his pockets, found a handkerchief, and passed it over to her. She looked at it, and then at him, as if he'd offered her an annuity for life instead of a piece of cloth. "I wash and clean it for you later," she whispered.

He shook his head.

"Because," she said, "life. I look at my life and ask, what is life, anyway, and I think, Batya, life is tissue paper. Strong, ha! Like tissue, I am protected by tissue paper."

I imagined long nights in a smoky Serbo-Croatian café, arguing what life was. Or long days in a Center City condo.

"Thin, like tissue. Over, like this," and once again she snapped her fingers. "My sainted mother is one minute frying breakfast and next . . ." She lifted one hand, as if to snap her fingers one more time, then she sighed, and put the hand back down.

Both Mackenzie and I nodded sagely. We agreed. Life

was tissue paper, but now she had genuine cotton in her hand. Make of it what she would.

Apparently, the baby was also voting with its feet—whether on the tissue or cotton side of life, we couldn't tell. Batya looked startled, then put her hand on her belly. "Jumping all the time. The shock . . ." Then she looked at us. "Is not right, he shouts at his mama. My baby never will shout at me. Not allowed where I come from. Child respects."

We both maintained our solemn expressions of agreement, but I wondered if Mackenzie, too, was considering how carefully Batya cast the shadow of suspicion on Leo Fairchild and, as an alternate, the bride-to-be who had brought the death flowers. If, indeed, there was anything suspicious about Claire Fairchild's death, the housekeeper was making sure she was in the clear.

And why not? Her mental ledger sheet had no downside to Claire Fairchild's demise. It was all plusses: no I.N.S., no deportation. Plus, a legacy. Death had all the advantages.

"Help me," Batya said, pushing forward in the chair. Mackenzie all but catapulted out of his chair and took her arms. "I mean with problem." She nonetheless accepted the hoist. Once she was standing, she brushed off her belly and faced us.

She reminded me of the *Venus of Willendorf*, that Paleolithic carving that supposedly represents the first woman, or at least, the first work of art of an idealized naked woman. The exaggerated, enormous breasts resting on a very pregnant belly, and the rest of the body nearly inconsequential, mere methods of moving around that enormous fertility.

The Venus of Philadelphia spoke. "Help tell me what I do now."

"Do you have family here?" Mackenzie asked.

Batya bit at her bottom lip. "Aunt. She watches my baby,

but is no room there. I sleep on floor when I go. Still, better than here, with ghosts."

Perhaps Claire Fairchild had been telling the truth and she'd posthumously reward the woman's years of loyal service. I hoped so. Unless, of course, Batya had arranged the woman's end.

Batya pointed toward the back of the condo. "I mean help me with that. What I do about that?"

"About what?" I asked, just to prove I was also in the room.

"Come," she said, leading us down the hallway to a bedroom. "Mrs. Fairchild's room is mess. Is all right if I clean? Looks bad for housekeeper to leave mess."

The bedclothes were pulled back with a sense of rush and emergency, but that seemed all that was amiss. Otherwise, it looked like a chronically ill elderly person's room. Apparatus, bottles, and comforting aids, like special pillows.

The bed was like a hospital bed in that the back portion could be angled up, and it was in that position now. She must have had it that way to talk with her visitors.

The hospital theme spilled onto her night table, which looked like a pharmacy display, overflowing with pill bottles and pill dispensers. I saw a large segmented one that had the days of the week on it, and it wasn't the only pill holder. The tabletop was crowded with her medications, but also with small vanities—a lipstick, a hairbrush, a compact, plus predictable necessities like a tissue dispenser and water carafe, and the telephone that hadn't been used but nonetheless summoned the paramedics. A water glass lay on the floor, a still-wet spot showing around it. It must have been standing on the night table, en route to the telephone.

"What's this?" Mackenzie asked.

"Her compact," I said. "For face powder."

"No!" Batya raised her arms. Hands off, she was saying

without words. "This thing, Mrs. Fairchild, she breathes in it so doctor knows how she is."

"How? Does he come visit for checkups?"

She shook her head. "No. She does it a lot, and the telephone, she says, it goes through telephone to him."

Mackenzie stared at it for a long while, as if whatever had happened was recorded on it. "I'd like to know. . . ," he said. "I wonder if . . ."

Batya looked worried. "Is important thing. Scientific. I never touch."

He nodded, then smiled at her and looked around. The oxygen tank idled on the floor near a basket filled with magazines. As Leo had unfortunately noted, she didn't seem much of a reader. I didn't see a single book in the room, but a TV set on the far wall faced the bed. The remote control was still on the spread, and Batya pointed at it and waited until Mackenzie said it was fine to remove it.

"Was she using oxygen when the paramedics came?" Mackenzie asked in the lightest of voices.

Batya looked stumped and shook her head. Then she spoke slowly. "I . . . no. No," said more emphatically. "Strange. Should be on her face at night. Night is worst for her breath, when she sleeps."

"That is strange," Mackenzie said in that agreeable voice that made Batya and C.K. part of a team.

I didn't find it strange that she hadn't been on oxygen. Claire Fairchild had died before she settled in for the night.

"Mrs. Fairchild would be angry at mess like this."

My definition of a mess had a lot more slack built into it than Batya's did. But I wasn't the housekeeper, still afraid of what the late Mrs. Fairchild would think of the scene, and my ego did not ride on such things.

"People think lazy housekeeper, such mess. But the TV, they say all the time don't touch anything."

"That's at the scene of a crime," Mackenzie said, as always making the word have no hard edges. When he says it, *crahm* sounds nearly edible, and not at all frightening. "Police weren't here, were they?"

"Men came to take her away."

"Paramedics took her to the hospital."

"She is dead already when they come."

"Yes, but . . . they weren't the police. Still," he said, "it's okay to leave things alone for a bit. Take a rest. Relax."

"Is okay I make the bed? Mrs. Fairchild, she—"

"Why not? But don't touch anything else yet."

She nodded gravely and moved, slowly, toward the bed, obviously eager to smooth the covers. "Nothing else," she said. "Nothing else, then Mr. Leo, he cannot say I take his mother's things."

"Good idea. Everything will take care of itself in a while," Mackenzie said kindly. "You have other, happier things to think about, like your baby."

She blinked and looked down at her beach-ball body and I thought she might cry, but instead, she took another deep breath and nodded while she fussed and pulled and straightened and smoothed the sheets and covers.

I felt sorry for the life that had driven her out of her home and homeland, sorry she was now so alone in this new world. Sorry that her job and husband were both gone and, along with them, whatever safety she'd envisioned for herself and her children.

Nonetheless, while Batya smoothed the last inch of cover, I tried to memorize everything I could see, to burn a mental image of where things were placed and what things they were. To be the camera.

As if it were a crime scene, because I was positive it was.

Eleven

"WELCOME TO THE RANKS OF THE UNEMPLOYED," C.K. said as we left the late Mrs. Fairchild's building. "Well, except that you're not, teach."

"Unemployed? Are you saying that just because—"

"She's dead? You weren't going to say that, were you? Just because she's dead doesn't mean she isn't still employing us? Who is she, Elvis? She's gone, the investigation's gone, and we're outta there. As is, it's going to be harder 'n hell to get paid for what we already did. Leo doesn't sound like the easiest guy on earth, and he obviously wasn't happy with his mother's decision to hire us."

"Can you walk away from the whole thing like that?"

"What else am I supposed to do? The woman is finished with problems and questions, unless the afterlife is a much more anxious spot than we've been led to believe. An' she definitely can't write checks anymore." He stopped in front of a hole-in-the-wall restaurant and read the menu posted in the storefront window. "Are you as hungry as I am?" he asked.

"Look here, Mackenzie. She's gone, but we're still here."

He stood up straight again. "Indeed. Here and alive and hungry as hell."

"About our budget? Our carefully worked out mutually agreed-upon eating plan? And today of all times—right after you tell me we aren't going to be paid for the job we just did."

"What say? Just this once? Even though this menu's Greek to me. Place smells good."

I glanced at the menu. "This is Greek to everybody." We had gone over our new finances a dozen times, and had come up with the current income and outgo plan. Due to Mackenzie's more regular hours, now that he was no longer chasing crazed killers around on their time schedules, dinner together was a predictable almost-daily event, and somebody had to think about it. We took turns being responsible for producing something edible.

The new budget did not allow for lots of meals away from home or even cooked by other hands and brought into the home. In exchange for these additional domestic duties, we agreed to drop our standards of cuisine to anything that didn't cause permanent damage to the central nervous system.

Truth is, I'd come to enjoy both my turns and Mackenzie's, though most times, we split the chopping and broiling or whatever needed to be done. It was a good time of day, close to my favorite, when we'd gone our separate ways and were back together to talk about where our travels had taken us.

"Pretty inexpensive," Mackenzie said. "The prices are in English."

Tonight was officially my turn. Was it my ethical responsibility to remind him of that, or of our promises to be fiscally wise at all times?

I decided it was not. He was an exceptionally smart man, and surely he'd considered those factors already and didn't need my input. Besides, I had a hunger headache and was still upset about Claire Fairchild, and not a little upset, too, with the way Mackenzie had blithely dismissed the entire matter.

We went into the small room, fragrant with olive and lamb-scented steam, and my stomach and I realized the encounter with Sonia Lawrence had detoured me from lunch and I hadn't had a chance to eat anything since half a bagel at breakfast, except the pretzels that were a constant at Ozzie's office.

Ambience was not this restaurant's forte. Once, this had been a living room, which should have made it homey, but it was bleak, with the look of a newly deserted home. I had the feeling the owner had blown all of his decorating funds on a few pints of paint.

We sat at a table covered with a white cloth with a square of white paper atop it. That was festooned with a small vase with a droopy rose, the one that bloomed after the last rose of summer. We were the only customers, and the restaurant appeared a one-man show. The owner/host/waiter/chef practically danced over to us and presented us with menus, and I was glad we'd brought a little action and cash into his life.

I was tempted to order everything listed, but contented myself with pastitsio, that lovely confection of ground lamb, pasta, and many fat calories posing as a sauce.

Mackenzie ordered fish in a garlic sauce, and once we'd been served bread and a dish of olives and feta and neither of us seemed likely to keel over from starvation, I cleared my throat.

"You aren't, are you?" he immediately asked.

"I have to."

"You won't give it up?"

"It isn't right."

"You've got to understand that most times, you aren't going to know the end of the story. It's an important idea to get hold of. Most times, you do your piece of investigatin', turn it in, and then you're on to a new question. You don't know how it's used, who was found guilty or set free, or whether the wife actually divorced the guy who's been hidin' his money away. We're only chapters in somebody else's story."

"Something isn't kosher back there, Mackenzie," I said. "That's all I could think while we were there, and that's all I can think now."

He examined the pathetic rose, not meeting my eyes. "No reason to assume that." His breath denuded the flower of two of its remaining petals. In an act of botanic kindness, he looked at me directly and spared it further damage. "It's a job. Was a job. It's over."

"The woman was healthy—except of course for the emphysema, but people last decades with that. She was faking illness. I don't believe in coincidence."

He drank a hearty gulp of his water. "Should have ordered ouzo, if I didn't have to study later on. You know, sometimes I think about all the studyin' ahead, the years of it, an'—"

"We at least have to tell the police about . . . her. The fiancée." There was absolutely nobody in the place except the two of us. The proprietor, who was reading a newspaper at the far end of the room, had spoken only broken English, but I still couldn't bring myself to be indiscreet and say her name. "Isn't it the law or something?"

"The law for us is the same as for anybody else. Nothing special granted to us, so the decision is based on what you think a right-thinkin' citizen should do."

"Okay, then, as citizens, shouldn't we—"

"Manda? Listen up. If you boiled all those things we found about the woman down, we'd still only have hearsay, speculation, and gossip. The accidents? Maybe she's attracted to men who push too hard—riding the motorcycle, sailing around the world."

"Leo Fairchild is certainly not a—"

"Maybe she's ready for a change. An' maybe she's shown

some less than totally honorable behavior. Or maybe she really did try to start a business, or try to repay loans, even if she failed. But a beautiful woman gifted by admirers is as old as history. Not your feminist ideal? Okay. Not mine— but not illegal, either."

"There's something shabby about her ethics. All the playing around with her name, and the trail of dead bodies—"

"Like I said, accidents. Suicide, maybe. Not murder, or she'd be locked up now."

"Unless she's too damn pretty and clever."

"My mama used to talk about girls who had 'bad reputations.' She used to warn my sisters how once you had a bad rep, it was yours forever, and what could be worse?"

I knew that refrain, and in fact, it was the first common bond I'd heard of between our sets of parents.

"You're buyin' into it, is that it? And you want to tell the police—before there's evidence of any crime whatsoever— that Emmie Cade has a bad rep?"

"You make it sound so . . ."

"Don't get swept along by a whole lot of bad-mouthin'. Didn't you tell me some story about your bein' a slut?"

I nodded again.

"It made me so hopeful, too," he said with the shadow of a grin. "Who knew it was all a figment of somebody's imagination?"

Emmie Cade's story was different. Years and years of bad behavior.

"You want to toss suspicion on her for no good reason? Why not wait till we find out what happened? Why not wait till after the autopsy and the pathologist's report? Then—if—sure."

"Will there be one? If the doctor said heart attack—"

"He wasn't in attendance and she didn't have a history of

heart disease particularly, so yes. I believe so. Why not wait?"

I nodded.

"I mean more than a few minutes."

"Not too many minutes," I said. "Enough of them and Leo Fairchild will be married to that woman."

"And?"

"Isn't it obvious? Besides, I more or less made a promise to help Claire Fairchild about this marriage. To help her stop it if it put her son in danger."

He moved the small silver vase from between us and leaned forward, smiling. "Interesting way of looking at it. Ozzie would have a good laugh at that interpretation of our roles. But tell me: Why are you so sure she was killed?"

"Because I came to see her, and Leo got suspicious, and somebody's secret was going to be exposed."

"Ah," he said softly, leaning back in his chair. "You've managed to feel personally responsible. Consider this: If you believe you triggered events, how did that happen?"

"The way I said."

He shook his head. "Too vague. What I'm askin' is, who knew we were hired, aside from Mrs. Fairchild and the two of us?"

Even before he'd finished that sentence I realized where he was headed, and I wasn't willing to travel that road with him. It'd only make me feel worse. "You can't think Beth . . ."

"I have to think Beth, because who else is there? If she didn't tell Vicky Baer, for whatever reason, then how did the information make its transit around?"

"It didn't necessarily start with Vicky Baer. She came to talk about giving a shower for Emmie. Obviously, Emmie herself told her that she was getting married in two weeks." The awful thing was, I could envision Beth telling Vicky Baer because she thought what I did was "cute" and might make her own subtle sales pitch that much more engaging. I can arrange everything, she'd be saying in essence—even a sister who's sleuthing around the Main Line. She would never do anything that she perceived as potentially harmful, but why would bragging about your sister's job be a bad thing? She'd undoubtedly said something, and Ms. Baer thought back to all my remarks about her old friend, and put two and two together. Those excellent schools she'd attended insisted you knew that much math.

And then, likely as not, indignant on her friend's behalf, she told her, and Emmie told Leo.

I must have looked still more depressed, because Mackenzie changed tracks and tried to make me feel better. "The most logical explanation is that Claire Fairchild told Leo when he confronted her about—"

"Me," I said. "My fault. I should have had a better cover story, but I didn't know I'd need a story, and of course, I had no way of knowing the woman didn't read."

"Doesn't matter now. So maybe she told him, he told Emmie, and she did or didn't tell her old friend. Or it started the other way."

"But if Leo was the one who found out, in that fight with his mother, he probably wouldn't be stupid enough to tell his fiancée. I mean, I assume he didn't want the two women in a permanent state of war."

"Unless his mother told him about what happened in San Francisco and he got scared, too. Wanted her to know he was on to her."

That produced an olive-eating silence until finally, only a small container of pits remained. The feta and bread had long since disappeared. I couldn't think of any logical response, and all I wanted to say, again and again, was: It wasn't right.

"Here it is and it's beautiful, is it not? My two best, best dishes! Enjoy!" The owner chuckled as he presented us with enormous platters. The aroma of nutmeg drifted up from mine, and Mackenzie smiled and inhaled deeply over his garlicky entrée.

"There's Batya, too," I said. "She overheard everything."

"But she wasn't being investigated, so your theory—"

"Maybe her motives had nothing to do with me."

"Gets you off the guilt-hook, then, right?"

"Well ... I'm bothered about who called the paramedics, aren't you? She's the only possibility."

"Why would she lie and say she didn't, then?"

"So she could lie and say she didn't know Claire Fairchild was dying."

The chef-owner hovered nearby, waiting.

We complimented him on the aroma, then tasted, and recomplimented as he continued to stand there. He poured more wine into my already-full glass, convinced Mackenzie—not a difficult job—that one glass of wine wouldn't prevent studying later on, and again awaited a verdict, which was again positive.

The food was delicious, but if he insisted on being an active part of every dining experience, I could understand why the place wasn't thriving.

Finally, he left us alone.

"Something rotten happened there," I said. "You know how to find things out. You were a homicide cop all those years."

"I'm not one now. I have no legal—"

"You're clever."

"You have an idea, don't you?"

"More a gut feeling somebody did that woman in."

He stopped, a fork filled with flaky white fish doused with the stinking rose—I could smell the garlic from across the table—midway to his mouth. "How?" he asked quietly. "She was alive after everybody left. So how?"

"I don't know. Something slow. A poison?"

"There are symptoms with poisons. Symptoms not meant for the dinner table."

"Something biological warfarish. Something the government's afraid terrorists will use."

"Like what?" He didn't even look up from his food when he asked that. He didn't care.

"There must be those things—look at the anthrax deaths—or what are we all worried about protecting ourselves against? Claire Fairchild went from relative health to zap, dead—"

He sighed. He over-sighed, so that if there were a far balcony, the theatergoers would know he was tired, possibly peeved, and definitely not interested. "Forgive me," he said. "I love you dearly, and among the things I love about you is your mind, which comes up with surprise after surprise, as now. But for the rest of dinner, could we shelve this and talk about reality?"

"As if—"

"Reword that. Let's talk about urgent matters."

"Those matters are two days away," I said. "Claire Fairchild is dead now." It was much easier thinking about a dead near-stranger than contemplating the visitors ahead.

Ever since they'd announced their "All-U.S.A.-Scattered-Offspring Visitation," I'd felt like one of those metal hunters at the shore, poking in the sand and sifting out the worthless from the treasures. Not only did every remark about past affairs of the heart resurface, but so did odd bits and pieces, descriptions and explanations of his family from which I built an image of parents who seemed an acquired taste, like cigars or octopus sushi. Mackenzie called them *eccentric* and *colorful*, but anyone who's read books by Southern authors knows to duck when those adjectives are in the vicinity. *Eccentricity* mutates into *lunacy* when it crosses the Mason-Dixon, and *colorful* families are genetically suspect and dourly *dysfunctional* in Yankee-land.

We grow eccentrics in this climate, too, but then we lock them up.

For starters, C.K.'s parents, who hadn't even given him a first name, were themselves named Boy and Gabby. More properly, Boyd and Gabrielle, but nobody called them that. I frankly cannot imagine a grown man in Philadelphia being called—allowing people to call him—Boy.

Perpetual Boy or not, Mackenzie Père sounded less dotty than Gabby, and their couplehood was always described in the most glowing of terms. C.K. forever referred to his happily mismatched parents when I'd get nervous about our differences. To him, they were the gold standard of how opposites can attract and keep on attracting.

Boy was described as an outdoorsy sort of man, fond of hunting and fishing, bad jokes, and lamentably conservative politics that Gabby in no way shared.

I wasn't apprehensive about their eccentricities on my own behalf. It was how those interesting deviations from the norm were going to mesh with my parents' familiar yet strange ways. My father was shy, taciturn, an observer, a city boy who considered stamp collecting a sport. He'd never hunted and never wanted to. His politics were liberal, thoughtful, and soft-spoken. He loved his family passionately, but was not a demonstrative man.

My mother was listed as an Independent, and her political philosophy mutated according to whatever annoyed her at any given moment. She wasn't shy about sharing her views—or changing them fifteen minutes later. She was also an inveterate toucher and hugger, and even normal Northerners had been known to step back and be astounded by one of her unprovoked hugs.

My mother was coming north to crack the whip and get us in line—and that meant the line down the aisle. None of this shilly-shallying and delaying. Bea Pepper was on her way.

My father was coming north because my mother was, and when the word *wedding* floated through the ether, what he thought about—but was too polite and quiet to say—was the enormous Mackenzie clan and what it would cost to manage such a guest list. He was not a wealthy man and he was all for taking things as slowly as possible.

Mackenzie's mother had never even hinted that she'd like things to move more swiftly—at least not with me—and who knew what Boy Mackenzie wanted, aside from a shotgun and a fishing rod?

The fathers didn't seem likely to get along, and the mothers seemed even less so. But their arrivals were forty-eight hours away. Somehow, it would all work out. That had become my new mantra, but at the moment, my mantra's batteries had run out.

"You look so worried," Mackenzie said. "Shouldn't be. They'll love you to death. They're all for having fun and celebrating whatever's around to celebrate. That's undoubtedly how they wound up with eight children." He reached over and put one of his hands atop mine, the one that had his grandmother's ring on it. "No reason to be concerned," he said softly. "Everything's going to be fine."

But his words were southerning up, which is to say, mushing down, spun and liquified in the blender of his own apprehensions.

And why shouldn't he be nervous? Why shouldn't we both be? Why on earth were we supposed to believe that stupid mantra—It Will All Work Out—when nothing whatsoever had, so far?

Mackenzie was wrong. Dead wrong. It was easier and more productive to think about Claire Fairchild. There was nothing I could do about the Parents' Visits. That would be its own disaster, or it would not.

But Claire Fairchild had suffered the ultimate disaster, and I could do something about that.

I smiled at my fiancé, my love, my partner. I smiled and realized how easily looks—including mine—could deceive. Because I wasn't going to let go of whatever Claire Fairchild's death might mean, or my part in causing it, no matter what Mackenzie thought.

Yes, I was his partner, in life and in work, but neither relationship meant I was supposed to be indistinguishable from him. I was myself, and I'd do whatever I thought was right.

He smiled back, his face full of love and trust.

I wasn't sure I liked me at the moment.

Twelve

ONE OF THE OFTEN-OVERLOOKED GOOD THINGS ABOUT teaching is that it's very Zen, an ongoing lesson in living in the minute. To do even a mediocre job, and to avoid all hell breaking out, a teacher has to be present in mind as well as body.

That sounds easy, but if taken seriously, it's anything but. Being on, being alert, being aware of what's happening in twenty to thirty separate bodies and minds makes for an incredibly difficult job even without the mandate of wedging culturally important information between the audience's ears. Imagine what pay and benefits Actors Equity would demand if their member performers had to hold the stage, being alert and on for five to six hours per performance. *Hamlet* each and every school day.

But the good side of this is that it means the teacher's mind can't wander and obsess, even if really important nonclassroom matters loom, like planning how to prepare for meeting the senior Mackenzies. Making A Good Impression. This translates into the mundane quandary of what to wear. Certainly not the otherwise perfect white silk blouse the teacher currently has on, not tomorrow and not perhaps ever again, because ten minutes earlier, her pen leaked navy blue ballpoint gorp, a splat the size of a cat's head over its right sleeve.

And this particular teacher could not, at the moment, think of a single other item in her wardrobe.

She might have thought about how messy the loft was and how much scrubbing and tidying she'd have to do tonight, and she knew her mother certainly wished she would. But luckily, there was no opportunity to think about such concerns. She had to Be Here Now And Always.

I was also too busy paying attention to the classroom to ponder the meaning of the note in my mailbox this morning, complete with smiley-face, of course. *Dr. H.,* it said. Sunshine had reverted to plain English for The Supreme Boss of Us. That *Dr.* part was an ongoing mystery. Nobody knew in what field that doctorate had been pursued, or what offshore diploma mill had produced it, because he showed no special learning—not even basic smarts—in any area yet plumbed. But no surprise, Sunshine believed in it and accorded it the full dignity of a normal abbreviation. After that, the note degenerated into pure Sunshinelish. *1ts 2CU—f2f b43@ bk. OK?*

Sunshine's notes forced me to sound them out the way a kindergartener might. "Onets—*wants*—two—to—Oh, C.U. To see you. Face-to-face be . . . no. Before three, about book." The effort exhausted me and only the *OK?* didn't require effort. Hers was the longest, least efficient, short-hand I'd ever seen.

It had to be about Sonia Lawrence's difficulties with *Lord of the Flies.* If I needed further proof of Havermeyer's lack of a brain, and I did not, here it was. Any half-wit could have told her that even if we were at war with evil, understanding the enemy, recognizing the impulse toward it would be a good thing, the equivalent of arming our side.

Couldn't he have simply said thinking was a good thing? On second thought, how could Havermeyer, who'd never dared to entertain an original thought, say that? I'd have to do battle, senselessly. I'd win. Havermeyer was wary of me, ever since I'd caught him playing doctor instead of behaving like the one he claimed to be. But the idea of having to waste breath and energy on something this stupid exhausted me in advance.

Not that I could really think about that, either. I owned nothing suitable in which to meet my future in-laws tomorrow. I had a mess of a loft that would tell the world, or at least the senior Mackenzies, all that I didn't want them to know about me, at least not until my wonderful qualities put my less-wonderful aspects into perspective, and I needed a haircut and didn't know if I could get an appointment during tomorrow's lunch hour.

And my parents were flying in to make sure there was a clash of cultures.

Not that I was thinking about them, either. I was a teacher. I had to be alert and on throughout the day.

We were dealing with antonyms, and that's what was on my mind. What is the opposite of looking forward to meeting your in-laws?

To give a hypothetical example of what a conscientious teacher simply cannot consider while she is in front of a classroom: If a woman is about to meet her future mother-in-law who—have I mentioned this?—designs and makes her own clothing, even, sometimes, to the point of dyeing the fabric and/or weaving it—then what should that hypothetical young woman wear? Should she be tailored and professional looking when she knows said future mother-in-law is fond of a former Miss Swamp who undoubtedly wears bangles, bustiers, and white patent go-go boots? Or should she instead try to anticipate and echo her colorful mother-in-law to-be? Make the older woman feel comfortable, the way a good hostess might by dressing so her visitors think they've picked the perfect outfit themselves. Should she worry about the workmanship and check all seams and feel really, really bad that she has no idea how to work a sewing machine?

Because if she did let such thoughts creep into even a sliver of her brain, her class might seize the advantage and win their case against learning any vocabulary at all. The S.A.T.s were under fire—that was probably the single current event my students recognized—and for all they knew, they said, the tests might be history and irrelevant by the time they'd apply to colleges. And they'd have wasted all this time learning words!

"It isn't like nobody understands me," a cute young thing said. "I mean, I've been talking my whole life and if I don't know *ambidextrous*, who will care?"

"Yeah," the boy the next row over said. I checked the chart. Brad. I had to memorize their names, forget about Boy and Gabby and focus on the classroom. Brad obviously had the hots for the cute young thing, even if winning her involved talking about vocabulary. "It's not like I have these big blank spots when I talk, you know. Like I'd have to shut up because I didn't have that vocabulary lesson."

There's a dark part of me that loves to watch them rally their forces and shape logical arguments, even when their defense is ignorant nonsense. But sooner or later, you have to stop it, even if you aren't obsessively thinking about all the things you haven't done or taken care of that's going to cost you points with your future in-laws. "We're learning how to think," I said. "We're also talking about analogies, about seeing the relationships between words and ideas. . . . There will still be S.A.T.s, but with more emphasis on your writing. So how about learning a few words with which to express yourself?"

They regarded me with compassion and pity. I was so far removed from their concept of sane behavior and ideas, they looked as if they were planning an intervention to get me the help I so desperately required.

Meanwhile, my inner couturier had gone over the edge and was screaming in many languages, pacing in tight circles inside my brain. How about that linen outfit? Needs ironing. Tonight, then, after I clean and polish and straighten. Won't wear it to school, because by the time they arrive late tomorrow, it'll look as if I'd slept in it.

Or maybe I would indeed sleep in it and have a head start and an excuse.

Is black better? Is black always safe? Or too . . . New York. They're from Louisiana. They won't get it. But my black slacks didn't need ironing the way the beige linen ones did.

"Who's ever going to even say *ambidextrous*? And why would they if they can say 'I can write with both my hands,'" the boy—I checked the seating chart—Daniel—on the other side of the cutie pie—I checked the chart again—Allison—said. Dueling hormones for the fair Allison's hand. If they'd only learn the word *ambidextrous*, they'd know they could each have one of her hands.

When would I have their names memorized? It had never taken this long, had it? "Either hand," I murmured.

The other good news is that even as you're failing to be a decent teacher, and you aren't really there, the sheer force of adolescent will and obstinacy drives the hour on, heaves it through the slow lurches of the classroom clock until this session's over. Either they'd learned *ambidextrous* or they hadn't, and I'd settled on ironing the linen outfit because then I could wear a celadon summer sweater Mackenzie had given me for my birthday. He said it matched my eyes, which it doesn't, but his mother would have to approve of something her son had chosen. Maybe that would include me, too.

THE MORNING SEEMED INTERMINABLE. ACTUALLY, IT WASN'T an illusion. It just barely terminated itself after about five years. When I'd exhausted my patience with my inner-wardrobe mistress, my attention again ran sideways, into a pit called Havermeyer Is On My Case Again.

I should probably be ashamed to say that this item fired fewer brain cells than my choice of clothing had. But then, I'd been coping with Havermeyer for years, and I was completely new at the daughter-in-law thing.

Experience pays. What I've learned about the headmaster and perhaps all truly stupid people in power is that somewhere in the center of their bombastic hearts, they know they're dumb. They deserve a bit of sympathy, because it must feel rotten to be in constant danger of being shown for the fool and fake they are.

It should be against the law—against the Constitution—for an idiot to be in charge of innocent children's destinies. But given the situation, and the tenuous state of our jobs and the economy, we protect and defend our young by using guerrilla tactics against Our Leader.

I've learned that my best defense is an offense, and I bamboozle him by using his own methodology, i.e., emphatic stupidity.

I don't question or await his answer. Instead, I agree with him, right from the get-go. I behave as if I know what he's about to say, which is, amazingly enough, precisely what I wish he'd say, and nine times out of ten, he silently retreats and changes his position so that he can agree and even, perhaps, believe that's what he meant all along. Why not? It isn't as if there's any bedrock of conviction or philosophy for him to tap into, test ideas against.

And so at noon, finding him idling away the time in his office, I decided to get the meeting over. "Thanks for grabbing this problem by the horns," I said as I entered his office. It's an odd room, decorated with Latinate diplomas from unrecognizable institutions. I wish there were time to study them, but he's made sure they're out of clear-reading range. Besides, I had to stay aggressive. "That woman means well, as we both know, but really . . . can you imagine?"

He'd gestured for me to sit, and had taken his seat again, behind his massive, empty desk. I considered how warm he must be on this balmy September day. He wore a vest no matter the season, and I was convinced it was only so that he could dangle his pseudo Phi Beta Kappa Key across his shirtfront. Now, he cleared his throat.

I rushed in before he could. "She's so worried about adolescents reading about evil that she's going to leave them unable to recognize it. And where would we be if we censored young minds that way? The author's a Nobel Prize winner—isn't that a sufficient credential? He's part of the canon, now."

I was pretty sure my principal thought I was now talking about artillery. That war on evil, perhaps.

"It's a good thing this happened early in the year," I rattled on. "This way, a tone and precedent—especially in the light of the higher standards you're implementing here—is set for the future." He waited a few moments, then nodded very slowly, as if he were still learning how to lower and raise his head. "And I hope it's not out of line to say how impressed I am with your swift and efficient handling of the entire situation."

The hook had been set. I could almost see it in the fleshy part of his cheek. It was safe to pause for breath now.

"Mrs. Lawrence is concerned about her daughter's—"

"Feel free to reassure her that you've alerted me to that and I'll take special care of—pay special attention to—her daughter. And again—thanks so much for handling this. I'm positive that with your reassurance, she's already calmed down." I was halfway out of my chair by the last words.

Havermeyer looked more and more troubled, but he, too, stood, and nodded in his slow, heavy-headed manner.

I put my hand out to shake his, and he nodded again, shook my hand, then pulled back. "Did you know you have a—" He pointed at the ink blot. I was tempted to do a Rorschach with it, but before he could remember that this wasn't how he'd intended the meeting to go, I looked at the mess on my sleeve with exaggerated horror. "Oh, no! I'd best take care of that. Maybe it's not too late! Thanks for pointing it out," and I was out of there.

Except I was buzzing—my cell phone, bought for the after-school life, was buzzing.

"You are sooo popular!" Sunshine chirruped as I fled into the hallway. "But did you know you have a boo-boo on your—"

"Please," a female voice on the phone said. "I need to talk to you."

I covered my free ear with my hand and began the ascent to my room, where, perhaps, I'd find quiet. Most lunches—except mine—had been eaten, and now, kids were everywhere.

"I know you probably don't want to—or don't care, but I have this horrible feeling—"

"Who is this?"

"Emmie Cade. We met the day before yesterday. I need to talk to you."

I was midway up the staircase and I paused, nearly causing a major collision with a young man racing up behind me. "But, I . . . but we—how did you find me?"

"You told us where you taught school. And she—Mrs. Fairchild—told us—told Leo, really. He was so worried about who you might be that she told him what she'd done, why you were really there."

I had no idea what to say. Was I even supposed to talk to her? According to C.K., our business with the Fairchild family—current and future members—was finished. Our client was finished, too. There was nothing further we could do for her and nothing to discuss.

But when I didn't say anything, she rushed back in. "He thought—forgive him, but Leo thought you were suspicious. He knew his mother didn't care for books, so he didn't believe your story and he thought maybe you were a con man—a con person. That's why she finally told him the truth. About your investigating me. And he told me."

And now she was telling me. Why?

"I thought he must be wrong—and then I checked today, and here you are, really a teacher. So even though she said—and Leo said he checked, because she told him the company you work with—I don't see how you can teach school and actually investigate anything—"

"Surely you didn't phone me to discuss time management, did you?"

Her voice lowered almost to a whisper. I was in my room now, and I closed the door, though I couldn't have said what I thought I was keeping out. "I have to talk to you. Otherwise—please?"

"With Mrs. Fairchild dead, I'm—we're—no longer involved, so I don't see why—"

"No, please."

"If you have something important to say, say it now. I'm really busy—"

"It isn't something that feels right on the phone. And to be honest, it'll take a few minutes. I could meet you anywhere, anytime. Please? My life's at stake here."

She was ridiculous. Dramatic, silly, and preposterous. She was taking her Romantic Poet image too seriously, but playing the damsel in distress didn't suit her. She was the one to fear. She was the one who left casualties in her wake.

And I was the one with the Mackenzies barreling toward me tomorrow, and much more than one after-school session's worth of preparations and stocking up ahead of me.

"This is not a good day," I said. "I don't have any free time whatsoever."

"I wouldn't ask, honestly." She had a lovely, melodic voice, even when she insisted it was under strain. I amazed myself by feeling sorry for her—then felt sure that's what she wanted. "But if I don't see you before the police—"

"What police?"

"*The* police."

"What do the police have to do with anything?"

"The *police*!" As if repeating the word with ever-more emphasis would give it context. "I'm sure they'll want to talk to you, and I need to talk to you first, because she hired you and I don't know what all—"

"Stop. I don't understand what you're saying, and you're saying it too fast. Why are the police going to talk to me?"

"Because—because—" She sounded near tears, or perhaps in them already. "I thought you'd know, you being on this investigation, and—"

"Ms. Cade. In about five minutes, my classroom will fill up with twenty teenagers. Try hard to make yourself clearer. The police are going to talk to me because . . . ?"

"They—the somebody, whoever it is who does things like that—"

"Like what?"

"Test. Do things to—to dead people."

"A pathologist?"

"Yes. I think so. That's it, I think. They—he—said something's wrong in her bloodstream. In her."

"Like what?" Something slow-acting that allowed those hours to elapse? I hadn't been serious when I'd said it.

"Barbiturates."

A medication. Not a poison. An accident, not a murder. The woman had prescription bottles filling the top of her nightstand. She must have grabbed the wrong one. "Too much of one of her medicines?"

"It didn't sound that way. Besides, she had that box with the dates and little places for morning pills and noon pills and nighttime pills. They were all counted out in advance. Help me." She sounded as if she were calling out from the bottom of a well.

I realized I had pulled my head away from the phone, and I was shaking it, as if to quell the urge to reach out and rescue her. Her defenseless "help me" echoed, and I understood how good she'd be at seducing me over to her camp. I didn't want to be there.

I didn't want to know what she wanted of me, why she had to see me. You don't have to meet and plan things out if you're going to tell the truth. That's one of honesty's main advantages: It saves time.

I wanted to tell her she deserved whatever she got, and I was not going to be her next comrade in crime, or a stepping-stone to her next victim.

I looked forward to talking with the police and turning over the flyers and the news story from California, and whatever else had been faxed to Ozzie's office yesterday after we left. I wished I could tell her that I knew enough about her already to want to stay miles away, but all I actually said was, "I'm too busy to meet with you."

"But—you can't do this to me! I won't let you—"

Let me! I didn't wait to hear what she wouldn't let me do, what she might threaten. I said good-bye.

It took me a while to shut off the phone. It's hard when your hand is shaking.

Thirteen

I HADN'T BEEN LYING—I DID KEEP A SPECIAL EYE OUT for Melanie Lawrence. Judging by the maternal concern for her sensibilities, I thought she might be somebody I'd missed, an introverted, shy, socially backward child who'd been dangerously overprotected and monitored, and I was ready to help her maneuver her way through this brave new high school world. The important thing was not to blame the sins of the mother on the child.

But I hadn't missed her, and if ever a girl looked as if she didn't need my help—or anyone's—it was Melanie. She was the amazingly self-assured creature I'd noticed the first day. The leader of the pack. The girl and the mother's worries didn't mesh, mainly because the girl was so much of a diamond chip off the maternal block, a petite blonde with features so regular and pleasing, they were just this side of computer-generated. She sat through class surrounded by friends, attentive herself, smiling and nodding acknowledgment of points made in the discussion of the opening segment of *Lord of the Flies*, and adding a few well-spoken comments of her own. She was going to grow up and run the world, or at least a megacorporation.

Lord of the Flies was, as always, a great book for discussion, both rich and unintimidating. "What do we know at this point about these boys?" I asked. "What do we know about Ralph?"

"Strong."

"Good looking," a girl said, and when the boys laughed derisively, she sat up straight and said, "It says so! It says that's one reason they picked him as leader."

"Not that smart," a boy said. "Piggy's the one who figures out what to do."

I kept checking my seating chart. Had to learn names more quickly. I wished kids came in more colors and patterns. It would be so easy to remember who went with a paisley face or plaid hair.

"Mean!" a tiny girl—Olivia—said softly. "That whole thing of calling him Piggy when he asked not to be."

"Then is everybody mean?" I asked. "Didn't everybody laugh when Ralph called him Piggy?"

A moment's silence, people looking side to side, checking out one another until a boy—Tony—shrugged and said, "You know how it is. Going along with the group."

Good. Whether or not Sonia Lawrence approved, we were moving toward a discussion of group psychology, and her daughter didn't seem in danger of toppling over from the weight of the topic. "Any other signs of these boys being ready to go along with the group?"

They were right there with me, having made note of the choir in its matching uniforms and their obligatory voting for their leader. "And Jack," I said. "What do we already know about him?"

"He's dangerous," Melanie said. "He has a knife. I was wondering why he had one. But he's ready to use it, too."

I decided to stop worrying about Melanie.

"He'll use it," a girl nearby added. "Because he lost face when he didn't kill the pig."

"He said so," one of the boys added. "He said, 'Next time.'"

"Have you thought about how you know these things?" I asked. "How the author made you know that without telling you directly?" No response, but they weren't rolling their eyes, which was a plus. "Have you ever heard the term *foreshadowing*?" They didn't groan the way kids do when they're asked to look at the craft behind the story captivating them.

I felt something akin to a tickle in the heart. This was going to be a good class. We'd have fun and learn a few things along the way—and that *we* included me.

This was all the more remarkable because it was the last period of the day. Post-lunch for them. I'd again missed my own. Pre-freedom for all of us. This hour is generally subject to both impatience and torpor, which is not a great combo, but here they were, working together as a group, and their sparks of intelligence ignited an active discussion that lasted until the bell interrupted, announcing the end of day.

As though the bell tolled for me—my mind instantly switched to the next hurdle: getting ready. I envisioned a marathon race, a movie in fast-forward as I cleaned and ironed and manicured and even marked papers and made up a quiz for Friday, so that I'd be ahead of the game and have time for Gabby and Boy. I'd had such a good time last period that I'd barely had time to think about the impending visit, which was high testimony to the quality of my ninth graders. But now, the Mackenzies' road-weary car— it had already visited four others of their scattered offspring—crashed into my classroom and my brain.

The room emptied. A few boys nodded discreetly as they made their exits. I took that as high praise, a thumbs-up. I was going to be allowed to live. "This was fun, Miss Pepper," Melanie said as she left. "But—" she leaned closer.

I felt a shudder of worry. She was going to mention evil. She was going to echo her mother.

"I think you'd want to know that you have this big ink

stain on your sleeve," she said. "It's a real shame. It's a pretty blouse."

I was most assuredly not going to worry about her anymore.

And then the room was empty, except for Olivia, still placing her book in her backpack. I watched with mild amazement, because no able-bodied living human, aside from a mime, moves that slowly. I knew she spoke normally, she'd participated in class, and I wondered if she had a neurological problem. "Olivia?"

She looked up—slowly. "Sorry," she said. "You can go. I . . ."

"Need some help?"

She looked startled, inappropriately frightened by my question, then silently shook her head.

"Are you all right?"

She switched her head shakes to nods.

"Then I have to lock up, so—"

"Could I stay a while? I won't touch anything."

How could I explain that this was not the day to deal with idiosyncratic desires—or serious mental problems, except for my own. She was tiny and she looked windblown, inside the room, as if a secret storm had set her quaking. Much as I hate admitting it, it's never a great sign, and surely not a normal sign, if a student isn't eager to leave my room.

"Wish I could let you, but I'd be in big trouble if I did that," I said. "What is it? Are you well?"

She nodded.

"Then is something frightening you—something out there? Somebody?"

She sighed and shook her head, then she stood up abruptly. She was small and boyish, almost hidden—or hiding—inside her baggy clothing. "I'm sorry. I'll leave now."

"Tell you what," I said. "Would it be all right if I walked out with you? How do you get home?"

"The bus. On the corner."

"Would you keep me company? You're on the way to my car."

She blinked, then shrugged. "Okay, I guess."

She'd be safe and save face, because everyone would assume she was in some kind of trouble—with me. Why else would anyone be near a teacher when she didn't have to be?

I steeled myself against all manner of real and imagined Olivia-demons, but absolutely nothing threatened or seemed out of place. No stalkers, no cars idling, no derogatory calls, not even an embarrassing whistle or insult, and finally, the bus arrived and Olivia climbed on.

I turned away, glad for the anticlimax, and nearly smacked into a petite woman it took me a moment to recognize.

"Oh, no," I said. "I told you on the phone—I'm in a rush. Not today. There's nothing to say, anyway."

"Please. I'm desperate!"

I believed that she'd once been an actress. A good one, too—and she still was. "Maybe some other time."

"There isn't any other time. I'm sure I'll be—they're going to—please. I feel as if . . . my whole life—you have to help me."

"Help you?" I didn't know what to say. Help her? What was wrong with this picture? Claire Fairchild was dead. Emmie Cade's husband was dead. A former fiancé was dead, too. The people who got close to her needed help, not her.

"You think I'm evil."

Evil. Such an old-fashioned word, a pre-Freudian word, but obviously back in popularity. This was the second per-

son in as many days to present me with the idea of evil. "I
have no opinion of you," I lied. "I don't even know you."

"You were investigating me. Maybe you still are. I'm
sure you've heard bad things, but they aren't true." She
spoke softly, but *they aren't true* sounded strained, as if she
wanted to scream them. "I have to convince somebody that
they aren't true." Her calm façade crumbled as she spoke,
and she waved her hands, pushing off her phantom "bad
things."

I was painfully aware that we were standing on the corner, smack on the busy sidewalk of a midtown street, and
students who passed stared openly. "This isn't the best
place," I said softly.

"Where is, then?" she said. "I waited outside here for
you. I only—I feel as if—"

Her stammering felt fake and annoying. In fact, I
couldn't stand the entire situation. I had things to do, a life
of my own and no time to be segmented and pulled apart.

"It has to be now." Her voice had regained calm and a
new solidity. "Now."

"No, it doesn't. I'm sure you have your reasons, but I
honestly cannot—"

"If somebody was poisoned, and you could save them,
but you were really busy right now—and I don't doubt that
you are—all the same, would you wait until it was conven-
ient for you to see them? They could be dead by then!"

But the nonhypothetical person was already dead. Odd
she should pick the poison analogy.

And maybe this business was not for me. Could you imagine either Nick or Nora ignoring the damsel in distress—or
the femme fatale—whatever this shape-shifting woman
was—because they had to prepare for their in-laws? I sighed,
reconsidered, and admitted that my priorities were slightly
skewed. "Can you be quick, please?" I finally asked. "I wish

I were exaggerating about how pressed for time I am, but I'm not."

"I'd like to think that I'm as important as any other case you're investigating," she said quietly.

I was flattered. In her eyes, once I left the schoolhouse, zap, I was instant P.I.-woman. "You are, of course," I said, "but the truth is, this isn't my case anymore. Our investigation is over. The client died."

"That's just it! It isn't over. Can't be, with that—what they said, and you never had time to find out who I really am. You only heard bad things."

I pulled back a step.

"Didn't you?"

"Tell me what's on your mind. I don't have time for games, and I'm going to my car in five minutes." I checked my watch and made sure she saw me doing it. It also reminded me that I truly meant what I was saying. Ready, set, go.

She looked around, clearly wishing for a more intimate spot and for time to present her case. "If we could find a—"

"Can't. Here and now, or not at all. Five minutes—less the time we're wasting."

"It's that I don't know how to say it because I don't know what's going on."

"You need to talk to me but you don't know what to say?"

"How to."

"Try. One word, then another. The way you usually would."

She blinked, then she looked down, at the tips of her chic, polished shoes. "People don't like me," she said, head still lowered.

I might have expected this of a teenager. Or the poor child Lily, who'd tried to kill herself because of perceived unpopularity. Or from me, those months in sixth grade, but not from an adult, and a near-stranger. "I'm not a mental health worker. I can't help your personal problems."

"You're proving my point. You don't like me, either. Do you? And you don't even know me. I'm not talking about not being invited to the prom. People like me that way—but then something happens. Like it did with Leo's mother. People—for no reason—get bad ideas about me."

"Hey, Miss Pepper! Don't you ever go home?" a student called out as a gaggle of girls walked by. I waved and returned my attention to Emmie Cade's poor, pitiable-me routine.

She hadn't turned to see who'd spoken and didn't react to the mild interruption. She was completely engrossed in her own woes.

"Why are you telling me this?" I asked, although I had a working theory of what she was up to. She knew we'd found out about her various and sundry dead consorts, the mystery surrounding her recent and untimely widowhood, and this was damage control. A helpless, girlie variety of same.

"Mrs. Fairchild told Leo she'd heard bad things she wanted to check out. Bad things about me. But what? Why? Who said them? I'm an ordinary person, trying my best. Bad things happen *to* me, but that can't be what she meant. I've had bad luck with men, but now, with Leo, I thought—" She tilted her head and looked at me, her expression pure needy appeal.

That was probably the method she'd used so effectively several times already. Maybe with guys, she threw in more eye-batting and perhaps even a tear.

She read my face—or, at least, my lack of response—and her expression melted down into resignation. Despair. "I'm afraid you heard something damaging to me," she said, her voice soft and tremulous. "I'm afraid that since Mrs. Fairchild died so unexpectedly—"

"When a person's killed, it's generally unexpected." It was mean to say that, to watch fear return to her face, but I hated what she was trying to do with me.

"And I'm so afraid! What will the police think when they know she suspected me of . . . I don't even know what. But that she was investigating me—and then this happens." She blinked fast, as if holding back tears, and shook her head briskly, telling her own self not to cry. "The worst part is—I don't know why this keeps happening. Why don't people like me? Why do they think such awful things?"

I had no answer. Or, more accurately, I thought the answer was lodged in a cliché somewhere—where there's smoke, et cetera. When she was always the last person standing—and when so many had fallen—one had to worry. But even I, Amanda Cruella, wouldn't say that out loud. She looked so fragile now, and even though I knew it was a practiced pose, part of her repertoire of endearing stances, I was sure a harsh word could shatter her.

"What should I do?" she asked. "How do I stop this? How do I set the record straight?"

"I honestly don't think there is a *record*, but I guess if I were you, I'd wait until somebody, somewhere said something directly to you. And then I'd be honest."

"Can't I hire you? You could find out why this keeps happening to me."

"I'm sure there's a serious conflict of interest there," I said, sure of nothing of the sort. It felt as if there should be a conflict—but with whom? On what basis?

She accepted the idea. "Then could you help me just because—because I'm a decent human being and I'm in trouble?"

"Calm down. You aren't making sense."

"Why did she suspect me? What did she suspect me of?"

"Who?"

"Mrs. Fairchild—your employer. What were you investigating?"

"You."

"I know that. Leo told me. But why? What did she think? What bad things did she hear? From whom? How?"

"It doesn't matter now."

"It does! Who else heard whatever it was? And why is this happening? I left San Francisco because it had started back there. There was this . . . buzzing. That I'm a . . . that I did horrible things. I ran as far as I could get, but three thousand miles away—it's happening again. This behind-my-back—but as fast as I turn around, nobody's there." She looked wide-eyed and terrified, even though her words were fairly well organized. I didn't trust her or her claims of being afraid.

"I'm sorry you're going through this, but I do believe that ultimately, the truth, whatever it is, will out."

It was her turn, after pressing almost too close to me the whole time, to step back now, and turn herself into a vaguely amused sophisticate. "You believe that," she said slowly.

I nodded.

"It's so naïve. I'm surprised. I thought you were savvier. Understood more about the world."

"Look, whatever it is—" I felt awful sounding as if I didn't know about the rumors. She might be guilty of a multitude of crimes, but somebody else was, in fact, spreading the word. Somebody, or several somebodies—the post offices had been scattered—had mailed damning notes to Claire Fairchild. Had worked to craft them, to find the information, to post them. Emmie Cade's suspicions were grounded in reality. What I didn't know for sure was whether the accusations were grounded in reality as well.

"It's only rumor, you say. Sticks and stones and all that. Ignore it."

"How can I?" Her voice rising, she reached out as she spoke, as if to grab my hand, to literally pull me over to her side. I stepped back and she caught herself, and clasped her hands together. "Mrs. Fairchild is dead." She sounded slightly out of breath, as if she were exercising. "She took medicine that killed her. She doesn't go out much. She doesn't shop. Somebody had to give it to her, then, right? I was there that night, and if they think I already . . ."

I waited.

"In San Francisco, my husband drowned. All the papers kept saying was what an expert yachtsman and sailor he was, and that's true. But they didn't say he was also an expert drinker. Not a drunk, not an alcoholic, I think, though I'm not sure, but a man who binged socially. It's easy to keep that under wraps when you have money and own your own company, even though it was pulling that down, too. I didn't really understand about it until after we were married, but I had hopes we'd get it more under control. We didn't.

"Instead, we got better at keeping it a secret. He'd get tipsy at parties, but then we'd leave. I'd drive or we'd take a taxi, or hire a limo service, and maybe he'd finish his drinking at home, where nobody except me would see it. He didn't always go into his office, even when he was around, and things there were sliding, so when I suggested that he was drunk that day . . ." She shuddered. "Why would I lie? His friends knew. Nobody suspected anything terrible then. It was sad—but not that much of a shock, even. They knew what had happened—and then it all turned around. His first wife, I think. She hates me. I understand. His kids hate me, too. Somebody, anyway, started these rumors, and suddenly the papers quoted people as saying—even people who'd been drunk with him lots of times—that he was a great guy, a regular pal—fun to be with, which he was, and that they were shocked about the drowning because he was such a good sailor."

"You're saying he fell overboard drunk?"

"Of course. And that's what the law thought—thinks—too. He wasn't wearing a life vest, and that's presented as highly suspicious—if you saw those news stories, or maybe you actually did, if you were checking out my past."

I didn't respond.

"Why is that suspicious? It's embarrassing, but not evil. He was—we were—I was in the . . . in our bedroom. I was below. He wanted to get another bottle of wine. He was . . . amorous. People don't wear life vests then."

"There were all those people—"

"Nobody around us. Just me and Jake in our own room. And that's taken to be suspicious, but if you understand the situation . . ."

I was listening to her as skeptically as I could manage, but also wondering whether listening at all was a good or stupid thing. Would Mackenzie compliment me for gathering additional information or would he say he couldn't believe I'd wasted so much time? Much more than five minutes had passed. He'd made it clear that we'd be lucky to be paid for what we'd already done—I had to remember that this semi-career was all about money—and we surely wouldn't be recompensed for standing on the corner talking with the prime suspect.

"I'm not a bad person," Emmie said. "I'm not saying I've been the most careful, or . . . or—" She waved her arms again, as if one of them might catch the missing word. "Sensible woman. I was . . . I don't know. Wild. And I made dumb choices. And sometimes I took the . . . easier way. If somebody offered to help me out . . . maybe I shouldn't have, but it was never really bad stuff. I liked the wrong guys. Except for Leo, now. He's different. He's solid. And, okay, I've done things that weren't . . . I was not a perfect little good girl. Or big girl. But none of that means I did the kinds of thing they're saying."

"Maybe they aren't saying anything. Or more likely, maybe nobody is listening to whatever somebody's saying."

"Mrs. Fairchild was."

"She was hoping I'd find nothing. She liked how happy her son was."

Emmie looked at me sideways, her mouth curled. "She hired you to check me out. That's not what I consider real friendly."

That reminded me of my own future mother-in-law, and I checked my watch.

"It's making me ill," she said. "I can't sleep without drugs—I can't eat—it's making me crazy and sick. That woman—that Batya—she says I killed Claire Fairchild with this little bunch of flowers I brought for her. Poor woman——I think she's snapped."

"I'm sorry," I said softly, and I meant it. I didn't know how people tied their lives up in knots this way.

"Can I talk with you again? Will you help me? Is there some way you could find out who's spreading these rumors?"

I knew they were more than rumors. They were newspaper reports, her actual track record. "I'll—I'll think about what's appropriate," I said. "And now I absolutely—"

"Thank you! Thank you for listening."

No matter how many doubts I had about whether she was a liar and a murderer, there was something undeniably winning and sympathetic about her. Mackenzie had reminded me that even the newspaper story was innuendo and supposition. "The Truth" as an absolute was nowhere to be seen, so maybe she was being victimized on a grand scale.

Or maybe she was an experienced—almost a professional—manipulator. Actress, seasoned fortune-hunter, experienced seductress. A siren, and I was a sucker. I made my way to my car, thinking only, now, of Gabby and Boy, Bea and Gilbert, and how I was going to handle the next few days. Countdown had begun, and I had enough to do to fill every one of those twenty-four hours.

Mackenzie should be home by now, cramming as much reading and classwork in as possible tonight so that he wouldn't feel pressured when his parents arrived.

We'd have time to talk while we cleaned together, later, but I wasn't sure I could wait that long to tell him about Claire Fairchild's unnatural death, and Emmie Cade's bizarre curbside appearance. In fact, I knew I couldn't. I unlocked the door to our loft and called out, "Study break time! Drop the books because you won't believe what—"

Three tall people stood up.

Impossible. Mackenzie had hired actors to scare me out of my wits. This was Wednesday. They were coming tomorrow. *Thursday.*

The two tall strangers grinned at me. They stood in the middle of the mess and chaos of my household, smiling. Or perhaps silently laughing at the pathetic situation.

I blinked.

They were still there.

"Noah's girl—" the balding one said.

"Clarissa," the Technicolor one added.

"Clarissa was invited to visit a friend, and Noah and Angela were driving her upstate, so we left a day early. No traffic, either."

"Besides, we were so excited about meeting you, honey! Come over and give a hug." She wore a shiny scarlet peasant-style blouse and dangling green and scarlet sparkling earrings, and she opened her arms wide. Her nails matched her earrings. Including the sparkles.

When he'd called his mother "colorful," I hadn't realized he meant it literally.

"Poor baby," she said. "You've got this huge blotch on your sleeve, did you know?"

"Meet the folks," Mackenzie said.

Fourteen

EITHER HIS PARENTS CALLED AHEAD FROM THE ROAD, OR Mackenzie had suddenly become prescient. It was not in either of our natures to rush home from school and shop, straighten and polish, and yet, once my vision stopped flashing and crackling and my synapses returned to their usual connections, the tidiness of the loft registered.

I tried to not look surprised by anything. Not the untimely arrival of the senior Macks, at the passable condition of the gigantic room, or at the miraculous apparition of tortilla chips and salsa dip on the table.

C. K. Mackenzie's stock shot through the roof, rose so high, the entire world economy snapped back into high gear.

"She's just as pretty as you said she was," Boy Mackenzie told his son, giving him a congratulatory whomp on the shoulder. Boy's boy had found a good 'un.

I knew it was a compliment, and I knew I had to look pleased, but I really didn't love being talked about—in fact, being weighed and measured and judged—in the third person while I stood there, still encircled by Gabby Mackenzie's arms.

The woman was a world-class hugger. I could barely find the breath to smile in response to Boy's appraisal of me. She finally released her grip, but held on to my arms. "She certainly is that," she said. "Pretty as can be."

I wondered where they thought I actually was and when they'd decide to speak directly to me. "Thank you," I said softly, absolutely hating this. Visions of Miss Swamp filled my head, with me next to her as the "before" image. My lipstick had worn off hours ago, and I hadn't combed my hair since lunchtime. It didn't bear thought. At least I could blame the ink stain on fate, not bad grooming. "And now if you'll excuse me, I'll change into something clean and—"

"Nonsense!" C.K.'s mother said, leaning back—still holding me—and smiling broadly. "You look fine."

I did not look fine. Or *fahn*. They were Southern. Of course they'd say I looked wonderful. I had to ask Mackenzie what they said when they were alone, what proportion of any conversation was close to sincere and how much was automatic pilot. Of course, despite his rapid acclimation to Philadelphia, he was still a Southerner, too. He'd lie graciously along with his folks.

Meanwhile, he was looking at me with controlled eye signals that I interpreted to mean, "What did you mean when you came in the door, babbling?" while I was trying to blink, in code and eye squeezes, "Claire Fairchild was murdered!"

Good thing nobody tried our codes in wartime. Didn't work. We looked like people with eye disease.

I took a deep breath and filed Emmie Cade and Claire Fairchild away until appropriate, and focused on my future family members. I let go of trivialities like murder and murderers, and made room for my hitherto unsuspected inner Southerner. At once, sharp edges softened, the light in the loft grew golden and life simpler. I gestured for everyone to sit down again, settled myself near Gabby Mackenzie, smiled, said, "Help yourself to this lovely looking salsa"— said it more than once, to tell the truth—and then said, "Tell me about your trip! You've gone so far and done so much, you must have had all sorts of adventures!" The exclamation points that dotted each sentence's end came from a surprising and inexhaustible wellspring of acute hostessing and, to my amazement, each little ! sparked smiles and conversation, so we were off and running.

Gabby was well nicknamed, but unlike my father, Boy was an equal partner in storytelling. They finished each other's sentences, interrupted, corrected, laughed, and continued on, so that their combined narrative of far-flung children, grandchildren, homes, pets, and picnics broke the ice and, by some sleight of hand, pulled me into the great swarming mass of Mackenzies where, to my surprise, I almost felt comfortable.

But Claire Fairchild's death intruded, despite my best wishes. And Emmie Cade's paranoia. Murder will out, or at least seep its vivid stain into an otherwise pastel, pleasant conversation. What had happened to Mrs. Fairchild in the middle of the night? Who had happened?

And when I forced myself away from them again, back into the present and the warm family glow—my parents intruded themselves. This was not a mix that was going to work. Not even if Gabby and Boy spoke nonstop, which, apparently, was pretty much what they did. My mother would know they needed to catch their breath sometimes, and she'd be ready to pounce with her two cents.

She wasn't mean-spirited, and she meant well, but without knowing her specific agenda (though I feared it involved Handel, bouquets, and the phrase "I do"), I knew that introducing her would be like putting a tree limb into the spokes of a moving bicycle. Trees and their limbs are nice. There are, nonetheless, situations they don't help.

"You've got to hear this, Manda," Boy said, pulling my focus back into the room. I hoped my expression hadn't been too remote. "Porter's boys have these dogs, these dogs that—"

Gabby burst out laughing. "Stop, stop immediately, you

terrible man! I can't bear—they are the worst behaved, most adorable things—"

I should make it clear hereabouts that I have, from time to time, thought Mackenzie's accent rendered him nearly unintelligible. But he tries. And he's been in Philadelphia long enough to have clipped off some of those open-ended vowel sounds that once clouded his words. For my part, I'd retrained my ears and I can make out what he's saying most of the time, although the more emotional he gets, the blurrier his syllables become. Most of the time, that doesn't matter. As long as I'm sharing the emotion, who cares what he's saying?

But his parents were another matter. I had to assume everything they said—and they said so very much—mattered. I would only seem intelligent if I understood why they laughed so often, and it was in my best interests to comprehend what they were telling me about this family I was joining.

Given my years of training with their son, I could understand them, but only by puzzling it through, which left me a beat behind. I felt as if I were running after phrases, grappling them to the ground, pulling off all the fuzz and sugarcoating and only belatedly saying, "Aha! Gotcha." And then, leaping up to gallop after the next batch that had gone sliding by.

Word-wrangling was exhausting. The good side was that it left me precious little time to think about Claire Fairchild and to appreciate my mother, whose words, however infuriating they could be, were spoken in my Yankee mother tongue.

"You would think," Boy said, "that they had enough on their hands with two sets of twins, so that they'd make sure their dogs behaved, because those kids surely don't. . . ." He smiled the whole time he said it, obviously enjoying his grandchildren's mischief. Perhaps, even the dogs'.

"Made me miss my babies, though," Gabby said.

This time when I captured the words, I did a mental double take. Babies? The woman was a veritable goddess of fertility, but her eight babies were strapping adults now. And if she meant her grandchildren, why miss them when she'd been visiting them? Maybe she missed the dozens back in Louisiana?

Mackenzie saw my expression. "These days, Mama calls her dogs her babies," he said. "Speakin' of lummoxy ill-behaved creatures."

Boy laughed again. "That's so they'll remind her of her real babies. Besides, the dogs mean well. Can't say that for the kids. On the other hand, the kids were pretty smart, and Gabby's babies—frankly, this might not be politically correct—"

"I'm not sure dogs are into that yet, Dad," C.K. said.

"Well, our two—they are mentally challenged, I swear."

Gabby waved her spangled fingers at him. "The poor dears."

"The poor stupid dears," Boy said.

"What are their names?" I asked, to make conversation. I was already deluged with names. Eight kids, six current spouses, three or four formers, and nine million grandchildren. Enough. But names were easier to follow than narratives.

"Cary Grant and Katharine Hepburn," Gabby said.

Of course.

"Finally named something for the actors themselves, not the roles they played," C.K. said.

His parents—or his mother, most likely—enraptured by the actors, had named C.K. and his siblings after the roles and personas they had played. They were always good people and, most often, super-rich, imaginary wealthy relatives with whom she gifted her children. My poor guy, named for C. K. Dexter Haven, the loveable wastrel in *The*

Philadelphia Story, didn't even get a full name. I must say, however, I'm glad she opted for the C.K. part rather than the Dexter.

With the dogs, however, she'd finally gone for the real thing.

"Poor Cary needs his medication twice a day, and I'm so worried that dizzy little girl will forget."

"He's epileptic," Boy said.

"Really? I didn't know dogs had epilepsy," I said.

"Not uncommon," Boy said.

"Poor baby," Gabby repeated. "I worry all the time Lizzie will forget the medicine and he'll have another seizure."

"Now, Gabby," Boy said. "Lizzie's taken care of your babies before, and she always does a good job."

"But we've been gone so long this time." She sighed.

"They'll be fine, Mom," C.K. said, and the talk drifted back to human Mackenzies.

I was running so hard after their words that it took me longer than it should have to realize that neither Gabby nor Boy ever gave a sign of passing judgment on their large clan, except to laugh at their antics. Not a flick of a mouth, a squint of the eye, an inflection in the words. They were amused by, or surprised by, or confused by, people— related to them or not—but I didn't see a frown of disapproval, or the heavy silences of disappointment. I didn't even feel the prodding finger of expectation.

I didn't dare think about this in contrast to my mother— but I couldn't help myself. She didn't precisely disapprove—but she always had an agenda, a next step, and was eager to move you on to it. So if she'd been here, and in fact, when she did arrive, instead of happily spinning wheels as we were now doing, instead of enjoying the fact of the engagement and the new relationships, she'd be pushing and pulling, tugging and entreating. Move on! Move on! Most likely, at such time as I actually do feel ready to marry C.K., immediately after he kisses the bride, my mother will step up with her imaginary clipboard and say, "Okay, now you're married. Time for children. How many? When?"

Maybe Gabrielle Mackenzie would be able to change the tempo, keep it easy the way it was now. I watched with pleasure as she used the whole of her arms to animate her sentences, and each time I was amazed by her dazzling, glitter-dusted fingernails. The woman had never had money, and without it and the help and comforts it could have provided, she raised eight children of her own, plus numerous strays and, according to her son, did it with laughter and few complaints. I hadn't believed him about the noncomplaints, but I was a believer now. She was a hardworking, kindhearted woman with a comic vision of life.

Even her fingernails were laughing, in their own way. Those hands that had scrubbed and nursed and tied shoe-laces and brushed hair and ironed and mended—those hands had been given their Emancipation Proclamation by their owner. Each red and green and silver nail celebrated its accomplishments and, at the same time, waved as flags of freedom, announcing that these hands were on vacation from soapy dishwater and scrub brushes.

I decided then and there that I liked her and, more than that, I admired her.

This was going to work out. At least when my mother wasn't around.

Gabby took a two-inch-thick packet of snapshots out of her pocketbook. "Meet the family," she said, passing them to me. She leaned close and pointed a spangled nail at a face and named it, one after the other. I tried memorizing what Noah looked like and what color hair Phoebe had, and which child belonged to which adults, but there were too many, and none of them looked related to the other. I tried the same method I used in the classroom, matching names with hair color, nose size, freckles, height, jug-ears and buck teeth—anything that marked a person's face as his own and none other. So Noah was dark-haired and relatively short and married to Angela, a woman who looked as if she ran miles every day; and Porter was a strawberry blonde—going bald—and tall and married, for the second time to the same woman, Myra, who was sharp-featured and dark-haired, and they had two sets of twin boys and two badly behaved dogs; and Lutie was slender and elfin and had surely been told lots of times that she resembled Audrey Hepburn, and had been married three times already, and was on the verge of a fourth merger, most likely also doomed, they calmly acknowledged. The marriages had been worth it, Gabby said, because they produced three equally elfin and exquisite grandbabies. "Her new beau is handsome. I'll say that for him. So who knows what kind of adorable baby they'll produce?"

I'm not saying it was a great attitude, or even a sane one. I'm simply saying it was refreshing and easy to be around.

I didn't even try for any of the dozens of children's names. They lived all over the country and weren't likely to drop in, so that could wait.

I murmured my admiration of each and every shot.

"A motley bunch, aren't they?" Gabby said. "Never could figure out why they all look as if we spotted them sitting by the side of the road and snapped them up and took them home."

And in truth, except for his rangy height, I couldn't see any resemblance between Mackenzie and his parents, or between him and his siblings as a group. I liked the idea of a tight clan of people who looked as if they should barely know each other.

Boy took a small notebook out of his pocket. "So here's the tally," he said with great satisfaction. "Two thousand, nine hundred fifty-four miles so far this trip. Decent mileage, too. Twenty-four on the highways—"

"Zero to five all the times he refused to ask directions and we spent hours and hours lost—you would not believe how many times," Gabby said, and then she laughed. If he was from Mars and she was from Venus, they'd found an intermediate planet where they could cohabit and enjoy the view all around them.

C.K. took his father's detour into driving adventures as a signal it was time to move on. Literally. "What shall we do about dinner?" he asked politely. "What tickles your fancy? I'm sure you noticed that we live in a trendy, cutting-edge neighborhood."

His animated parents went blank. Reading body language and facial expressions was easier than deciphering their speech, so I knew instantly they had donned polite Southern masks to hide the fact that they knew their son was protecting them from the ugly truth: This neighborhood, their faces said, was pathetic, but how brave of you to pretend otherwise.

We live in Old City, which was, along with Society Hill, where Philadelphia began on the banks of the Delaware River. In the nineteenth century it grew to be the center of manufacturing. When that moved on, people like us moved in, converted the warehouses, put in and supported galleries, cafés, and excellent restaurants. Our loft had once been the top floor of an Oriental rug warehouse. Today, an art gallery occupied the ground floor.

But I realized how provincial I was about it. I knew its value, and its place in the city's geography and history, but C.K.'s parents might see it otherwise. Their poor children lived in one room in an abandoned warehouse. They couldn't even afford the normal amount of interior walls. The neighborhood was sadly deficient in greenery, just like everything they'd heard about Northern slums. There was no front porch or garden, only skylights and oversized windows that viewed other former factories.

"There's a Spanish restaurant, a Turkish, sushi, seafood—what would you like?" C.K. asked.

"We did our research," Boy said. "Went to the Automobile Association, found out everything about this city. And, we read all about it on the Internet. So if it's all right, we'd like to go a little more native than your ideas."

"You want Pepper Pot Soup," C.K. said, "in honor of Ms. Pepper here. And an old Philadelphia tradition dating back to when General George Washington and the Continental Army were out in Valley Forge and near starvation. The cook only had scraps of tripe and some peppercorns, but he made a good enough soup to keep them going till they won the war."

A two-second and definitely suspect culinary-based explanation of the Revolution. "Pure tripe," I said.

He took that as verification, not as an insult. "Tripe was what saved the day," he said. "Everybody knows an army travels on its stomach."

Meanwhile, Gabby stepped back, as if horrified that she'd offended me. "We didn't make the Pepper connection, honey."

"No, no," I said. "It isn't my—"

"Hell, we didn't know about it at all," Boy added. "It wasn't on those Web sites. What is it?"

"Do you think the fact that it's made of an ox's stomach lining has anything to do with being left off the list of must-eats?" I asked. "We aren't known for our cuisine."

"Scrapple, then," Mackenzie said.

"Named for my aunt, Gladys Scrapple," I said. "Just joking. And that isn't what you want, either. First of all, it's a breakfast dish. And second—there is no second. No."

"Philadelphia is famous for good eats," Mackenzie said.

"You're—that's not nice," I said. "Just because you were raised in the land of fabulous foods."

"And you, in the land of—"

"Scrapple. As in scraps." I said. "The pieces of meat nobody wants, like ears and feet and gums and—"

"Oh, my, how . . ." Gabby was trying to be polite and gracious about eating animal noses, but she nonetheless waved away the idea with a flash of green and red fingernails.

"And—then it's spiced up and held together by lard," I said. "Are you really suggesting that isn't more yummy than beignets?"

"Crawfish étoufée?" Mackenzie said, grinning.

"Bananas Foster?" Boy added.

"Oysters Louisiana?" Gabby said.

"Hoagies," Boy said. "That's what we read about and that's what we came for tonight. Is there a restaurant like that in this neighborhood?"

Sometimes, there is a little extra-Manda sitting in the corner, laughing hysterically at the parallel life she intended to take. I'd wanted so to appear competent in front of my beloved's parents. We'd made extensive plans for their arrival. Beth was even at this moment orchestrating and prepping for an exquisitely designed meal for the next evening. I had intended at the very least to have clean and organized hair, and no stain on my blouse.

I suppose all that translates into a need to feel in charge of my destiny, or at least in control of something. But here I was, stained, mussed, and taken by surprise. I gave in to it. I accepted reality.

Gabby and Boy—and C.K.—were from the land of laissez-faire. I decided to let go and enjoy the evening. Be Southern and thank you, Scarlett. Tomorrow would be time enough to be hyper-aware of what I wasn't thinking about, but should be.

Hoagies would be fine. Different colors of cholesterol sliced and oiled and stuffed into a roll. What's not to like?

"Great, then," Gabby said. "We're off to the races, and darlin'"—she gave my shoulder a friendly, nonpainful pinch—"while we munch, you and I can talk about dates."

"Dates?" I was engaged, I didn't date anymore, and surely she— no. Couldn't be.

"Here's what I was thinking," she said. "Lutie's having her wedding back home, so why not combine the two? I know it's her fourth and your first, but that shouldn't matter, should it? It's still a wedding, and that way, everybody's already gathered together. His family's rowdy, I hear, but you know, ours can get that way, too. And with your parents in Florida, almost next door, and the savings of a double wedding . . ."

I barely heard the rest of the details, and there were lots. Gabby Mackenzie had figured it all out. My audio portion returned when I heard her say, "I already have my dress— the cutest thing. Made it myself and did a fine job, if I say so myself. I hope stripes are all right. You like chartreuse or fuchsia? You're not going to get all fussy about color schemes and things like that? You know, when—who was it, Boy? The first of our boys to marry—"

"Noah," he said.

"Right. When Noah was getting married, I read that the mother of the groom is supposed to do two things: Keep her mouth shut, and wear beige. But darlin', do I have to tell you I do not fit that pattern?"

I thought maybe I'd just curl up inside my head and stay there.

". . . how about it?" she said.

I looked up through the skylight, wishing to lodge a formal complaint with whoever was in charge up there. The one who was laughing himself silly. I know I'd said I'd relinquish control, but I only meant about my hair and my blouse. Not my wedding—an event I wasn't ready for, in any case.

I half turned, and caught Mackenzie's expression. He's good at hiding his feelings, which served him well as a homicide detective, but either he'd changed with his new life as student, or his mother had the power to melt his adult traits the way my mother could with me. In any case, he was watching us, his mouth half open, its shape somewhere between a smile and a cry for help.

"It sounds wonderful," I heard myself say. "And so thoughtful of you, too! But the fact is—"

What's the fact? Quick, quick!

"My sister—you'll meet her tomorrow—is already planning the wedding. That's her profession, you see. It's all set."

Mackenzie's mouth was now three-quarters open.

"Wanted to surprise you all," I said. "Didn't we, darlin'?"

He nodded. "We were goin' to tell all of you, Amanda's parents as well. Tomorrow."

"Well, that's wonderful, then. When's the big date, then?" Gabby Mackenzie said, completely happy about everything.

"Christmas," Mackenzie said.

My turn to stare, mouth hanging open.

"We're both on vacation from school then."

"Christmastime." I nodded, amazed I could still move my head, because it felt as if a brick had just been tossed against it.

Not only had I started actually marching down the aisle, but worse: I'd given myself the push. I'd been intent on manning the barricades through my mother's visit. I'd planned to spend every minute in active, alert resistance, explaining why marriage was impossible at this time. I was ready and able to defend my right to refuse, to establish my own timetable for major life steps, to hold my ground till she retreated.

I might as well phone and tell her to cancel her trip.

She'd already visited. She was already here.

I had become my mother.

Fifteen

C.K.'S PARENTS APPARENTLY HAD BOUNDLESS ENERGY, and our hoagie and Italian ice fiesta lasted too late for a working day. By the time we bid adieu and Gabby and Boy headed off for their hotel, C.K.'s voice was strained as he muttered calculations about when he could fit in the missed reading he'd intended to do this afternoon.

I had great pity for him, but an equally urgent need to tell him about Claire Fairchild and Emmie Cade. I'd worried earlier about whether he'd be upset about the time I'd spent with Emmie. Instead, he was upset about the time I was going to take telling him about it. But through his yawns and despite his loving looks toward his books, he made a phone call to a buddy he'd worked with in homicide.

I heard him talking softly for a long while, with lots of half-laughs and many names, some of which I recognized, and then he said, "I'll be here. Yeah, till late. Thanks," and hung up.

"Tom's checking," he said. Then he yawned and settled in at the oak table that serves as an auxiliary desk. It has the best light in the house with its overhead lamp, and it's closest to the coffeepot, so it's his main post, and at this hour and this level of exhaustion, he was going to need all the help bright light and caffeine offered.

He tried to study while we waited, and I tried to allow

him to do so, but I didn't succeed, and therefore, neither did he. Just because we couldn't yet talk about Claire Fairchild's death with any assurance didn't mean there was nothing left to discuss.

"Do you think your parents liked me?" I asked.

He looked unduly surprised by my question, then he pulled out all the stops and flowed with fulsome Southern praise and reassurance. "Of *course* they did. Wasn't it obvious? What about all that laughing, and hugging, and literally clutching you to their bosoms? How about all that talk about your bein' their new daughter and all? Those welcome-to-the-family lines?"

He was so emphatic that I didn't believe a word, which meant I had to ask for lots more words. I had to ask about how "truth" was defined in the former Confederacy, and what percentage of a Southern smile could be considered sincere.

He finally drew a deep breath that might have also been a profound sigh, and once the air had circulated through him down to his feet and back up and out again, he said, "And should Southerners trust Middle Atlantic sincerity?"

"We're not as nice, Mackenzie. So sure."

"Like about dates? Like about weddin' dates?"

"Oh. That."

"How's that? I could barely hear you."

And I could barely muster up a complete voice. I sounded like a mouse in an animated cartoon. "You think your mother took it seriously?"

"You kiddin'? She marked the date and, like she said, she already has the dress, so I think we're gettin' married during winter break. An' she absolutely cannot wait to talk with your mother."

Despite the warmth still clinging from the day, I felt chilled. I looked at the man under the hanging lamp and knew that I loved him, and that he was the person I wanted to be with.

Everything up to this point felt familiar. Meeting, dating, dating more, living together. Even being engaged was more or less part of the continuum—a sort of intensified going steady.

But marriage! Terra incognita. I had wanted to wait until I'd thought the word through long enough to fray it, make it a comfortable fit, and I would have, except for my big mouth.

"I think it's a great idea," Mackenzie said. "An' why not? I mean what I'm saying, despite my roots in the South." Even so, he looked enormously relieved when the phone interrupted further discussion of our impending nuptials, and he answered it before it completed its first full ring. This time he mostly listened, nodding, making *um-hmm* noises, saying things like, "An' I thank you for that," "Who could have heard?" and "Interestin'." And then, after a pause, a chuckle, he said, "We'll be even. No, I mean it this time," and he clicked off the phone.

"Yes?" I asked. "That took forever. Is the poison's name the longest word in the English language? Or was that your mother telling you how much she really didn't like me?"

"It was phenobarbital."

"Who?"

"It was Tom, tellin' me the drug in the bloodstream was phenobarbital. A pretty common, legal drug."

"She took so many different pills—did she simply overdose on that one?" I remembered about the box and the premeasured amounts going into every cubby, but despite such aids, people get confused, disoriented, and accidentally overdose.

Mackenzie shook his head. "Not possible. It's used for a lot of things—including as a downer for overcharged speed

freaks, amphetamine junkies. So it's on the street, and anybody could have gotten some without going through a doctor. Officially, it's used, short-term, for things like insomnia
or anxiety—kind of a tranquilizing sedative—but it depresses the respiration, so somebody who already has
respiratory problems—well, it's obvious. It'd never be pre-
scribed, because it does what it did to Claire Fairchild.
Slowly stops the breathing altogether and permanently."

"So, it truly was murder, not a heart attack and not an
accident."

"And not missed this time," Mackenzie said.

"What does that mean?"

"The obvious. Lots of deaths like this get missed. The
doctor decides it's natural and nobody checks. Person's
buried, end of story. Pathologists love to say: 'If there was
a light burning on every grave of a murder victim, our
cemeteries would be illuminated brightly at night.' "

I was chilled by the image and its meaning.

"Okay, now?" he asked, and with great show, he pulled
the text closer to him and picked up a highlighter.

But it wasn't okay yet. I replayed what he'd said and
found myself stuck on something he'd skipped right over.
"Insomnia."

"I could use some insomnia," he said. "Maybe then I'd
get this reading done."

"Emmie told me she can't sleep. She takes something."

"Manda, there are so many sleeping pills . . . half the
world can't sleep when they want to. Now me? I could. I
could right now within ten seconds, but I have to study
instead. 'Sides, think about it. Would she tell you outright
she was on a drug to sleep if she'd poisoned somebody
with it?"

"Have you met her?" I asked.

He looked puzzled, and shook his head. "Why?"

"Just wondering." I'd been sure he was so blinded by her sweet and innocent façade that he couldn't believe any wrong of her. I was determined not to be, but now I wondered whether my refusal to judge her on face value was pushing me in the opposite direction.

"Tom said it's used for kids with seizures, and far as I know, we don't have a kid on our list of suspects. Fact is, we don't have a list. Further fact is, whatever happened and how is none of our business. An' Tom said he'd let me know if and when anything significant comes up. This," he waved toward his textbook, "this, however, is now my business."

"Wait," I said. "One second more is all. Something you said . . ." My tired brain tried to sift through piles and mismatched scraps, but levers and gears felt rusted out, or perhaps buried under hoagie layers, and I pawed through my mental archives at less than warp speed.

"I really need to—"

"There's something I should be remembering."

"About phenobarb?"

"Maybe. No. About who takes it—wait—"

"You keep saying *wait* and I do, I am, but nothing happens."

"That's what *wait* means." I controlled the urge to say *wait* again, because it was so close, almost there—and then it was—"Batya's child is sick."

"She had that baby today?"

"There's an older one. A sick one. Her aunt takes care of him. She told us, remember?"

"What does bein' sick mean? Kids get sick. He could have a head cold. He could have an allergy to seafood. He could have a harelip or typhoid fever. Listen, Manda, I've done my bit—against my better judgment. I found out what there is to know, and now, I can't talk anymore. I ei-

ther read this stuff now, or skip dinner with the folks tomorrow."

I ignored the threat. It was hollow, anyway. "She kept
saying sick baby, or the like. It sounded more serious and
chronic than a head cold."

"An' Batya struck me as a hysteric."

"She's got big-time problems. She's a virtual prisoner
there."

"Was. But about her child? Did she say he has seizures?"

I shook my head. "She said something about the cost of
his medicine."

"It could be nothin' more than chicken pox."

"She had motive, Mackenzie. Mrs. Fairchild said she was
leaving her money in her will but pretty much giving her
nothing while she was alive."

"Stupid tactic," he muttered.

Batya put the pills in their proper cubbies. It would be so
easy to substitute the murderous medication for a regular
prescription.

It would be easy for anyone to do so. I was back to square
one. And speaking of that, "Who called 9-1-1?" I asked.
"Did you ask? They have records, right? They always know
who called it in."

He blinked and looked up at me, frowned, and seemed to
reel in my words, as if they'd missed their mark but were
still hovering in the ether, awaiting delayed entry to his consciousness. "Oh, right," he finally said. "The doctor called
it in." He put his elbows on the table and his attention on
the page of his text, looking excited and challenged, like a
champion swimmer about to make the plunge.

I stood up as an act of good faith. "I promise to shut up
in a minute, but you need to explain, because there wasn't
any doctor there."

He looked at me with distant recognition, then once

again seemed to climb out of the book and rejoin me. "This is it, then?"

I nodded. I even meant it this time.

"There's this gizmo people with chronic lung disease use. Circular gizmo connected to the phone line. We saw it next to the bed, remember? You thought it was a lady's compact."

"She breathes into it, Batya said."

"She opens it up and breathes into one side of it and, through the miracle of modern medicine, the person monitoring it on the other end can analyze the velocity of her breath and know how her lungs·are doing and what she needs in the way of medication."

"That's amazing. I mean that seriously. It tests how well her lungs are working through the phone lines?"

"Far as I understand these things. She has to do this a few times a day, and if the results are confusing, they'd ask her to try again, and that night, apparently the test breaths showed a downward spiral—less and less velocity."

"So it took a while. It took a long while for that drug to slowly stop her breathing."

"Guess so."

"And she probably didn't fully recognize what was going on, so it wasn't as if she called for help."

"But the doctor did," he said. "When the tests come back that way, they retest, and then they call the patient, they phone, because the medication needs adjustment, but, of course, nobody answered the phone."

"She was probably unconscious by then."

"Or dead."

"But where was Batya? Why didn't she answer the phone?"

He tilted his head. "You're really set on her, aren't you? Tom said there isn't a phone in the maid's room. Apparently, Mrs. Fairchild was afraid she'd call Romania, or wherever she's from. Plus, Batya says she was asleep by that hour."

"Or awake, but not interested in saving Claire Fairchild's life."

He ignored that. "And Claire Fairchild always kept the ringer turned down low. She could hear it, but it didn't carry. When the doctor got no response, he phoned 9-1-1. Now you know everything I know and pretty much everything the police know at this point and when they know more, you'll know, too. But that'll be it. Tom said if I cared all this much about a homicide, why'd I leave? I've used up my bargaining chips for a while." With great deliberation, he put his finger on a line of text and leaned forward to read it. But he looked up for one moment and said in a serious, weighted voice, "Let go of it. It's a police matter now, and we don't have any other option." He didn't wait for me to agree or promise or say I understood. He returned to his textbook with a relieved sigh.

I kept my thoughts to myself, but they kept me up even after I'd said goodnight. I registered the barb about our not needing further information about Claire Fairchild, but I couldn't understand how Mackenzie could just turn off interest in something like this, could be content to be that chapter in somebody else's story.

Maybe it was because I'd met everyone involved and he hadn't. Or maybe I was too new at investigating, becoming intimately involved in someone's life and concerns and then, at some externally determined signal, stepping back. Way back—out of sight and out of mind.

I wasn't built that way. Instead, I lay in bed staring at the high ceiling, thinking about Batya, Emmie, and Leo's stack of grievances against one ill elderly woman, trying not to think how easily any one of them could have killed her, and trying as well to ignore all that and build a case for what I wanted to believe, irrationally or not, which was that none of them had done this.

It was a long time before I could stop seeing brightly lit cemeteries and fall asleep.

Sixteen

I WAS EXHAUSTED THE NEXT DAY, AND NAGGED BY TRIVIA such as the realization that I'd never ironed my linen suit. Even as I thought it, I also thought "who cares?" I'd already made a bad first impression. More importantly, I was surrounded by matters of life and death and love and marriage—and adolescent educations—and my wardrobe choice was a shameful concern.

And yet it was stuck in my mind, like a yellowing reminder on a corkboard.

I entered Philly Prep with one unworthy goal: to leave it as quickly as possible. Perhaps I could manage a brief nap at home before I faced the dual-family nightmare evening.

"Oh, you!" Sunshine called out. I'd gathered my meaningless notices and flyers, relieved to see there seemed no follow-up or second chapter to Mrs. Lawrence's flap about *Lord of the Flies*. "You popular thing, you!"

I looked around to see who she could mean, and she giggled. No other teachers were in the office at the moment. "You, silly! The word on the street is that there's a blogger or five saying good things about you!"

"Blogger?" Was this the verbal equivalent of her appalling shorthand?

She waved an *oh, go on with you* gesture, as if I'd committed a witticism. "*You* know. They think you're sharp, so you must know about Weblogs."

"Who thinks . . . no. I'm confused."

She giggled again. I was an endless source of amusement to Sunshine, and I wondered why it annoyed me so much to be the generator of such joy. "Can't say who," she said. "I promised. So let's just say—"

I knew she was going to invoke a small avian creature. She didn't care how shopworn her clichés were. Blogger might be new, or at least new to me, but it would soon be old and she'd still be cherishing it. And now—

"A little bird told me. They think you're cute, too." And she giggled again. "You could be Miss Blogg of the year! If there only were one!"

"When you say 'they,' who do you mean? I don't want names, but are we talking about students?"

She nodded emphatically. "Lots of them have these Internet sites, you see, kinds of journals where they write their opinions of things and people—like you. Back to school and all, that's what they wrote about, and they like you."

"So far," I said. "We're four days into this semester."

"First impressions count!" she trilled.

"What else do they put on these sites?"

She shrugged. "Anything they want to. Just like any other diary."

"A diary everybody can read."

"And doesn't that make it fun?"

I thought that made it not a diary, but never mind.

"They talk about themselves, what they like . . . I had one for a while about my kitties because they're so dear. And each day I'd say cute things they did. And about my unicorn collection and when I found new ones and all, and I'd list links with other really good unicorn sites or blogs I really enjoyed. Things like that." She looked lovingly at the line of tiny creatures on the divider. "I put photos of them up and all . . . but then I got this job and, well, you know,

I wouldn't say it to them, but I . . . kind of outgrew it, I guess."

"Blogging," I murmured. "Live and learn."

"Absolutely!" she said as if that was the newest, smartest phrase she'd ever heard.

I was popular! Finally! Blogs and bloggers liked me. I guessed that was nice news and I used it to keep me skating over the surface of the day. I had no intention of getting involved with my classes, as I was saving my emotions for the evening ahead.

The entire morning I accomplished this unworthy goal, ending with the juniors, who were about to embark on a research paper. I've done the "do not plagiarize" spiel so often, I went onto automatic pilot.

"News alert," I said. This part was indeed new, and I had to pay attention to what I was saying. "There's a spiffy program I can and will use that checks the entire Internet to see whether any sentence of your paper that makes me suspicious was copied. New technology for an old problem."

They looked stunned and disheartened. I wondered if my fans were in this class, and how soon I'd be voted out as a favorite of the gods. Favorite of the blogs, I should say.

"High tech or low, the penalty's the same. If you don't acknowledge the original source, you fail. So let's go over how to take notes and to give credit where credit is due." I heard a collective sigh, but I didn't feel a moment's qualms about making it hard and even painful to steal someone else's ideas. "If people don't footnote and attribute quotes and ideas, there's no way to check whether what you're being told is true or not. And this applies to the miracle of the Internet as well. Check their references before you accept whatever is written there as gospel truth. It's too often rumors or one person's opinion. Check the source."

And after a familiar demonstration of note taking and record keeping, it was lunchtime.

I decided to spend the hour out of doors, in the park across the way. I'd find a sandwich or the pretzel vendor. The day was sunny and crisp, with the sweet tang of impending autumn. A day to cherish and press into a keepsake book, and I wanted to be part of it. My need to leave had nothing whatsoever to do with the Square's proximity to Claire Fairchild's condo.

I was obviously not the only person heading for the great out of doors, and it took a while to merge with the lunchtime exodus. The stop-and-start human traffic and, perhaps, the clusters of whispering and giggling girls gave me time to remember that it was imperative that I speak with my sister.

Once outside, I stood near the school building at a polite distance from the students pouring out, and I made my call. As annoying as they are, I was once again grateful for the invention of the cell phone, which kept me from making my personal calls in front of the office staff. Even though Sunshine would never scowl, tap her foot, and check her watch the way our former secretary, or warden, had, I did not want her privy to my web of lies.

Even before I spoke a single word, I felt winded, as if I'd already jumped hurdles. Beth was sweet and serene. She'd pick our parents up at the airport in two more hours and, in the interim, she'd whipped up delicacies that would earn her toque at Le Cordon Bleu. "They'll love, love, love it all," I said. "Just the way they adored their hoagies last night."

"Where? Who? You said they were arriving today. Why were they here last night?"

"It had to do with Noah's daughter's sleepover, so don't ask." I told her the entire sordid tale, starting with my surprise introduction and rushing as quickly as I could toward and over my amazing, damning gaffe.

Beth squealed, and I knew she'd be applauding if she

weren't holding the phone. Actually, I realized, those peeps, squeals, chuckles, and whoops were, indeed, the sound of one hand clapping.

"Would you tell Mom and Dad, then?" I asked. "I mean, before we all get there? So it looks as if you're breaking a brand-new secret?"

She agreed. "But Christmastime? Why then? Places are booked solidly and—"

"Beth, I don't care if it's in that mansion. Maybe it can even be postponed, or forgotten. And if not, it can be in our loft, which is not booked for the holidays. Or City Hall. I don't want to go to Louisiana and be half of Lutie Mackenzie's fourth wedding into a, quote, *rowdy,* unquote, family."

"Have you told Sasha yet?"

My friend Sasha was still partying her way through Great Britain. "You're the only person, aside from his parents who—"

"Better tell her soon. It's hard to get decent flights during the holidays."

"I cannot believe you're already working on the guest list," I said.

"Okay, okay. Just trying to make things easier on you."

"I realize that." I didn't mean my sigh to be as loud as it was.

"Don't worry about it," Beth said. "Let me see what I can do. I'll work on it this very afternoon."

I had no doubt she would. They would. I imagined my mother hurling her bag onto Beth's guest room bed, rolling up her sleeves, and digging in to Beth's library of sites for overblown events while my father asked, dolefully, "How much does that one charge?"

"They have an enormous family," I reminded her. "Eight kids, six—no, there's Lutie's intended—seven spouses, thirty-seven grandkids, uncles, aunts, cousins . . ."

"You might want to reconsider their offer. I wouldn't mind a trip to New Orleans."

"Then go. You don't need a family wedding as an excuse. And Bethie? Tonight? Expect a Technicolor explosion. Gabby Mackenzie has never heard the word *neutral*, not in colors or opinions or temperament."

"Sounds like I'll like her."

She would. I did. That didn't ease my growing discomfort.

I headed across the street to the Square, thinking about anything and everything except the idea of being married four months from now. And thinking about weddings, how could I not wonder about Emmie Cade and Leo Fairchild's? Was it still scheduled? Were they being sidetracked by being suspects?

I walked through the crowds of students and citizens soaking up the September sunshine, and headed toward the farthest corner from the school. I told myself it would be the least populated. It was mere coincidence that my goal was only thirty-five steps away from the Fairchild building—I could, in fact, see its balconies from where I stood. The objective was a quiet, only partially occupied bench. Olivia didn't seem to take up even the space a small person might.

"Mind if I share?" I asked through the pops and bursts of sound and laughter filling the rest of the park.

Olivia didn't look up. She shrugged. Not precisely a warm welcome. One of her hands held her lunch, still in its plastic Baggie. She looked like inert matter, as privately desolate as she'd appeared at the end of school yesterday. I settled for the shrug, and sat at the far end of the bench.

She took out her copy of *Lord of the Flies*, put it on her knees and, using only one hand, carefully found a page. Then she held it open with that hand while the other continued to cradle the untouched sandwich bag.

I felt pulled into her bubble of silence. It was more than a stillness. The withholding of sound and the effort to keep something bottled up thinned and charged the air surrounding us.

She stared at her book. I was positive the show of needing to finish her assignment was a pretense. Olivia's entire being announced that she was the kind of girl who'd always have taken care of her homework. And in fact, when I really looked at the open book, I realized she was almost at the end of the novel, well ahead of where assignments would have put her. But her message was clear: Company was not welcome. I thought about finding the pretzel man, but talking with Beth about the evening ahead and wedding ceremonies had quelled my hunger. In fact, I felt as if food might make me ill.

That meant I had nowhere to go except, perhaps, to that building steps away. I tried to remember whether I'd actually promised not to, then laughed at my attempt to be legalistic. I didn't have to have promised. Claire Fairchild's death was now officially a homicide and out of our hands.

But during the course of the long night before, I'd wondered what Batya was going to do, or had done, and how she'd now support herself and her children. More than that, I wondered whether Leo Fairchild was privy or partner to his mother's supposed bequest and/or the I.N.S. threat she'd held over the housekeeper's head.

"Thanks for the rest," I said. "I just needed to sit a moment." I saw a splat on the book, and Olivia slammed it shut, then reached up to fiercely brush her index finger across her right eye.

She was wearing a delicate yellow T-shirt and flower-sprigged short skirt, and all the same, she felt dark, something with the power to absorb even the brightness of this day. Her ache was almost palpable over here, on the other side of the bench.

I felt an impotent rage, knowing I couldn't fix whatever made Olivia's life feel so frightening and hard to bear. I was only her teacher. I crossed her life's path five of the hundred and sixty-eight hours in a week. Something much more significant than I weighed her slight body down. However, maybe knowing somebody wished they could work miracles would help. "Olivia?" I whispered.

She looked at me for a slice of a second, then back down at her closed book, speaking so softly, I had to work to make out her hesitant words. "I . . . don't . . . understand . . . why people are so . . . mean."

"Do you want to talk about it?"

She looked at me again, her eyes wider, and shook her head. "No. No. I meant—I mean—the *book*." She looked away again.

As an English teacher, I should have been thrilled that assigned reading was having such a powerful effect. It was a magnificent, rich book, and its message heartbreaking, especially in this dangerous new world. For one frightening moment, I thought perhaps Sonia Lawrence had been right and this book was too much for these students in these times.

Then logic returned, and I could in no way buy the idea that William Golding had driven Olivia to stay in my classroom after school, and to sit alone during lunch, crying.

That, however, was what she wanted me to believe, so I sat weighing respect for her privacy and need to mourn whatever it was in her own way against my concept of responsible adulthood. "The book," I finally said, "is thought-provoking. Yes, people can be cruel. We all have the potential to be that way. To be uncivilized. But we also have the potential to be kind. To think things through. To not act out of blind fear. It would be heartbreaking if we didn't have the ability to keep an eye on what's right and wrong, to choose not to go along with the crowd, not to bend under mob rule." I leaned forward, to try to really see her.

She didn't move, except for her eyes, which glanced at me, as if to make sure I was real. "I sound like a jerk," I said. "Sorry."

She didn't say anything, didn't deny my jerkdom. At a time like this I almost missed Sunshine—or my future mother-in-law—both of whom, with profound insincerity, would have pooh-poohed, told me I was anything but a jerk, and insisted that, in fact, my platitudes had been enormously helpful. "Can I help you in any way?" I asked. "I would really like to."

She shook her head rapidly, her eyes wide with fear that I might do something, anything.

"Okay, then. But take that as a permanent offer. At any time, if you change your mind and think of something I could do—or if you want to talk . . ." She sat impassively, a plaster statue depicting resignation, loss, capitulation. "Okay?"

She finally nodded with great insincerity.

I had no choice but to move on through my day, although I no longer envisioned myself as skating on the surface of anything. I felt like someone who'd stumbled badly and had one leg through the ice.

The lunch hour was barely underway, I was not welcome on my park bench, I was practically face-to-face with Claire Fairchild's building and I didn't think I'd actually taken a vow to have my curiosity surgically amputated. I worried about Batya, too, about her impending delivery date, about her illegal status, and about whether Leo would honor his mother's financial promises. I couldn't see what would be hurt if I simply stopped by. A friendly, innocuous courtesy call.

There. I'd successfully argued my case with me and I'd won. Guilt-free, I made my way to the lovely old building, where I was greeted with yellow crime-scene tape across Claire Fairchild's once elegantly austere front door. If Batya was in there, she was now truly imprisoned, but of course, she couldn't be, and wouldn't have been, ever since the tape went up yesterday, when the dead woman's blood showed traces of barbiturate.

C.K. was supposed to have been told of any new information, and this seemed new enough. I pulled out my cell phone and called the man.

"Mackenzie here," he said softly.

"The door's taped up."

"Manda? We're at Carpenter's Hall, listenin' to a talk about the First Continental Congress. I mean, they are, my parents. I'm outside to take this call. But this is where it started. This is where they talked about splitting with Britain. Can't this wait?"

"I don't think so. Claire Fairchild's apartment is a crime scene now."

"It was always a crime scene," he said. "Ever since a crime was committed there."

Sometimes his wit eludes me. "But, Batya—she was staying here."

"Tom called," he said. "Cell phones are a mixed blessin'. Gets harder to escape work—and that isn't even my work anymore."

"Tom called and you didn't tell me?"

"I didn't want to talk to that ditz secretary, an' I know she doesn't interrupt your teachin', so I thought it could wait while I played tour director."

I understood that his attention and interests were elsewhere. I didn't care. "What did he say?"

"Tom?"

"Who else would I mean?"

"We've been hearing about and from Ben Franklin and Thomas Jefferson and John Adams, who had a lot to say."

"*Tom.*"

"There's an A.P.B. out for Batya. She's disappeared."

It took me a moment to process that. "Batya?"

"Right. Once again, the butler, more or less, did it."

"But disappearing doesn't necessarily have anything to do with what happened to—for all we know, she's in labor somewhere."

"Her aunt says she doesn't know where she went. Took the little boy, too."

"But her aunt would never tell—she's illegal. She'd be deported."

"And turns out you were right. Her little boy has seizures and takes phenobarb."

"That still doesn't mean she'd—"

"You're suddenly her defender? Yesterday, you were giving me reasons why it had to be her. So you were right. Why change positions now?"

I couldn't have rationally said why, except that Batya was no longer an academic puzzle, something to be figured out. She was a woman whose motives were based on grave problems, and life in prison would only increase the weight of problems on the next generation. "Still and all," I said, knowing how weak I sounded, "she in no way seemed— she was so concerned about keeping the bedroom untouched—"

"Odd that she knew it was a crime scene, wasn't it?"

"That was a language problem. A TV-watching problem. Not proof of anything."

"I have to get back to my parents. I should tell you this: Before she disappeared, Batya tried to refill a prescription that didn't have any refills left."

"Not—" I gave up on blanket denial. "Phenobarb?"

"She said her aunt had lost the last batch."

I was silent long enough for Mackenzie to ask if I was still there. "So that's it," I finally said.

"Pretty much. She can't get far with a toddler and ultimately a newborn. I'll see you later."

The image was horrifying and bizarre, but I thought she could get far. Women had children at home, or with midwives. Women like her would shelter and hide her.

I wondered why I found it comforting to envision her evading justice.

I made my way back toward the school, through clusters of students, nannies, toddlers, and a scattering of the elderly, most of whom normally wait until the Square clears of teens. Midway through the park, a blur on the far periphery of my vision spun around and came toward me at a near run.

I didn't want to see her. I'd already struck out, dramatically, in my attempts to help Olivia, and then, to offer help to Batya.

I didn't want to see a person I didn't want to help in the first place, but there she was. Emmie Cade.

Seventeen

"I WAS GOING TO COME TO YOUR SCHOOL LATER ON—after school—to ask if you were going to, but look—bumping into you now. Great! Saves time, I guess."

I unspooled the sentence, looking in vain for its core. I felt suddenly and totally exhausted, physically burdened, as if heavy weights had been strapped across my shoulders.

"So can you?" she asked.

I shook my head.

"No? You can't?"

"I don't even know what—"

"Help me! Take me on as your client. You said you'd find out if it was allowed."

I'd forgotten all about that, and with great apologies, I told her so.

She looked like a child told that Santa was a myth.

"It doesn't matter now, anyway," I said.

"But it does. They're already—the police, I mean—everybody's being questioned and even Leo—even he's acting as if I . . ." She didn't look poetic today. She was wearing clothes, not a costume. In place of long lace sleeves, a blue denim shirt, and jeans. Her skin, especially around her eyes, looked strained.

She leaned closer, her voice now a hoarse whisper. "I can't let this ruin my relationship with Leo. I won't. I need your help—I need to find out why I keep being—why—"

She seemed unable to complete the thought, to say out loud what pressed so painfully on her mind.

"Say whatever it is. Putting it into words won't make you guilty of something you're not."

She straightened her posture, inhaled, and said in one long breath, "I don't know why people think I'm such a bad person when I'm not." She exhaled again. "When I never was."

I couldn't help but notice that while her mouth had managed to brave saying it without breaking, her eyes were moist by the end of the sentence. What a tear-filled, no-lunch hour I was having. "Please—you know what I mean," she said. "Don't you?"

I nodded, even though I wasn't sure, and the only thing in my mind was that old joke: "Just because you're paranoid doesn't mean somebody isn't out to get you." Is it also possible that where there's smoke, there's really only fairy dust or fog?

"And it's your business to find things out."

I was about to tell her about Batya, and then I reconsidered. I didn't care what the police believed or how obviously everything pointed toward the housekeeper—I still wanted to know about the anonymous notes. Why, in fact, people did seem to hate Emmie, suspect her of multiple crimes. That would be a new case, a brand-new investigation having nothing to do with the murder. "The police haven't been bothering you, have they?"

She shrugged, nodded, shook her head, and completely confused me. "Everybody," she said. "They haven't said anything to me in particular, but they did ask me a lot about poor Jake. And even about . . ." She lowered her eyes, looked down at her hands. Her eyelashes were amazingly lush and long, throwing shadows on her cheekbones. "About a man I was once engaged to. I can't imagine how they did that much background on me hours after Mrs. Fairchild died—" She blinked, fighting back tears.

I knew how they knew so much so quickly. We'd turned over everything we had: the news stories, the anonymous notes. This presented a new ethical question. Could I accept her as a client if I was the one who'd gotten her into trouble by providing information the police would otherwise have no ready way to know?

Awkward did not begin to describe how I felt. Another situation in which A. Pepper not only failed to help but actively made everything worse.

"I apologize," I said. "I meant to find out about this situation, but something urgent came up. I promise I'll check into this. Are you all right meantime?"

Her laugh was closer to a quick, hard bark. "I can't sleep or eat, Leo barely looks at me directly because"—she shrugged, ready to foolishly trust me with whatever she knew—"because the medicine they found in her bloodstream . . . I had pills like it for insomnia. Leo knew it. We'd been . . . I've been staying with him. Now, it's so awkward . . . I mean, if there's no trust, if a man thinks maybe I killed his mother!—I'm going back to my place for a while." She hoisted the tote bag straps up higher on her shoulder. "A little space between us. Maybe for the best."

Leo was her perceived problem. Leo's lack of faith. She had a powerful innocence—or fabulous acting skills. Whichever it was forced me to acknowledge that the police were probably right, and Batya was guilty. Which also meant that not only had Emmie not harmed Claire Fairchild, but that it was possible she hadn't ever deliberately harmed anyone.

I noticed a generalized movement of the students across the way, as if they were swaying, en masse, toward the school building. I checked my watch. The bell would ring in three minutes. "I have to run," I said.

She shook her head. "I still don't get it how you can do two jobs, but I guess it's obvious you can." She sounded wistful, perhaps because of her own spotty work history. "You'll call me, then?" She fumbled around in her bag and found a pen and a piece of paper and wrote down a number. "That's my place," she said softly.

I nodded.

She looked down at her toes, today shod in utilitarian running shoes. "I'll probably be there a while." Head still lowered, she walked away.

I turned to go, then reconsidered and ran a few steps to tap her on her back. "I have a question."

She pivoted, eyes wide.

"What's with the names?"

"I don't—"

"Your names."

"My *names*?"

"There are so many of them. Why is that?"

She looked surprised, then, stymied. Her pretty brow wrinkled above her nose. "I guess, if you're going to help me, you need to know whatever you need to know, but the names don't have much meaning. I mean, I could explain each switch, but it's so boring, starting with never liking Mary Elizabeth." She closed her eyes and did a mock shiver. "It wasn't ever me. It's a Goody Two-shoes kind of name."

"Bore me. Lots of people dislike their names—but you've disliked a whole series of them."

"All I did, mostly, was play with the name itself, use nicknames, so I was Maribeth at one point, and Betsey at another, and I think Liz for a short time, but that didn't fit, either."

"Emmie, there are—"

"Oh, yes. M. E., the initials, too. I nearly forgot."

"But how about Stacy? Weren't you Stacy Williams for a while?"

She grimaced, and nodded. "I dropped out of college and got married to a guy named Billy—William Stacey—and so I was Betsey Stacey then. I'd always dreamed about going on the stage, or being in movies, but that wasn't the right kind of name, and Billy didn't want his surname used that way, so I turned his name around. Stacy Williams. That sounded right but, in the end, it was the only 'right' thing going on in my life. I didn't get anywhere with the acting— of course, we were in Atlanta, not exactly the center of the world of drama, and then, the marriage ended, too."

She looked at me as if I now understood some arcane secret, as if she'd said enough. She hadn't.

"You were going to explain all the names."

She lowered her head. The word "woeful" snaked through my brain. "When Billy walked out—"

I was surprised to hear that her husband had ended the marriage. I'd assumed that those choices—that everything— had always been in her control. The new understanding troubled me and suggested other untested assumptions on my part, and that idea, potentially upending everything I took for granted, was dizzying.

"I was pretty much a mess. Not my favorite time," she said, trying for a small smile that, instead, upped her "woeful" quotient. "And I certainly didn't want either my actual married name, last name Stacey, or that stage name that was his name in reverse. I moved to Austin and changed back to my maiden name—lots of women do that, so I was Stacy Cade. Then I fell in love with a great guy named Geoff Collins. We were engaged and then . . . then his motorcycle turned over and . . . ." She sighed, and shook her head. "It wasn't legal. We weren't married, but I didn't know what to do, how to show how much I cared, and so I used his last name when I came to California, and I was trying to act again. Stacy Collins, and after a year or so, I met Jake and I became Stacy King. After Jake . . . after him, I felt as if all the names had been . . . part of my string of horrible luck, so I dropped Stacy and King and went back to being Mary Elizabeth Cade, except . . . I still can't stand that name, so M. E. is a nickname, do you see? I told you it was boring."

Interesting how history is seen by its various players. Her story rang true, but all the same, every suspicious overtone had been wiped away along with mention of repeated survivor's inheritances. If she believed that version of her past, let alone if it actually was accurate, I could understand why she'd be confused by her bad reputation and the dark cloud of suspicion that had relocated with her.

"And now," she said. "Now, with Mrs. Fairchild dead and Leo so worried and . . . I have no idea what all his mother said to him that evening, about me, what she heard, or thought, but he looks at me as if . . . as if—"

The bell rang. I don't know if we were saved by it, but I was relieved. My tidy mental household, where facts and truths had all been hammered into place and I knew the territory blindfolded, was abruptly being renovated, leaving me dizzy and tripping over certainties. I needed to think. I quickly made my farewells.

Unfortunately, a classroom is about the last place on earth to enjoy peaceful contemplation. Emmie Cade's sad trek to Claire Fairchild's condo faded from my mind as the classroom filled. This group was starting the semester with a writing unit, and I was trying to make playing with words as enjoyable as possible.

"I want you to write an argument," I said. "That doesn't mean a quarrel, it means I want you to take a side on an issue, and write something that would convince your reader of your point of view." We'd counted out, and now I said, "Everybody who was a *one* is on the *it's a good thing* side, and all the *twos* are on the *it's a bad thing* side. And here's the idea you're arguing: Would it be a good or a bad thing for a sophomore to win the lottery and wind up with one hundred million dollars."

"Good!" the sophomores said in unison.

"No fair if I have to say it's a bad thing," said a boy who was made mostly of freckles.

"Why should we have to pretend to believe one way when we don't?" a sulky girl in the back asked, so we talked about thinking about what our opponents might believe, and thereby being able to anticipate and answer their statements. "It gives you an advantage and stretches your mind—and makes you wilier in the future. Consider it mind reading. And I promise, even if you're on the side that says winning all that money would be a bad thing, and then you go out and win a hundred million dollars—you'll be allowed to keep it."

They divided into groups of yays and nays and collectively brainstormed for the next fifteen minutes. "See how many points are made and with which ones you agree. Take notes. Then you'll organize your thoughts and write up your own argument, based on those points."

I knew I could relax when I heard the "it's a bad thing" group generate ideas. In fact, they sounded like Cotton Mather—anything enjoyable was inherently bad. The "it's a good thing" group was having a heavy debate about whether a person that rich needed to complete high school and how many pairs of shoes any female had a right to own.

While they debated, laughed, protested, and made notes, woeful Emmie Cade pushed back into consciousness and I tried to unassume, to see her as she was, to base my view only on facts, not opinions or loaded words I'd read.

It was nearly impossible, which was a frightening truth in itself.

The good news—and I sorely needed some—was that

when the bell sounded again and the class ended, I realized that for the past few hours, I hadn't had time to obsess about the evening ahead.

The ninth graders settled down with enough chatter to make me think they were forming a community. They'd come from several feeder schools, so the speed with which they seemed to have cohered was heartening.

Unless, of course, this was its own little *Lord of the Flies* community in the making.

I wondered where that thought had come from—and then I saw Olivia, who suggested that while no man is an island, perhaps an undersized adolescent girl might be. She looked as isolated as she had out in the park, but a thin veneer of fear had been added.

It was too soon in the school year to be this concerned about a child. Too soon in the story, as if we'd skipped the introduction and the buildup, ruined the tension, and leaped directly to the nail-biting climax.

I wished I could approach Olivia, waggle my finger, and say, "You know the rules forbid grave emotional distress the first two weeks of school. There are too many other things to attend to at that time, Missy, so reset your mental state to the 'normal' setting immediately."

Things were degenerating on the fictional island of boys as well, but that was according to plan. I broached the meaning of the bespectacled character of Piggy, carefully never saying words like *symbolic*. "Where does he fit in with the boys?" I asked. "What do you think is his role in the group?"

And after a minimum of searching, they suggested that he was civilization. He knew the rules; he advocated proceeding logically, taking things a step at a time, preserving themselves by building shelters, by taking a census of who was there.

"Then given that they're so proud of being English, of being civilized—why is Piggy having such a hard time?"

"Because he isn't attractive," Melanie said. "He doesn't look like a leader. I'm not saying that's right," she quickly added, "but all the same, I think that's a part of it. And he doesn't fit in." She said this last line with great assurance. Melanie had the look of a girl who would fit in—or make the rest of her peers fit themselves to her mold.

"Anything else?" I asked.

"What he wants, what he says they should do isn't as . . . exciting or fun as what, say, Jack wants."

"Good point, David." I'd had no trouble memorizing his name. Few eyes actually twinkle, no matter what poets say, and few are actually turquoise, but David's did and were. He was also observant and intelligent and it would be tempting to call on him all the time, to hear his opinions, of course, but also so see the turquoise twinkle trick. "It's more fun to be wild, to give in to impulses."

"For a while, at least," someone else added, and the discussion flowed on about the meaning of the names, the specifically named Jack and Ralph, the derogatory nickname for Piggy, the merged names of Samneric, and the generically named "littluns," about the fire that's set and burns out of control.

It went so well that I believed Havermeyer's hyperbole. Our standards were rising. This was probably the best and surely the most enjoyable class I'd ever had.

Olivia remained conspicuously silent, although she listened and watched and had read more of the book than most of the class. And then, a few minutes before the end of the hour, we got to the beast. "What is it, do you think?" I asked. "Will the hunters find it?"

And then, Olivia, her posture abruptly ramrod straight, her hands flat on her desktop, spoke out clearly and forcibly. "There's nothing to find. There's no beast. They're the beast.

It's whatever they don't understand. Whatever they're afraid of. That's what they turn into a beast."

And having said her piece, she sat back in her seat and, without showing any sign I could have defined, seemed to once again withdraw into the position of a distant observer.

The class rhythm of easy, rapid-flowing conversation halted. Some of the children looked surprised, as if in the course of the hour they'd accepted Olivia as a mute, and they'd just witnessed a miracle.

No one, perhaps with good cause, seemed able to pick up on her idea and run with it. "That's a good observation," I finally said. "Do you think it's true off that island, too? Do we turn what we fear into monsters and beasts?"

And once again, I fell in love with my ninth graders. I hoped this lasted, that when their hormones fully kicked in and they felt more familiar that they didn't try hard to "fit in" by imitating the older classes' studied apathy. I hoped they'd always be eager to discuss ideas, even painful ones that questioned their own prejudices.

I wondered what Melanie Lawrence's mother would say if she had been in the room. Would she have understood why it was not only good, but important, for our children to grow up able to think, and to consider ideas that were possibly foreign, or threatening? That if they did that, perhaps they wouldn't turn those fears into their own beasts, to be hunted and killed?

Probably not.

At the thought of her mother, I glanced at Melanie herself, and caught her smiling pleasantly at Olivia and yet somehow projecting a forceful negativity—a deliberate nothingness. As if poison came out from that smile. I couldn't understand how she was creating that impression, but I could feel its result, and I knew I'd have to find language for it because I didn't like it and wouldn't tolerate it.

Olivia, meanwhile, studied her fingernails, purposely or inadvertently missing the stare-down.

And then the bell rang, and the class looked like so many jack-in-the-boxes, tops off. Even Olivia gathered her things and would have left with the rest of her class, albeit at the back of the pack, had I not put a hand out to stop her. "Could we talk a moment?" I asked.

She drew a deep breath, as if I presented a challenge, or a trial. "If it's about . . . how I was, I'm okay now."

"That was an exceptionally insightful comment you made, about fear and how we handle it."

She looked at me directly for the first time. "Miss Pepper, I'm okay now. Thanks, but—there's nothing to talk about. I'm transferring out. I decided today, and talked to my mother during last period, and she says I can."

"No! Why would you? The semester's barely begun and—"

"I know how it'll be. It'll be just how it is. Nobody will talk to me."

"But why?"

"Because . . ." She shook her head. "It just is, and it won't stop."

"How can you know something like that? There are new people here, new friends to be made—"

"It was this way all summer. I thought it might stop. We used to be friends. I helped her a lot with her math homework."

"You and . . . ?"

"Melanie."

Perfect Melanie? Always smiling, popular, protected by her mama? If I hadn't seen that blank nothing of a stare this afternoon, I wouldn't have believed Olivia at all. I shuddered at what was going on and what I miss and what I didn't know how to fix.

"We went to the same camp in July, and this boy—this

boy she liked, he liked me, and from then on, she said we weren't friends anymore, and she got all the other girls to not talk to me and—" She blinked furiously, her unnatural calm gone. "Everybody likes her. I thought maybe when I came here, it would be different, but . . ." She shook her head. "She told the math teacher she thought she saw me cheating on a test this morning. Nothing's different."

"Couldn't we talk this through? Get both of you together and—"

"It's worse now," she continued, as if I hadn't spoken at all. "As soon as she got home, she blogged me. She's still doing it. People who didn't know me, even, they read her blog and . . ." She shrugged.

"Does she tell lies about you?" Maybe we could stop it, then.

She looked as if she was deciding, as if she didn't quite know. "Not lies, really. No. Things like . . . I'm stuck-up. I think I'm too smart. I guess that's because I helped with her math homework. I dress bad. I'm not loyal. I steal boyfriends . . ." She shook her head again, this time with an expression of amazement. I thought of her and then of Melanie, and understood why she'd have trouble believing she could "steal" someone away, but I could also see how appealing she would be when her face wasn't creased with worry lines, her posture not bent into a slump.

"I still think that surely, there's something we could do to make things better. We can't let someone drive you away— we can work things out. We're civilized people!" I heard myself echo the pathetic claims of the soon to be savage, murderous English boys in *Lord of the Flies*.

She looked at me directly, as if she, too, had heard the echo, and in a quiet voice, said, "Melanie is like Jack, the hunter, the wild boy people want to follow. I'm Piggy."

"That's fiction. We can learn from that—we're supposed to learn from that—"

"There isn't anything anybody can do, except what I'm doing. I'm going to go to the public school near me. It's big. She's not there. It'll be better."

There are societies and religions that consider being excluded the ultimate punishment. The loss of community is basically a death penalty.

Young girls were experts in the trade. Boys might go out and fight, but girls were probably the ones who'd thought of shunning as a penalty in the first place. We could protest and protect, we could teach sensitivity—but I wasn't convinced it would change much, because the process was subtle and below the radar of most adult eyes. So there was no way I could tell this diminutive girl that her ninth-grade worries were trivial or meaningless. I could still feel aftershocks of the year my enemy labeled me a slut, and remember how relieved I'd been to enter a different junior high from the one my tormentor attended.

"I'm so sorry," I said. "It's cruel and stupid."

She put her copy of *Lord of the Flies* on my desk. "I finished it," she said. "I wanted to know how it turned out, but now I'm sorry I do." She looked at me directly for the first time, I thought, and she seemed to grow an inch or two. "I hoped I was wrong about how I thought it would turn out. I hoped Piggy would get out of there alive. But that isn't how things work out, is it? Hoping is worthless, and it doesn't save anybody."

I took her hand and held it. I wanted to hold on to her, keep her, fight her battles for her, and knowing I couldn't do any of those things didn't lessen the wanting.

"The difference between fiction and life, Miss Pepper, is that Piggy couldn't escape to another island. I can."

I watched her go, and this time, it was my eyes that were damp.

Eighteen

THIS WAS FAR FROM THE FIRST TIME I FOUND MYSELF yearning for a mentor—a wise headmaster to whom I could turn for advice and counsel—but at Philly Prep, such an idea was ludicrous. Maurice Havermeyer was going to see Olivia's sad trajectory out of our school only as an entry on the debit side of his ledger, and therefore, a major failing on the part of a faculty that should have strapped her down and kept her paying tuition.

I sought instead the wisdom and companionship of Rachel Leary, the school counselor who was once again large with child. Children, actually. She'd been told she was having twins. "Tell me you're here to give me a back rub," she said as she packed up files.

She'd bid us all—except Dr. Havermeyer—adieu last June, sure she was going to be a full-time mother for a while, but the economy had slumped right down on her household, and her husband was looking for work, so she was back. At least until maternity leave kicked in.

"Did you come here with a problem?" She sounded fearful.

"I came here to steer you out of the building." The problem had been resolved, for better or for worse. "But how about an issue to mull?"

"An issue that doesn't have to do with Stan finding work and the mortgage getting paid and what we'll do about child care with three kids under three—or anything related to that?"

I promised.

"Or about college applications and interviews?" The nightmare season for high school counselors.

I promised again.

"Or—"

"This isn't about Havermeyer, either."

She chuckled. "How did you guess the third side of my grief triumverate?"

As we carefully made our way down the staircase, I told her about Olivia.

"I don't know," Rachel said when we reached the empty entry lobby. "That's a horrible situation that's unfortunately not exactly rare. We can try sensitivity training."

"Her class is reading *Lord of the Flies*. It's almost a blueprint for ostracism and ganging up on somebody—but it hasn't stopped anything from happening. Although, of course, we haven't finished it yet."

"It won't, nor will the sensitivity training, if you ask me. It's hard to change behavior when it's intentional. It's not like being unintentionally or stupidly sexist or racist—it isn't as if her tormentor doesn't know and delight in the fact that she's making life miserable for that girl. But I can help set up a program, at least get them talking about it. It's subterranean, though."

"I thought Melanie was the sweetest thing. Actually, she is sweet, and smart and good in class."

"See what I mean? It takes deliberate action on their part for us to even see what's going on—and then, intervention, likely as not, makes it worse."

"That's what Olivia said."

"Smart girl," Rachel said as we left the building. "And much as I hate to say it because it's ethically and morally and every way wrong and it shows a huge failing on our part—but I think she's made the right decision. Sometimes, if there's poison in the air, the best idea is to head to where you can breathe."

Piggy's other island. I suspected she was right, but that didn't make Olivia's departure less depressing.

"Did you know the students are making book on when I deliver these guys?" she said. "The high flyers are going for an unscheduled in-school delivery. A sort of live action you-are-there sex ed class."

"And an effective way to encourage safe sex."

She chuckled. "Havermeyer would love it."

"Finally. Something no other school can boast, besides absolute mediocrity."

I HAD SHOWERED AND SHAMPOOED AND WAS LINING MY eyes when the phone rang across the room. Macavity pricked his ears, as if finally, somebody was calling him. "It's not for you, dear cat," I said. His eternal optimism was touching. Who was it he thought might phone? "Relax."

And I relaxed, too, once I realized it wasn't either my parents or my future in-laws on the other end. Then I grew tense again.

"Hey, Amanda," the voice said. "Joan here."

"Hey yourself, Joan. How's everything?" We speak a few times a year, so—why now, when I was wearing panty hose, wet hair, eyeliner, and precious else? And why hadn't I found the portable phone instead of this one, which had me chained to the kitchen wall? I didn't want to be rude, so I ran through "I-can't-talk-right-now-but-I-do-love-you" exits, like making a lunch date, or calling her back tomorrow.

"I apologize for the delay, but I got it," she said.

I had no idea what she meant.

"You forgot?" Her voice rose a full octave on that final syllable. My failing memory was a huge and audible disappointment—*I* was a huge disappointment and I'd also probably hurt her feelings. And then I realized what this was about. Joan worked at Shipley. I'd asked her to investigate Vicky Smith Baer's transfer, mostly so I could find out where she'd come from, and then I'd know a school Emmie Cade had attended.

I also realized that what had seemed important three days ago no longer mattered. Mackenzie's contacts had come through speedily and, in any case, Claire Fairchild was dead and the investigation over.

"Of course I didn't forget!" I lied. "I'm astounded that you were able to find the material so quickly!"

"I wanted it to be faster, but the woman who's in charge of the archived files was out with the flu and when she returned, she was overwhelmed with accumulated work—and she's the kind of administrative assistant you do not want to tangle with."

"I know the type."

"Finally, this morning, she found the files. Then it took me all day to call Ohio Cliff, to get a little clarification."

"It's okay, really." I would never tell her it didn't matter anymore. She'd tried so hard.

"No, I know things must be urgent in your new line of work."

"Honestly, Joanie, I'm delighted you were able—" This could go on forever, and even though I had time—an hour, in fact—this particular back-and-forth wasn't overly interesting. "What was it you found out? And why did you have to call the school in Ohio?"

"I thought—I hope it was okay, Manda. It's just that I checked Victoria Smith's file. She transferred to Shipley in November." She paused, for dramatic effect, I thought.

I gave her the prompt she so audibly yearned for. "November."

"Well, that's it. Juniors who are getting ready to apply to

colleges and take S.A.T.s and just . . . be juniors don't switch mid-semester when there's no emergency. And there wasn't any note about a problem, except one note saying that her current grades were not to be taken as the norm. That she'd gone from being an A student, on the hockey team, and all-round epitome of prep school girl—it didn't use those words, of course—to a pretty bad student. She had C's and one D. And I noticed that her parents didn't move with her, and that there hadn't been a death in the family, so I snooped further, and there was a note from the admissions director saying she should be admitted at this unorthodox time because she was in an unusual situation and a change of scene was all that was required. So that's when I remembered a woman at Ohio Cliff I met at the conference, and I—I hope it's okay and it didn't foul anything up for you—I phoned her."

"And?" I was getting chilly, wished I'd snagged a shirt or robe en route to the phone. Also, I thought Joan had already made her point, but I listened on.

"I failed miserably. When I asked about what that message meant, she wouldn't tell me. She said it was confidential material and she couldn't see the relevance to anything all these years later. I just wanted you to know I tried."

"And succeeded. Completely. You found everything I needed."

"I guess I thought you wanted more. I know I did, after I saw that note. I mean the girl went to class, so it wasn't that she was pregnant, which is one reason to leave your old school midyear. I think they're just covering their behinds. Not that anybody would sue a dozen years later, but who actually knows? She said it had nothing to do with the school or faculty or administration, and in her opinion, everyone acted precipitously. 'Time would have taken care of it,' she said. As if that means anything. But I kept talking and hoping she'd get more specific. All I got in the end was that 'girls will be girls.' It was something about popularity and cliques and not belonging. Nothing that should have produced flight. I'm sure it was just what we see here—and you probably see at your school, too—"

Joanie was sweet, and a dear friend, but once you pushed the "on" button, it was difficult stopping her. "Teenage girls," she said. "Moody, unpredictable. So she exercised her woman's—young woman's—prerogative to change her mind. Probably angry with her family because they wouldn't let her stay out late. Who even knows? I am constantly amazed here, and you must be, too."

"Yes," I said. "Certainly. About boys, too."

"Right. Of course. Our boys astound me, too. But I suppose I can understand Ohio Cliff's reticence, because you never know what's going to turn itself into an accusation that the school somehow failed the child. In any case, I'm happy to say, I couldn't find any evidence of any more problems once she was here with us. She was a good student, in fact."

Her voice had become pleasant background buzz to me, like crickets on a summer's night. I wasn't sure about that woman's prerogative, or pure moodiness.

Then I realized that Joanie's pace had slowed. Stopped. She'd been waiting for a response. "So I'm sorry I couldn't get any more," she said, wrongly interpreting my missed cue as disappointment.

And once again, I told her not to apologize at all. And then I swung the conversation over to how she was doing with the new school year underway, and finally to why I couldn't talk as long as I wanted to, what with the big dinner tonight. "Mackenzie's going to pick me up in . . . a few minutes," I said, lying about the time for expediency's sake. I actually had almost an hour till we sallied forth to pick up his parents at their hotel, but for once, I wanted to dress and dry my hair at leisure.

"I'm so sorry. I didn't mean to keep you. Your in-laws! You're getting *married*!"

And that, of course, is not an item to be lightly dropped into the end of a conversation, so we spoke on. She offered unsolicited old-married advice about mothers-in-law ("Beware!" being the condensed version), and I asked about the exploits and achievements of her three children, and how the new term was going at her school.

And at mine. "I think it's going to be all right. I like a lot of the new kids and they seem—for the time being—actually interested and motivated. And I was told that I'm getting good notices on their blogs."

I was showing off, demonstrating not only my reported popularity, but my up-to-the-minute mastery of contemporary adolescent technology. Joanie was suitably impressed—and confused, so then I had to explain what little I knew about Weblogs. I was, however, truly intrigued by them because they seemed important—the next thing after telephones for keeping up nonstop teen communications. And that was, given Olivia's experience with them—and mine—a good and a bad thing.

Finally we reached the psychologically apt time for a polite farewell. Once again, I thanked her for her help, and then, after we made a date for an after-school cup of coffee two weeks hence, on a day she didn't have to carpool, I could graciously, politely, hang up.

It's conversational etiquette that makes Mackenzie roll his eyes and mutter—till I object—about how long it takes women to say good-bye. It's one of the few aspects of his personality that depresses me, because it means he doesn't understand part of the basic rules of civilization. If it were up to him, telephone exchanges would be about information and nothing more. Over and out with military precision, and that of course wasn't the half of it. Anyone who works with teens knows that.

But even having completed the call according to my inner rhythms of social interaction, I didn't feel finished with it. I stood near the phone, thinking I now knew something, but I couldn't access it. If I stood still, I might catch it. So I stood a minute in my sheer-toes panty hose, hair drying in berserk patterns, trying to pinpoint that thing, that something that was so close—and then almost into consciousness and then it was there—it was *that* close—

And the door opened. "Hey, Manda?"

I needed one minute more to get that thought into range, so I put up my finger in the universal signal of "hold it," and C.K. stopped talking.

But not everyone did. "Our feet are killing us, so we thought we'd save time and come directly here instead of—whoops!"

Although her greetings had begun before she was visible, now, Gabby Mackenzie was inside the loft, which is, after all, one large cube, with only bedroom and bathroom partitions. And there we stood for a painfully long second, both of us wide-eyed with disbelief.

"Oh, my," I heard from a male voice that was not my beloved's.

My beloved, in fact, laughed out loud, which might be grounds for removing him from the category of "beloved" altogether. But I couldn't give much thought to that, because I had turned my back and was running, hands clapped on my rear end, toward the sanctuary of the partitioned-off bedroom.

One thing about the experience was that it cured me of all concerns about what I'd wear when with my in-laws. As long as I wore something, I'd be ahead of where I was now.

Nineteen

By the time we were en route to Gladwynne and dinner, I'd gained proper attire and hairstyle, but had long since lost or abandoned the thread of the idea I'd been pursuing. No matter, I decided. If I have questions, Emmie herself will answer them.

And then my niece and nephew, sister and brother-in-law were hugging me, and Horse the dog was bumping his head against my knees for attention and my parents and Boy and Gabby were cheek-kissing, hand-shaking and hugging, and round and round in every possible combination people demonstrated that an impending marriage trumps everything.

I relaxed into the confused merriment. Why not? We were an island of loveliness filled with happy cooking smells, the beautiful surrounds of Beth and Sam's house, their adorable children, and almost equally adorable dog. It was, in fact, close to the picture of comfortable domesticity that's always supposed to be either a bore or a sham, but certainly wasn't in this case. I knew this from careful and cynical long-term observation. And like a delighted audience at this performance of marital possibilities, the two sets of parents cheered.

I didn't think I'd ever seen my mother this happy, and it made me the slightest bit sad for all the times I'd been annoyed by her matrimonial nagging. Her hints and prods had been irritating, infuriating, and often ludicrous, but they were from her heart, part of a sincere belief, however antiquated and ridiculous, that to be married was to be safe in some way she passionately desired for her daughters.

Now, thanks to my unintentional announcement of a marriage date, she considered me safe. Her work was done, and on this, the seventh day, she rested.

And though I'd promised myself not to think about it this evening, my mother's contentment inevitably contrasted with my memory of Claire Fairchild, who also only wanted her child to be safe. A wave of sadness took the edge off the bright evening.

But not for anyone else. By blundering into a wedding date, I'd defused the potential tension of this evening, and the two sets of parents, so dramatically dissimilar, were united and excited about seeing this through in style. I thought I'd be building conversational bridges all night long, but there was no need. I could have left the building and the party would have raged on.

I looked at my mother in her little black dress, the one she insisted be a part of every woman's wardrobe, her proper patent pumps, and her mother's marcasite initial pin. She'd have looked like a Puritan preaching to a lady of the evening, had both she and Gabby not looked so delighted with each other's company. Gabby, towering over her, was laughing at something my mother had said. She looked like a tropical bird in the emerald brilliance of her dress—scoop neck, bouffant sleeves, skirts flouncing with blue and red embroidered tracery—the sort of thing Marie Antoinette wore when pretending to be a milkmaid, except for the strappy red high heels.

Even the fathers, Mackenzie, and Sam had found common ground, and all four were nodding in agreement with a topic I couldn't begin to guess.

My sister, supervising her own daughter who was carrying a tray of endive piped with what appeared to be crème fraîche and caviar, caught my eye and gave the thumbs-up sign. And then Sam poured champagne all around, and Mackenzie and I were toasted with only one minor glitch when my mother called the groom-to-be "Chuck" and Gabby did a double-take.

Joy reigned in Gladwynne. Poor Olivia and dead Claire Fairchild and mixed-up Emmie Cade faded into the distance till they disappeared altogether.

Dinner was a fine medley of barbecued lamb and crisp green beans and more wine and much laughter with Gabby, mother of seven married children who'd had thirteen weddings amongst them, regaling the table with tales of outrageous mishaps and mismatches. My mother looked worried by the stories at first, and then gave up and laughed along with everyone else.

Even the children, sipping apple juice in wineglasses, behaved, and when they started to fade, I took them upstairs. My longstanding role as spinster aunt included reading them bedtime stories when I was around, a perk I intended to keep. Now that Alexander was of an age to have favorites, each session followed a long negotiation. "Not the poop book again," Karen insisted. "Or else I get my own story."

I didn't have time for two books, and finally, they agreed on *Best Friends for Frances*, which seemed appropriately about siblings finding out they could be friends. I hadn't realized or remembered that the book was concerned with Frances's response to being excluded, but reading about it brought Olivia back into the room, the awareness of how much less aggressive and successful she'd been than a fictional badger.

Of course, badgers didn't have to go to high school. That made their lives easier.

Beth, afraid I was being trapped by her children, came upstairs, and together, we finished the story and tucked them in.

And ultimately, it was a traditional ladies-cleaning-up scene, with all of us vying for the "most helpful" award, but thanks to Beth's superpreparedness and modern conveniences like dishwashers, there was little washing, and no drying, and four women circling the kitchen until we divvied up the few chores. I was delegated to rescue the leftovers from Horse, which I did while we continued to talk about families, weddings, Beth's event-planning skills, and how cute the children were.

The senior generation was in the dining room, clearing the tablecloth and protective pads while I put leftover mint sauce in the refrigerator.

"I like your in-laws," Beth said. "They're fun."

"That they are. I can't believe how it's defused Mom. She's kind of rolling with whatever anybody says."

Beth raised her eyebrows. "Gabby is a bit ... overwhelming," she whispered. "But in a good way."

"She's such a happy person," I whispered back, although the two mothers were talking at such a feverish pace in the next room, they couldn't have heard us even if we were louder. "As if life's a super game, and she's on a perpetual winning streak."

I wondered if I could adopt some of Gabby Mackenzie's resolute joy, and then I accepted the fact that I was not made of the same material, and I closed the refrigerator, checking what new shots of the children or invitations Beth's refrigerator sported. Snooping, to be blunt. I saw a mildly familiar item. Vicky Baer's brochure. "What is she doing up here?" I asked. "The refrigerator is hallowed home ground."

Beth laughed. "I haven't actually had a chance to read it

yet, but I want to check out whether there's any crossover on there."

"Meaning?"

"You know. She consults all over the place, to all sorts of nonprofits, and I'm putting together a little dinner party . . ."

"May I suggest that subtlety isn't your strong point?"

"Come down from your ivory tower," she said, and that made me laugh.

"What's the opposite of an ivory tower?" I asked. "A mud trench? That's more like Philly Prep."

"I realized I know somebody at a foundation she works with," she said, "and I thought it might be nice, since they already know each other, to invite them both. In fact, I called her—Vicky—right before you got here, but she was out. A woman who barely spoke English answered. I do wish people who have trouble with the language would simply leave an answering machine on."

I made sure the wrap was tight around the last of the lamb and returned to the crammed refrigerator in search of a place for it. "So is she coming to your gala?"

Beth shrugged. "I only spoke—if you can call it that—to this woman, who said 'the lady is with the friend who is feeling bad.' It took me so long to get that, that I didn't have the energy to try to leave a message. I'll call her to-morrow. Check out the brochure. She's got an impressive business going."

I had zero interest in it. Besides, Vicky had given me one as well and it must still be wherever I'd shoved it, should I ever want to check it out. But Beth seemed to want me to acknowledge what a trophy she'd snared and how clever she'd been, to officially approve of her networking savvy, so I obliged her, opening and skimming through it.

Vicky Baer had indeed developed an impressive business. Or a sufficiency of people willing to lie and give her nice little endorsements. There were tributes about increased endowments, a revised and three-times-more-profitable fundraising plan, good service that didn't end with the contract, et cetera. I didn't personally recognize any of the sources, except Shipley School, but there were lots of them with the quotes, and then a sidebar list of still more.

This was a career I'd never have thought of, almost an oxymoron, helping nonprofits make money. Helping herself as well, I had to believe. And sampling just a few names, she'd pleased the boards of the KBS Foundation in Philly, and One Hundred Percent for the Children in D.C. I had a brief and nasty moment thinking that nobody would know if she'd made these places up. A King Henry School, that should have been in England, but found itself in Chicago; another, a more plainly named Prep school in Baltimore; and two in upstate New Jersey, right outside New York; The Family Foundation in Altoona; and The Learning Project in San Francisco for starters.

That's right—she'd bumped into Emmie while on business in San Francisco.

"I hope her success now extends to you," I said, returning the brochure to its refrigerator magnet.

I meant it. I was impressed. But I was also . . . I don't know what. Irritated by it. Something prickled, though I couldn't identify it. I wondered if I was jealous of her remarkable success, and hoped not. But I couldn't think why else her credentials annoyed me this way.

"One thing," Beth said softly. "You were honest with me the other night, weren't you?"

"About what? Of course I was. I always am, but what do you mean?"

"About Vicky. That she wasn't the one you were investigating."

"Absolutely not the one."

"Because you'd tell me, right? I mean, even if it's part of

your job, and if you found out I was walking into something bad—there's no code forbidding you to tell me, is
there?"

"My code of honor would absolutely make me keep you
safe."

She exhaled loudly, as if she'd been holding her breath on
this all evening.

I went back into the dining room to be certain that nothing edible was left in sight.

"You're amazing," my mother said as Gabby slid a
drawer closed. "How did you know where that went? And
before? How did you know where the table pads went,
too?"

Gabby winked at me. "Magic?" she said.

"Beth's magic, probably," I said. "She's the most logical
person I've ever met, so everything is in—"

"He didn't tell you, huh?" Gabby's mouth curled in a
tight, lopsided smile.

"Who? Tell me what?"

"My son," she said in the most matter-of-fact way. "Tell
you that I'm a witch." Her smile expanded till it half-
covered her face, and she laughed and pointed at me, at my
expression. "Guess not!"

"What—what do you mean?" My mother had her hands
raised, cupping the top of her head, all but drawing a
pointed hat up there.

"No, no," Gabby said, the half smile still on her face. We
amused her. "Nothing special. Ordinary witchy things. I
see things, commune with things."

We all saw things unless we were blind. And communed,
I had to assume, with something. But we didn't see through
solid cherry breakfronts, or commune with table pads as to
where they belong.

"I'm not like an Orthodox witch," she said. "I'm a sole
practitioner. No coven, no big rituals, and most of all," she

said, looking around to make sure her work was done, "not that stupid bad-spell stuff in fairy tales. That's not real. That's just evil propaganda."

"Of course it is!" my mother said, eager as ever to be prejudice-free. "But then . . . when? What?"

Gabby raised her shoulders and inhaled, then let out the air and relaxed. "I just have . . . powers, but I can't truly say when it comes on me. It's erratic. And between us girls, since the change, I think I'm mostly losing it. My grandmother said the same thing happened to her. I mean, look—it's down to knowing where table pads go." She shook her head, then smiled again. "Easy come, easy go," she said. "And now, let us get our poor hostess out of the kitchen, and join our gentlemen friends."

My mother glanced at me warily, quickly, then away. She obviously didn't dare to say a word or think it. Gabby might have one of her rare postmenopausal second-sight bursts and read her mind. Besides, for all her marital advice and warnings, she'd never once told me to avoid men whose mothers were witches.

We reconvened in the living room, where the conversation rolled back and forth between the out-of-towners about their mutual visits. My mother almost visibly took herself in hand and rose above her reluctance to play with witches, and mentioned possible outings. I moved still closer to my Mackenzie, who put an arm around me and smiled. He was one happy man.

"Your mother just said she's a witch," I whispered.

His smile faded, and he closed his eyes for a second. Then he sighed and fixed his blue gaze on me. "I was hopin' she'd skip that."

"It's not news to you?"

He shook his head.

"And you never felt the need to mention it?" It is hard to shout in a whisper, and my throat ached doing so, but I had no choice. There was suddenly an arid desert between us, littered with important things unsaid, secrets kept. I didn't dare guess what else lay there. The fact that he'd kept it to himself was much more serious than Gabby's beliefs. I was up on things. I knew that Wiccan was a feminist religion, a goddess religion, that it really didn't have anything to do with the dreadful stereotypes fear had created through the ages.

Although I wasn't sure anything much I knew applied to Gabby's iconoclastic witchhood that seemed to depend on a ready supply of hormones.

"You were complainin' this very week that you wished I'd never told you a thing about my past."

"This is a little different, don't you think? This would be like being frank with me about a genetic problem, or a history of . . . of—"

"Horse thieves?"

"Okay, not exactly, but—"

"She's an entertaining, loving lady, isn't she?"

"Is witchcraft what you meant when you always added 'but eccentric'?"

He raised one eyebrow.

"Okay. *One* of the traits you meant."

"She's Acadian. They're different, you know. Named for the great doomed lovers in Longfellow's poem, Gabriel Lajeunesse and Evangeline Bellefontaine."

"They're fictional. She didn't inherit this from them."

"They were family ideals. And do you remember the lovers' story? How they found each other again in Philadelphia?" He smiled, as if that made everything all right.

"Found each other in Philadelphia and promptly died," I said.

He looked at me solemnly. "My sisters do not have the gift."

"Let me be clear on this. Your sisters are not witches."

"Correct."

"And you? Men can be witches."

He shook his head again. "Apparently, the Mackenzie DNA includes antiwitch matter."

I couldn't help but wonder what other family secrets lay in store and whether I was at all eager to enter that store. I just hated not knowing something that central about his family, and worried now that Mackenzie had carefully censored his words, as if he needed to protect me from the truth, or protect the truth from me.

I didn't like either option.

I wondered if the surprise introduction of a witch in the family gave one an out from a wedding. I'd bet even my mother would accept that as an excused absence.

Twenty

"What a good time I'm having," Gabby said as the four of us walked to the car. It was still early. The dinner hour had been arranged for small children—and the originally planned arrival of the Mackenzies. The evening out here in the suburbs was lovely, with a faint whisper of autumn, a brisk edge to the soft night and, all around us, that wistful scent of the end of growing, of roses blooming for the last time.

"What a grand evening," Gabby said. "Lovely day."

"Evening's still young," Boy said. "Tell me it isn't true about this city rolling up the streets and let us take you out for a nightcap."

C.K. was grinning, contentment on every feature. He looked over at me. Apparently, he no longer cared about the stack of books he was supposed to be reading for school. He was definitely ready for more, but was letting me decide whether the good times kept rolling.

He was being a gentleman. A happy one.

Is there anything on earth more infuriating than being incensed with a man who's oblivious to it? "Sure," I said, because that postponed the argument I knew awaited us. I didn't want to spoil his parents' time, either. And it was early, just past eight P.M. "Anywhere. Your call."

"In that case," C.K. said, "there's a bar in South Philly that will provide not only drinks, but local color of a sort that will make you know you're not in Lafayette, Louisiana, anymore, folks."

We drove the Expressway in silence. Mackenzie turned on the radio and searched for the easy-listening station, the instant background noise because there wasn't any foreground. We seemed to have used up our chatter.

Gabby's need for polite sociability broke the silence. "What a darling family you have," she said.

"Thanks," I responded. "They thought the same of you." And then I set my hearing to "pleasantries," and let whatever was said blur into the background music becoming, if not white noise, then at best, pale, pale beige.

"Food delicious, too," Boy said, or something like it. "That lamb . . ."

"House beautiful . . ."

"Lovely . . ."

"Adorable . . . clever . . ."

"Even a lovely dog." That, of course, from Gabby.

Everything was perfect at Beth's. She had standards. She didn't get a mother-in-law who dressed like Merlin and recited chants.

"What dog have you ever met that you didn't think was lovely?" Boy seemed eternally amused by his wife. "This woman is a dog's best friend. Any dog. All dogs."

"Good creatures," she said.

And here I'd thought that cats were witch's familiars. Macavity had certainly taken to her immediately, but I'd ascribed it to his adoration of all things Mackenzie. Now I knew better.

"Do you think so, Manda?"

"Sorry," I said. "My mind was wandering."

"We could make a picnic Saturday? Everybody, includin' those adorable children of your sister's."

Saturday. Their last day. "Sounds great. I don't know Beth and Sam's schedule, but I'm sure they'd love it."

"How about Valley Forge?" Mackenzie said. "Toss in a little history." He had a future as a tour guide. Bars, picnics, you name it, he'd find the local angle.

"And their dog, too," Gabby said. "The park would allow him."

"Oh, Gabby," Boy said. "You're too much."

"I'm so homesick for the babies," she said. "And so worried Lizzie isn't going to remember to give Cary Grant his phenobarb both times. You know how she forgets things—and by the time we get home, he'll be having those fits again."

I sat up straight. "Excuse me?"

Mackenzie wasn't listening to me. He was into tour guiding. "Look," he said. "This is South Philly. See the row houses? All the same?"

"Like apartment buildings on their side," Boy said.

"Phenobarbital? For dogs?" I asked.

"New York's an island and had nowhere to go but up, but Philly could stretch out, and here you see it," C.K. said.

"Poor Cary's been takin' it for a while," Gabby said. "I just haven't been away all this long since then, and Lizzie's sweet but absentminded—"

"Her mind is pretty absent most of the time," Boy admitted.

"—and if Cary doesn't take it twice a day . . ."

I felt as if an electric prod had been applied to my brain. It zigged and zagged and pointed fingers and ran in circles shouting for attention.

Slow down, I told myself, as if I were back teaching the sophomores. Organize your thoughts.

Dogs. Medication. Vicky Baer's dog.

The ideas spun, chasing their tails.

Joan's call about Vicky Baer, nee Smith. Grade slump. Nothing the school did . . .

Olivia. Leaving school because of another girl.

Organize your thoughts!

The brochure.

Why the brochure? Why had it upset me? Her triumphant list of schools and foundations. Verbal bouquets from impressive clients all over the map. D.C., Baltimore, Altoona, Chicago, San Francisco . . .

"Cary will be fine," Boy said. "Not like you to worry this much."

"Mackenzie," I said, before he could point out other landmarks. "Humor me. Word-association time. What's the significance of these three cities: Baltimore, Altoona, Chicago."

"They all have an *a* and an *o* in their name."

I don't know how he does things like that so quickly, but I did know that wasn't the answer I needed. I sighed and folded my arms across my chest and even shook my head a bit to loosen up my thoughts, shake them out of the ruts they were in, get them organized.

I had it. "The *notes!*" I spoke as softly as I could, but I couldn't contain my excitement. "I knew there was something about that brochure—the anonymous notes came from the places Vicky Baer travels to!"

"Lovely. Except . . . so what?"

"So what? She sent those notes. That's what!"

"And? Mean-spirited, I'll grant you, but . . . I repeat, so what? Legally, what is that? Abuse of the postal service? Claire Fairchild might have been interested in that—if it's true—but she's beyond caring. Batya murdered her. Case closed."

No. It wasn't. Even if I didn't yet know why, I knew it wasn't over. And it felt urgently important that I line up the wild and unrelated messages flashing neon in my brain. Find the words to explain the electrical charges in my nervous system.

High school! Olivia. Leaving. Vicky leaving. Not the school's fault.

Sick dogs! Vicky left the dinner to take care of one.

No. Wait. My brain buzzed, the signs flashed randomly, all together, separately and I still couldn't make them out.

Phone call! She was going to take care of the dog after she took her phone call.

Emmie Cade had announced a wedding date that day. Was that the call?

Leo had already quarreled with his mother that day. Had found out about her hiring us. Told Emmie. Was that the call?

Pretending! Nobody knew Claire Fairchild was faking her illness then.

Shower! Something made Vicky visit Claire Fairchild that night. Was the idea of a bridal shower that urgent? Especially after she'd told me she wasn't all that close with Emmie, though they were old acquaintances, more than real friends.

Friend! Vicky's visiting a friend who was feeling bad. Right now. "Mackenzie." I put a hand on his arm.

"And here we are," he answered. "At the corner." I saw a beer's name lit up on a red brick wall. Accurate as ever, he'd found us a Typical South Philly Bar. It could occupy a display at the Smithsonian.

"No," I said.

He pulled into a spot a few houses up.

"No," I said again. "Turn around. We're wrong—everything we thought is wrong. The whole way we looked at this was wrong."

"This is it. I'm right," he said, looking confused.

"I mean about Claire Fairchild. Batya didn't do it, Mackenzie."

"Please," he said. "The police are—you know that. I told you—"

"They're all wrong, too! I know what happened now. Trust me. Turn around. We have to go to Emmie's right now." I looked at my watch. "And hope it's not too late."

"Actually, you're not making sense," he said, not unkindly. "My folks—we all agreed to a nightcap." He turned off the ignition.

"No! Turn it back on—I was wrong. I can't mess this up, too—she asked me to help her!"

"Who?"

"Emmie Cade!"

"No need to raise your—when? What about?"

"That isn't the point!"

"What *is* the point?"

"That you have to leave here right now and get to her—she's in danger!"

"Phone her if you're worried."

"What difference would that make? We have to go!"

"You're lettin' your imagination—"

"Ooooh, noooo," Gabby suddenly said, or moaned. She pressed both the heels of her hands to her temples. "I can't believe—I'm havin' the most terrifyin'—painful—vision—a girl—cryin'—something bad—somebody needs me. Quick. Somebody . . ." Her voice faded off.

"Oh, for Pete's—" Mackenzie said.

"Hits her like this," Boy said with audible admiration.

"She cries, she dies. . . ," she whispered rhythmically.

"Mother, please. It's not funny anymore."

The neon in my brain buzzed and flashed, all the words turning into danger signs.

"She needs, she—"

"Mother, those rhymes are—"

"Son," Boy said. That was all. Apparently, it was enough.

"This is craziness," Mackenzie muttered, but he started the car, turned the corner, then turned again, back into the direction of Center City and Emmie Cade. "Why, when all logic—" He gave up on the idea of logic. "You're going to be humiliated," he said. "This is about the least professional . . ."

I didn't answer. Neither did my ally, the witch, who sat muttering her pathetic rhymes, her hands still pressed to her temples. "Hurry," I said. "She's counting on our misreading everything. Don't play into her hands."

"Hurry, scurry," Gabby muttered.

Traffic was miraculously light—almost as if a witch were in control—and within fifteen minutes, we were in front of Claire Fairchild and Emmie Cade's building.

Way in front. We couldn't find a parking space.

"Tell you what. I'll wait in the car with my folks," Mackenzie said. "You can go up and check things out. Take your cell phone. Call if there's a problem."

What had happened to our partnership? What if something as wrong as I feared was going on and I was already inside the apartment? "At what stage in the problem should I call?" I asked, keeping my voice calm.

"I have to go with her. I have to see the girl in pain. Touch her—touch something of hers." Gabby Mackenzie still pressed her temples as if holding on to a vision, and her voice sounded as if it came out of an empty vase.

Mackenzie punched the steering wheel. "There aren't any parking spaces," he said.

"I'll make one happen," Gabby said, just as—right before?—slightly after?—a man walked out of the building jiggling keys.

"Damn," Mackenzie said as the man pulled an SUV out of a prize spot.

Damn was right. I looked at Gabby in amazement, then, in the two of us went, top speed, while C.K., still trying to save face and avoid going anywhere, pretended to be occupied with locking up the car and talking to his father.

Gabby and I entered the outer lobby. I found M. E. Cade's apartment number on a neatly printed list behind glass, and pressed the buzzer.

"They don't listen, do they?" Gabby said.

"Excuse me?"

"Like father, like son. Good as it gets, but—that tiny flaw. Don't take us seriously. Humor us, gentle us—and do what they think's right."

"Are you saying what I think you're—"

"Takes special powers now and then to get through to them."

"You *are* saying what I think you're—"

The men arrived. She didn't have to tell me to drop that conversational thread. We were buzzed in, and rode to Emmie's floor in silence, though Mackenzie's expression spoke volumes.

The future Mrs. Fairchild didn't occupy an entire floor the way the late Mrs. Fairchild had, and since the visiting clairvoyant apparently didn't do doors, I managed to go in the wrong direction twice, which was difficult, before determining on which door to knock. Only then did I allow myself to consider precisely what I was going to do with or about any of this.

Or admit, despite my supernatural backup, that I could be humiliatingly wrong.

The hallway was silent except for Mackenzie's whistle-hum, a faint and unpleasant sound he's apt to produce between his teeth, all unawares, when he would rather be anywhere but where he finds himself. "Nobody home," he said after a too-long wait.

"I know she's here. I'll prove it." Gabby pounded on the door, then nodded smartly.

And the door opened.

"That the girl in trouble?" Gabby asked me out of the side of her mouth.

I shook my head. "That's trouble itself."

"What's this?" Vicky Baer said. "Who are all of you?" She put a finger up to her mouth. "She's ill. Can't see anybody, certainly not a huge group of people."

Without a signal, without a word, Gabby and I pushed forward, moved Vicky to one side, and ran into the apartment.

"Hey!" Vicky screamed from right behind us. "Where do you think you're—"

"Emmie!" Like the panicked fool I was, I shouted her name even though I was sure she was already dead.

The living room was nearly empty. Little furniture and no body. Nobody. I ran through an archway, toward the bedroom, I assumed.

"Wait!" Gabby called, and I turned and saw her zoom through the open French windows, her arms held wide, and then, closed tight around a small figure leaning on, and half over, the balcony railing, like something dropped and abandoned there.

She looked smaller than ever, diminished. Boneless and liable to sink to the ground if Gabby let go, but Gabby didn't. Instead, she whispered something while gentling Emmie onto a wrought-iron chair next to a small table holding a bottle of wine and two glasses.

I flooded with relief to the point where I thought I might slide to the ground myself. She was alive. The terrible thing hadn't happened.

"Emmie's had too much." Vicky stood at the open doorway, hands on hips, Mackenzie and Boy behind her. Her voice so disapproved of what she saw, it felt curled down at its edges.

Gabby stood above Emmie, emerald sleeves billowing in the evening's breeze.

"I don't think so," I said to Vicky. "Claire Fairchild had too much, but Emmie hasn't had quite enough. What was next on the schedule? She was going to have a sudden impulse to jump? It wouldn't take much of a push. She's pretty small."

"You're out of—she's been drinking and ranting—"

I held up the bottle. "Nearly full. And neither glass really touched." Pity, I thought. It was good wine, going to waste.

Below us, a car honked and brakes squealed.

"I'm callin' paramedics." Mackenzie opened his cell and cursed softly. "Phone's dead."

"She's drunk!" Vicky insisted, but C.K. was gone, into the apartment in search of a live phone.

We were on the same side again. Partners.

Emmie showed signs of life. "Sorry," she said. "Sorry. Clifffffffff . . ." She sounded like a tire going flat. "Long time ago . . ."

"Who?" I asked, wondering where this man fit into her biography, but remembering, then, Joan's call. The school in Ohio from which Vicky Smith had fled.

"Says I ruined . . . sorry . . . teen . . ."

"Too drunk to make sense," Vicky said. "I'm going home."

"No, wait," I said. She wouldn't have, but Boy stood behind her like a closed gate. "What's your poor dog doing for medication these days?"

"Dog?" Gabby'd been idling, hovering over Emmie like a guardian angel, or mere mortal of the kind-and-concerned variety, not a proper witch at all. Of course, there'd been no need for magic. Emmie was alive. The word *dog* piqued the first sign of interest in the happenings.

"Why?" I asked Vicky. "Why Claire Fairchild? What did she ever do to you?"

Vicky eyed me blankly, her face a mask, and I knew. It had never been about Claire Fairchild. She'd been nothing more than a war casualty, *collateral damage,* that dehumanizing term that was easier to say than human beings killed by a war they weren't waging.

A woman treated as no more than a bump en route to a more important goal. A life dispassionately trashed as a device to frame someone else, a bullet to remove a rival. It hurt to believe it. "And Emmie takes the fall. Literally," I said. "That was your plan."

"I don't know what you're talking about. There's nothing mysterious about Mrs. Fairchild's death."

I hated that she referred politely, remotely to the woman she'd killed.

"She was dying," Vicky said. "No secret. She died. I don't see what you—"

"You don't die of pretending to be ill. You die when somebody substitutes her pet's medicine for your real pills."

"Your *dog's* medicine?" Gabby's voice again came out of empty tubing, echoing somehow on its own, and she was all action, her normal laissez-faire gone. She raised her arms toward the sky, her sleeves billowing, her nails twinkling in reflected light.

"Who are you?" Vicky shielded her face with her hands, as if Gabby physically threatened her.

"A witch," Gabby said in that inhuman hollow-pipe voice. "And I don't like you one bit."

"There's no such thing as a—" Vicky swallowed hard, and curled her mouth, but she didn't take her eyes off Gabby for a second, and when Gabby made two sets of claws of her spangled nails—that's all, not a word or a curse or a spell—I thought Vicky might faint. "You're insane!" She didn't sound convinced.

"Sorry, sorry, sorrrrr . . ." Emmie said in a whisper. "So long ago, shouldn't—"

"Shut up!" Vicky screamed, still keeping her eyes on Gabby, who made a sound suspiciously like a hiss.

"High school," I said. "And then what? Cornell? The boy she ran away with?"

"Nothing. Who cared?"

"You did. And then San Francisco—what? Bygones will be bygones, so you're polite to the widow and then what? Leo?"

"Din' know . . . Leeeeeee . . ." Emmie couldn't finish the name. Her head dropped further forward, and she was silent.

"Hang in there. Help's coming. Damn phone was in the bedroom—under the bed." Mackenzie was back. He went to Emmie, and I edged over and back to give him room and watch him try to keep her awake.

Below us, in the distance, I heard the whine of an ambulance. "Hang in there," he said. "Hear that? It's for you. It's help."

She flopped forward. Mackenzie bent to lift her.

"I'll let them in," Boy said. "She looks bad. Can you save her, Gabby?"

Gabby? The hissing spectator? Nonetheless, she looked at her husband whose I.Q. I was beginning to question, and nodded. An arrogant witch, or maybe they all were. Came with the territory.

"Stop acting as if she's a—"

"I can't read you your rights anymore," Mackenzie told Vicky, "but you'd better think about them, because the police are on their way, too." He got Emmie to her feet. "Don't give up yet," he said. "C'mon," and he walked her, slowly, toward the apartment.

"*Police?*" Vicky put her hands back up to her face. "You can't—I didn't do—" His back was to her, and she stopped, her mouth half open, her eyes suddenly tearing, and her words increasingly garbled. "You have to tell them I never meant for her to die! I only wanted—I only—you can't—it wasn't right—*again! She's* the witch. She ruins my life over and over again!"

"Don't you badmouth witches," Gabby said.

"Doesn't matter what you wanted," Mackenzie said, his back to her as he softly spoke to Emmie, and patted her cheeks. "Murder's what you got."

"What'll I do?" she wailed.

"Spend a long time in prison," I said, but just then, I saw Emmie Cade trip as she crossed the threshold into the apartment. "Watch out!" I called. "She's—" Gabby began, and both Mackenzie and Boy bent to catch her, bumped heads, then managed nonetheless to save Emmie from collapse before they stood up and rubbed their sore spots.

And all of us heard a terrifying squeal of tires and, from nowhere, down below, shouts.

I think I knew before I turned and saw the empty balcony that Vicky Baer was no longer with us.

It was over. Pretty much like that. The paramedics were delayed because of Vicky's leap, but they arrived in time, and there we were, locking up someone else's apartment.

No fireworks, no dark alleys, no punches, chases, gunshots, merely a witch and a zombie and, for me, a subtle shaking that wouldn't stop, and a terrible confusion about who, truly, the victim had been and when a crime actually begins. What do we do with hurts that started a lifetime ago?

I was glad Olivia refused to be cowed, that she'd move on, live her life. But what if Melanie kept showing up, kept removing what she held dear?

If you're Gabby Mackenzie, you say it doesn't bear thinking about right now. "It's all confusion, honey. All you can do right now is go through the motions of normal. Then, someday, things fall into place of their own accord."

That more or less made sense.

And if you're Gabby, you say that maybe it was all for the best, perhaps the least painful end for Vicky Baer, and you adopt her dog.

That made sense, too.

And, later on, when we were having a drink, silently and still in shock, and the men chose to recuperate in a guy way, walking over to the TV, where the Phillies were involved in extra innings, you take a deep breath and say, "So we did it, didn't we? A little witchcraft comes in handy."

That made no sense.

For starters, what had we done? Vicky Baer had jumped to her death, still feeling pursued by a fury named Emmie Cade. Did we pat ourselves on the back for that?

And Gabby's part of the *we* hadn't done a thing except stretch her hands toward the sky.

When I didn't respond, she prompted me. "Didn't we save the good one?" she asked.

I wasn't sure anymore who'd been the good one. "We saved the one who hadn't murdered Claire Fairchild. Who only hurt people unintentionally. Or because it was easier, or more lucrative."

"You said she was the good one."

"Since you mention that, I'm confused why I had to tell you."

"You care that I didn't know which girl was which? Big deal."

I also thought her incantations were pathetic rhymes, but she was going to be my mother-in-law, so I kept my mouth shut.

"Would you like it better if I called it women's intuition, which is just another name for paying good attention?" She shook her head. Tendrils of her snow-colored hair had pulled loose from the ornate updo and looked like punctuation marks around her face. "Men don't like that better. They ignore it. Puff up, pat your head, and say, There, there little lady."

True enough. I'd never invoke *intuition*.

"Like, say, that parking spot I made happen. It is possible that while you all blathered away about who was going where, I saw the man come out holding his keys. But maybe not. Maybe it was magic, and what does it matter? It worked out. I mean, God knows I'm sorry for that girl, but she killed a woman and didn't seem to give a damn. Not even now. She was going to kill another one. And—"

I knew what was coming, her priorities, what really got to her.

"—she endangered her doggie's life taking away his medicine. She had the last word this way. Played judge and jury and doled out her own punishment."

I hadn't thought of it that way, and now I did, while I sipped scotch. It helped. I was no longer as conscious of every nerve end in my body.

"So what do you think?" Gabby asked, breaking into my reverie. "Want to be a witch, too?"

"They don't do well in these parts. Think Salem."

"Oh, right," she said. "A pity what they did, wasn't it?"

"Plus, I think your son's onto your game."

She winked at me. "His father, too. Doesn't matter, though. It's like a middle ground where they can agree and still save face. And speaking of them, it's high time they paid attention to us, don't you think? I mean, you aren't even married yet and he's ignoring you. Can't have that." She clapped her hands, twice.

And damned if that instant a huge male cheer didn't rise up from the bar. "Home run!" the TV announcer shouted out. "And that's the game, folks, a nail-biter with the Phillies in eleven with—"

I looked at Gabby with new amazement.

She winked at me, and then at the men, whose mood had lightened considerably. "We won," Mackenzie said.

I looked at him. "We did indeed," I said. We had.

My partner, my fiancé, my love. My one-of-a-kind son-of-a-witch.

If you enjoyed Gillian Roberts's *Claire and Present Danger*, you won't want to miss her new novel

TILL THE END OF TOM

Available in hardcover in December 2004 from Ballantine Books

Please turn the page for an exciting sneak preview. . . .

One

MY MIND WAS ON STEINBECK; MY FOOT WAS ON A HAND.
I screamed.

No one responded, most definitely not the man on the floor.

I had wanted to escape the headmaster's annual interminable address to the student body. Neither his ideas nor his words had changed or improved over the years I'd heard them, and when I reached the limits of my endurance, I fabricated an excuse.

Put more precisely: I lied. "An emergency," I'd whispered as I made my way out of the auditorium.

A new wise saying: Be careful what you fabricate, because there he lay, a certifiable emergency, crumpled and inert at the foot of the wide marble stairs, a thin halo of blood around his head.

He was face-up, looking surprised, as well he might be given his position and the fact that his right cheek was indented, as if it had buckled.

My mind finally activated. I pulled out my cell phone to dial for help, although the man seemed well beyond any.

I saw movement out of the side of my eye, and turned quickly, fearing another shock, but it was only Mrs. Wiggins, the school's most recent—and again unsuccessful—attempt to find a competent secretary. She tiptoed out of the office, not exactly racing to my rescue. In fact, she approached so slowly that she was close to moving backward. She stopped altogether when she was a few feet from me.

I told the nine-one-one operator. "This is Amanda Pepper," I said, "a teacher at Philly Prep." I gave our address and the situation and ended the call.

Mrs. Wiggins remained as immobile as the man at the bottom of the stairs. "What—what—," she said, shaking her head as if to negate the evidence of her eyes. "What—"

"Please—go to the auditorium. Tell Dr. Havermeyer to keep everybody there. Explain what's happened."

"Who—do you know who that is?" Her voice was a hoarse whisper.

"Better hurry. The assembly's nearly over."

She shook her head again. Maybe she had a degenerative disease. "I'm not supposed to leave the office." She sounded the way a rabbit would, if it could talk. "I'm not even sure I should be out here, because what if the phone—"

"Mrs. Wiggins, this is an emergency." You had to spell things out for this woman, basic, primitive things, and although our recent rapid turnover of school secretaries was not a good situation, I couldn't help but hope it would continue, and that the Wiggins era was nearing its end. "I think this man's dead," I said as patiently as I could manage. "A lot of people are about to burst in here—police, paramedics, I don't know who all else. The last thing anybody wants would be for several hundred adolescents to converge on this spot."

"Police? But—why? Is this a crime? Do you—did you see something? Somebody?"

"They have to be called for accidents, too." I waited. So did she. "Go, Mrs. Wiggins. Hurry!" Even Havermeyer's seemingly endless drone, "Musings on the Possibilities of Life During and After High School," would ultimately conclude. "Hurry!" I said. "Do you want the students to see this?"

"Well, maybe you could—I could stay, and you could go tell—"

"Mrs. Wiggins! You're his secretary." I didn't care if that made sense. I had gone A.W.O.L. from assembly and didn't want to underline that fact. Besides, she was such a nervous, distracted creature that if I left her as sentry, she'd amble around the poor man and inadvertently ruin any evidence there might be.

She blinked, nodded, and moved toward the auditorium.

I searched for a pulse without disturbing the body. I wasn't sure what I'd found, possibly only my own fingertips' pulse, but he was still warm. I fumbled in my purse for a mirror to hold to his mouth. Meanwhile, I studied him, trying to figure out who he was and why he was at Philly Prep, let alone on the floor in this condition.

He was—or had been—an attractive enough middle-aged man. He had dark hair with the slightest threading of gray, and regular strong features. He looked to be in his forties or early fifties, and seemed surprised to be found in such an undignified and awkward position, one leg bent to the side, the other heel still on the bottom step, his arms flung wide as if, coming down that expanse of staircase on his back, he'd tried to brace himself and failed. But the hands that failed had been well tended. No calluses that I could see, and the nails were buffed and clean.

His suit, rumpled and twisted as it was, nonetheless spoke of expensive fabric and expert tailoring, and his feet were shod in beautifully polished Italian-looking soft black leather.

How had he gotten in without attracting notice? It didn't say much for school security, but aside from that, why would a man like this go upstairs? Everyone was obliged to be in the auditorium, so no one would have made an appointment with him for that hour. Maybe he was a parent who hadn't been informed of the assembly or who misunderstood the time of an appointment with a teacher or counselor.

I could understand Mrs. Wiggins looking horrified by the man's fall—but not her questions about who he was. She should have recognized him because he should have stopped at the office as the large sign by the front door requested. He looked like a man who followed the rules—at least, the easy ones.

Before I could find my mirror, the painful whine of a siren interrupted my search and speculations, and I gladly relinquished all further inquiries to the police and paramedics.